Bloodlust

Book Five

Blood Destiny

By

HELEN HARPER

You must take personal responsibility.
You cannot change the circumstances,
the seasons, or the wind, but you can change
yourself. That is something you have charge of.

Jim Rohn

Chapter One

The suffocating pain in my head just wouldn't go away. It didn't help, of course, that the bickering at the table was getting progressively louder with each disagreement.

"We're wasting our time with this." Scorn dripped palpably from Staines' voice.

I wondered idly whether, in my position as head of the task force designed to take down Endor, I could force the werebear to attend charm school. Maybe in Switzerland with a bunch of well-to-do teenage girls. Or perhaps Timbuktu.

"It's hardly our fault that he's not come back to this plane in the last week. Divination only stretches so far. We're not God, for goodness' sake."

I decided I'd send the entire delegation of mages along with him. They would be good at studying after all the years they had to spend at mage academies learning their art; in fact, they'd probably fit right in.

"Clearly," Staines sniffed.

"Her Most Eloquent and Gracious Majesty, the Summer Queen, believes that we should begin examining which planes this low-life human scum may be cowering in."

"And you're volunteering for that, are you? Starting with the first few hundred thousand?"

Beltran sent Lucy a withering look. "We're quite happy to narrow it down to a small list of possible demesnes and let you, as the brawn and clearly not the brains of this operation, investigate. It's about time the Brethren stepped up to the plate."

Just to keep things fair, I'd order the faeries to attend military bootcamp. Preferably in Siberia. Not that they didn't know how to fight, but they needed to be encouraged sometimes to follow orders and step up to the proverbial plate.

A pulsating vein began to appear at the side of Staines' forehead. I watched it, momentarily fascinated.

"Are you suggesting that we are stupid or something? Where exactly do the lot of you think that you would be without us right about now? Our strategies and tactics provided the single glimpse of an opportunity to take down this Endor."

"Strategy and tactics that came as a result of the Draco Wyr, not you. Besides," stated the Fae with a deliberate air of nonchalance, "you failed that time. Or had you forgotten?"

A deep rumble emanated from Lucy's throat. "At least we were there. You lot were hiding out in the woods."

"We were hardly hiding. If it hadn't been for our intervention in bringing the humans along, then imagine how much worse things would have gotten. I rather think we saved the day, in as much as it could have been saved. We don't have to be here, you know. We can quite happily stay in Tir-na-Nog and leave tracking down Endor to you. But we're not so heartless as to leave you without any hope of beating him."

"Not so heartless? Hold on a minute," interrupted Larkin. "When have you lot ever given a shit about any other species? You're only here because you want a piece of her," he jerked his head in my direction. "You're the most fickle, untrustworthy and soulless creatures out there!"

"You mean more soulless than the necromancer whom we're all here for in the first place? Really?"

"Don't speak to him like that!"

"I'll speak to him and you and anyone else who comes along in any manner that I please. What use are the lot of you magic men providing anyway?"

Max pushed his chair back. "Say that again."

"What use are the lot of you magic men..." the Fae began.

Blue light began to buzz and flicker around Max's bare skin. "I will destroy you."

"Destroy me? I don't think you even know how to create the simplest tracking spell, let alone something that can harm me." He smirked. "Well? Do you?"

"Is the Pope a freaking Catholic? Do bears shit in the woods?"

Larkin laid a calming hand on Max's arm. "Er..."

"What?" Max glanced down at his friend, who gave a pointed glance towards Staines. Realising what he'd just said, Max at least had the grace to blush ever so slightly.

Staines grimaced in disgust. "The faery speaks a modicum of sense. As far as the Brethren are concerned, we're just helping out." He looked at both the mages. "Let's face it, as a necromancer, Endor really falls under your sole jurisdiction. You should be counting your lucky stars that we're bothering to help out."

A vision of Staines walking gingerly across a room with a book balanced on his head while Max

—

and Larkin were in the corner flower-arranging suddenly popped into my mind. I let out an undignified snort. Everyone turned and stared at me so I pushed away the image and stared back, finally deciding it was time for me to enter the fray.

"If any of you wish to leave, then do so now. No-one will be held accountable if their respective organisations decide to pull out of this…" Waste of time? Utter catastrophe? Destruction of what could have been the rest of my happy life? "Council," I finished. I congratulated myself on my calm tone of voice.

They all just looked at me. I pointed over to my left. "The door's right there."

Nobody moved a muscle.

"Okay then. No more complaining about who should or shouldn't be here then. No more snide comments towards each other. No more bickering. You don't say anything unless it's going to help us find and destroy Endor."

Acquiesced silence bounded back at me. I noticed, however, that the vein in Staines' forehead had begun bulging again. Whatever.

"What is the status with the tree nymphs?"

Both Max and Lucy began to speak at once. I held up a hand to silence them, wishing I had thought to bring along some painkillers.

"Max?"

"We've placed wards around all of their main habitats. They are being maintained by a considerable amount of power that is depleting our…"

"Five words or less, Max."

—

His shoulders sagged. "No activity on the wards," he muttered.

"Lucy?"

She kept her face studiously blank as she answered. I guessed I was no longer considered a friend of the shifters then. I tried not to let it bother me. It didn't bother me. Not at all. Not one teeny iota. That sudden ache in my chest was definitely because of indigestion, not because the cloud of held-back tears was building up again at my heart.

"No sign of any nasties."

"Beltran?"

"The same."

"Have there been any reports from any other Otherworld species? Anything untoward whatsoever?"

They all shook their heads.

"Has everyone been warned?"

Staines cleared his throat. I nodded at him to speak. At least all that Brethren hierarchy shit was good for something.

"All the leaders, lords, ladies and councils have been notified of the situation. There are also alerts on the Othernet with numbers to contact should there be any suggestion that the necromancer has reappeared."

"Good. Re-route any calls that sound promising to me." I flicked a glance at Beltran. "How would you go about narrowing down the list of potential planes where he might be hiding?"

"It'll depend on who is already there and where we think he might feel comfortable. It's like finding a needle in a haystack, admittedly, but we need to

—

start somewhere."

I pursed my lips. "Agreed. As soon as you have a workable list, divide it amongst yourselves, the mages and the shifters to begin searching." I stared at them all, hard. "A minimum of one representative from each group needs to enter each plane together. If there is any doubt as to safety, then use your own discretion and bring more people. But if I hear of one, just one, infraction or disagreement or cross look, then I will be severely fucked off and I will personally deal with those involved myself. And they won't like it. We need to work together if we are going to track Endor down and beat him into fucking dust."

They all looked unhappy at that, but didn't disagree.

"Keep the Divination spells up, just in case he decides to suddenly show his face back here again," I instructed the mages. They jerked their heads in agreement.

"Unless there are any other developments, then let's meet back here again in a week."

For a split second, nobody moved. I glared at them all, irritation blazing out full wattage. Everyone stood up and began to leave. For a moment, I thought that the arguments were going to break back out again when Larkin stepped on Beltran's foot and a spasm crossed the Fae's face. But the mage apologised clumsily and Beltran instead made a gesture of irritated dismissal. Lucy took the long way around the table to make her own exit, pausing for half a second to drop a small note next to me, then left herself. All that remained in the room was the lingering odour of the mages' aftershave, which they'd probably only put on in such large quantities to piss off the shifters' sensitive noses, the blissful silence, and Lucy's note screaming up at me.

I stared at the small folded piece of paper. It had to be from Corrigan. It had been just three days since that awful meeting in this very room when I'd effectively dumped him in front of half of the Otherworld's great and good. Despite the imminent and very real danger that Endor offered, I'd been able to think of virtually nothing since but the look in his eyes when he'd realised what was happening. I'd gone back over it again and again, wondering whether I'd made the right decision or not by conceding to the Arch-Mage and the Summer Queen's demands. Half the time I thought I should have just told the pair of them to fuck off, the other half I didn't think I'd had any choice.

I reached out and gingerly touched the paper, then drew my fingers back as if burned. He had said he didn't want anything to do with me ever again. But I knew well that a bit of time and distance could calm frayed tempers. Perhaps he wanted to meet and talk out what had transpired between us, and listen to my side of the story. Or perhaps he wanted to reiterate that he thought I was a piece of low-life dirt not fit to grace the soles of his glossy wingtips.

I stretched my hand out again, trying not to pay too much attention to the fact that my fingers were trembling. This was ridiculous. I was a fucking dragon, for goodness' sake. I couldn't be afraid of a stupid piece of paper. More decisively this time, I picked it up and unfolded it, then stared down at the words scrawled there. Disappointment and relief warred inside me. The note was from Tom, not Corrigan. He wanted me to meet him outside the city on Thursday night to begin my transformation training. I'd only ever shifted into dragon form once, and that had been when my emotions were so out of control it was a completely involuntary manifestation. The dragon instincts had completely taken over my body and mind to the extent that I'd been too scared to give myself up to them again. But if we were going to have any hope of truly beating Endor, then I'd have to stop acting like a terrified little mouse and get with the program. Tom was going to use his years of shifter knowledge to help me. I sniffed, trying to tell myself I was completely nonchalant about the whole thing. No problem.

Standing up, I shoved the note into the back pocket of my jeans, scooped up my backpack and left the room, emerging into the busy restaurant floor of Alcazon. As soon as I did so, virtually every head turned in my direction and an abrupt hush descended across the space. My reputation was obviously starting to precede me. I straightened my back and glared at them all, wondering whether I was suddenly the object of the Otherworld's interest because everyone now knew my so-called secret identity or because they were all aware that I'd very publicly declined the opportunity to be the Lord of the Brethren's love muffin. Neither thought was a pleasant one, so I glared harder. The majority of the patrons hastily looked away. After years of attempting to keep a very low profile, I was not enjoying any of this attention at all.

I gritted my teeth and began to stride out, hoping I looked a lot more menacing and confident than I felt. I'd just about made it to the door, however, when a figure stepped in front of me. I scowled in irritation until I realised just who, or rather what, was barring my escape. My heart began to sink. I had a horrible feeling I knew what this was going to be about. A flicker of heat lit up inside my belly.

"You're in my way," I snarled.

The slender pale-skinned female inclined her head slightly, but the expression in her ruby red eyes indicated she wasn't about to get out of my path any time soon.

"I was hoping that we might have a word." Her voice was as icy cold as I knew her skin would be.

I pushed past her, trying not to shudder at the touch of her undead flesh. Unfortunately for me, two more vamps were now up ahead. So that hadn't been the royal 'we' she'd been using there then. Damn it.

"Will you join us at our table?"

I turned back towards her and mulled over my options. I could just ignore her and her bloodsucking friends completely. I knew I could easily bypass them if they really wanted to get in my way. I was very aware that every other being in the room was watching our little exchange, however. If the vampires were so determined to speak to me, then it was probably better to get it out of the way as quickly as possible.

"You can say what you need to here."

She lifted an elegant shoulder in a half shrug and a ghost of a smile traced over her lips. "Very well. We wish to procure your services."

"They're not for sale."

"We will pay you handsomely. You may not be able to hide your disgust at what we are, Miss Smith, but you would be surprised at what we can offer you in return for one little favour."

"In which case I'm sure there will be many others who will be more keen than I to help you out."

"Perhaps. But word of your exploits has reached our ears, and it seems that you have the necessary skills to solve our little problem."

I wasn't going to be able to wriggle my way out of this without threatening violence. Except I didn't think that would go down too well within the sleek environ of Alcazon. The trouble was, I thought I knew what she was going to say next. I played dumb though - there really wasn't much choice.

"What problem would that be?"

She blinked at me languidly. "A small matter of a missing vampire."

I knew it. Fuck. "Maybe they're dead." I paused. "Oh, sorry, you're all already dead," I said sarcastically. "Maybe they're no longer undead." Funnily enough, that was actually true.

"This vampire is a particularly strong one. There are few who would be able to take him down and we do not believe that he has passed. He is an important member of our little group and we would like to have him back. You will track him down for us." It wasn't a request.

"I'm pretty busy right now. I don't have time to go looking for one lost bloodsucker."

"You have met him before, I believe. When you came to our house and stole from us."

"I didn't fucking steal from you," I hissed. "Besides, I think you came off slightly better from that occasion anyway." The thought of Thomas and Brock still made my heart tighten in pain. "Why would I want to help find the guy who is responsible for my friends' deaths?"

"So you know to whom I am referring then?"

Uh oh. "I can only think of one vamp who I spoke to that night. The same one who appeared at the mages' academy soon after. Believe me, I have no desire to help you locate that prick."

And I didn't actually know where Aubrey was anyway. I'd not seen him since the last time I was here at Alcazon three days ago and he'd scarpered off. Goodness only knew where he was hiding now.

"As you have already mentioned, we are undead, Miss Smith. That provides us more than a little insight into the world of the deceased and all those who barter with it. Including say," she paused for a moment, blood red fingernails tapping the side of her mouth, and a malicious gleam lighting up her eyes, "necromancers."

Fucking hell. How did the vamps get hold of that piece of information? "So what you're saying is if I find your friend, you will find my necromancer."

"I think that is exactly what I'm saying."

I stared at her suspiciously. Did she know what had happened to Aubrey? It could hardly be a coincidence that it was me she had approached.

There had certainly been enough Otherworlders who'd become aware of his transformation to the world of the living to have let that little tidbit slip out. I sighed inwardly. My head was still hurting far too much to deal with this right now.

"I'll think about it," I grunted. Not.

"Excellent," she said, as if I'd already agreed to bring him to her immediately. "His name is Aubrey. He can be...dangerous if you get on his wrong side, but I'm sure you will manage it."

"I said I'll think about it."

She smiled at me coldly. "Here is my card. Contact me any time."

I stared down at the object she was holding out. Unsurprisingly, it was crimson in colour, with just a single telephone number etched into it in black. I took it from her, being careful just to pinch it at the edges. Who knew what nasty stuff it might have on it? I stuck it into my back pocket along with Tom's note.

"Great." I pasted on a very fake smile. "I have to go now."

"I will look forward to hearing from you.

Yeah, yeah. I stepped around her, careful this time to avoid touching her in any way. The two vamps up ahead had their arms folded and were staring at me expressionlessly. I was tempted to just shove them out of the way, but they moved to the side at the last second and allowed me to pass by without comment. Knowing that they, along with rest of the restaurant, were watching my departure, I forced a casually confident swagger into my step. I reminded myself not to forget to breathe and reached out for the door handle leading back to the outside world. Unfortunately for me, just before I could wrench it open, someone pushed it from the other side, and the edge of the door smacked right into my face, scraping against my nose and cheekbone, and sending involuntary tears springing into my eyes.

"Oh, I'm so sorry! I'm so sorry!" The blurry image of a waiter began to come into focus. Judging by the panic in his voice, he was worried about exactly what I was going to do to him for daring to try to open the door at the same time as me. Mack Smith, more monster than the monsters.

I tried not to show I was in pain and exhaled audibly in annoyance. "Don't worry about it." Then I stepped past him, and back out into the real world.

Chapter Two

My eyes were still smarting by the time I emerged into the daylight. A small hard knot of frustration had settled deep into my stomach. Talking about what everyone else was doing was all very well and good, but it was about time *I* actually starting *doing* something. However, until there was some kind of concrete information to work with, it appeared there was very little for me to actually do. I'd given everyone on the council tasks to undertake; it appeared that all I had to do was to wait until something came out from the fruits of their labour. It didn't suit me. I didn't want to spend too much time dwelling on what the vamp had offered, nor did I have any desire to wallow in misery about the things I couldn't change, such as my utter failure with Corrigan. And hanging around waiting for the inevitable problems that my transformation lesson with Tom was going to highlight wasn't particularly appealing either. Patience was clearly not my forte.

I could go back to Clava Books and help out there for a few hours. Certainly the ongoing bickering between Mrs. Alcoon and Slim would provide some entertainment, but after having to listen to the mages, shifters and faeries argue for the last hour or so, I wasn't sure I'd be able to cope with any more of that. I'd asked the pair of them to see what they could dig up about necromancers, on the off-chance any of the books the pair of them had access to could provide some clues as to Endor's whereabouts. After what was already two full days of digging, however, they'd not found anything yet, and I didn't really expect much would have changed in the last twenty-four hours.

I decided instead to try and clear the cobwebs from my head and go for a wander around to Balud's little shop. He'd been tasked with trying to find a weapon that might help defeat Endor. I could surmise by his absence at this morning's meeting that he'd come up short thus far, but at least it gave me some sort of vague purpose.

The sun was high in the sky and blazing down with the full heat of summer. Dappled shadows danced across the pavement with each passerby, and the streets were busy with the glowing faces of contented tourists. None of it was making me feel particularly happy. I strode along, taking elongated steps in order to reach my destination as quickly as possible. I resolutely refused to get out of anyone's way. The determination must have been visible on my face because virtually everyone maneuvered themselves out of my path. At one point, a sullen looking teenager seemed intent on playing chicken, heading straight for me and clearly refusing to get out of my way. When he was barely two feet from me, however, something in my face made him change his mind, and he hopped to my left with an elaborately heavy sigh. I knew I was being an idiot, but if I could control nothing else in my life then I was damn well going to control where I chose to walk. It was probably just as well that I arrived at the alleyway where Balud's shop was located before anyone decided to take me on.

As per usual, the little street was deserted. I stalked down to the door and rapped on it sharply. When there was no immediate answer, I knocked again. From within came a sound of clattering and muttered expletives. Well, at least the little troll was in.

When the door eventually opened, and Balud peered out, I remained standing on the doorstep, hands on my hips. "Didn't you get the memo?"

He stared at me, unblinking.

"Hello? Balud? There was a council meeting just now. Why weren't you there?"

He slammed the door shut. I only just had enough time to jump out of the way to avoid being thwacked yet again in the face. Okay. Perhaps I needed to calm down a little and be nicer. I knocked again, albeit more gently this time.

The door opened half an inch. "I'm sorry," I called in through the gap. "I've been having a bad day. Well, a bad week. More like a bad year. I didn't mean to sound so tetchy."

Silence answered me. I tried again. "I was just wondering if maybe you'd made any headway in finding something to defeat Endor. You know, the necromancer chappie? The one who might kill us all if we don't stop him?"

The door opened a fraction more.

"You did say that you were going to look for some kind of materials that might help us," I coaxed, "you know, being the best Otherworld weapons shop that the country has to offer, and all."

Clearly, flattery will get you everywhere. A small

gnarled hand finally snaked out and beckoned me inside. Grateful, I stepped over the threshold and the door banged loudly closed behind me. I jumped, startled.

"This might have once been the best weapons shop," the troll grunted. "It's not anymore."

I frowned. "What do you mean?"

He snatched up a glossy sheet of A5 paper and thrust it in my face. "Look."

My eyes scanned it. It was an advert for Wold's Weaponry. 'THE BIGGEST RANGE AND THE BEST PRICES' proclaimed the banner in capital letters. I smacked myself in the forehead. "The Batibat's shop is still open," I said, surprised.

It hadn't even occurred to me. Endor had forced the Batibats to work for him, including through this shop, as well as up at Haughmond Hill where Corrigan and I had confronted him. I'd had Alex investigate it to find out what information he could. In fact, the only reason that we knew anything at all about Endor's master plan had been from what the Batibat who ran the shop had told him. I'd just assumed that, by dint of our discovery, it would have been shut down. I was pretty confident Alex had already gotten all the potentially useful information there was to get out of her. And yet it wouldn't hurt to pay another little visit and see if there was anything else that he'd missed.

"Yes, little girl," spat Balud, "it's still open. And undercutting me at every turn." He waved the advert in my face. "How am I supposed to compete with these prices? It's outrageous!"

"Do you think Endor's still in contact with her?"

I mused thoughtfully. "It's unlikely he'd risk it, or let her into his confidence. But perhaps she's got some clue as to where he might be holed up." I should have gone to check on her before now. I was an idiot.

Balud looked at me as if to confirm the fact that I was crazy. "Did you hear what I said?" the troll demanded. "She's putting me out of business!"

"Oh, yes, that," I bobbed my head, attempting an air of brisk sobriety. "I can talk to her about it. Maybe ask her to look at her prices?"

"Or make sure she shuts up that shop and never tries to start up any kind of business ever again."

Somehow I didn't think that was how capitalism was supposed to work. I nodded slowly though. "Er, yes, I could maybe ask her to do that too."

Balud's eyes narrowed at me suspiciously. I smiled at him. "I'll see what I can do. Honest."

He grunted in doubtful acquiescence. "So what happened to your face?"

"Huh?" I was momentarily confused.

"Your face. You have a most arresting bruise."

"I walked into a door."

He raised his eyebrows. "Really?"

"Really," I said, mildly protesting.

He crooked his finger towards me. "Come with me."

"Well, actually I thought I might go now and check out Wold..."

"You'd forgotten she even existed until five minutes ago. She will keep for another half an hour."

I supposed he was right. Now that I had a potential lead to follow, however, I was itching to get onto it as soon as possible. Balud gave me a baleful look. I sighed. "Okay then."

He led me towards the back, then pointed into a small room off the side. "In here."

I pushed open the door. It creaked somewhat menacingly, and I looked askance at the troll. He rolled his eyes and pushed past me to enter. Shrugging, I followed him inside, attempting not to breathe in too deeply. The air was musty with the distinct aroma of mould, and it was so dark that I could make out virtually nothing whatsoever. I could hear the sound of scrabbling, and a curse, before the room was abruptly bathed in light. I blinked rapidly to adjust to the sudden change, then Balud was thrusting something into my hands. I glanced down. It was a small, cracked hand mirror.

He gestured at it. "Go on then. Take a look."

For once doing as I was told, I held the mirror up and stared at my reflection. Blimey. A large purple stain was making its way across the bridge of my nose and down under my right eye. It looked like I'd been punched repeatedly in the face. I poked at it gingerly, then winced.

"Wow."

"Indeed."

My eye seemed to be starting to swell up rather alarmingly. No wonder that teenager had veered out of my way so abruptly on the street. Even I had to admit that it made me look rather scary.

"I don't suppose you have any ice that I could put on this?" I asked.

"No."

"Not even any frozen peas?"

"No."

"A steak?"

The answering look was enough. I put the mirror down. Oh well. There wasn't much I could do about it now, I figured.

"I do sell a lovely range of balaclavas," Balud commented.

I flicked him a glance. He put up his palms. "Okay, okay, it was just an idea."

Harrumphing, I looked around the small room. "So what is this place?"

"My office. I have something here that you might find interesting. I was going to come by to the council meeting to show you, but then the flyer was shoved in through my door and I got distracted." He began shuffling around pieces of paper, scooping up first one bunch and then another. "It's around here somewhere," he muttered.

Motes of dust flew up into the air. I began to inadvertently choke and my eyes started to sting. Balud stopped what he was doing and peered up at me. "Do your eyes always do that?"

"What? Water? They seem to be doing rather a lot of it of late, to be fair."

"No. Not that." His voice sounded strange.

Puzzled, I stared at him. "What then?"

He continued to look at me, then eventually shrugged and went back to what he was doing. "Never mind."

"Balud..." I said warningly.

"Here it is!" he interrupted, triumphantly holding aloft a stained sheet of paper.

Curiosity gave way. I took the piece of paper and

scanned down it quickly. For a moment, I was utterly dumbfounded. "The Palladium? But that's what..."

"No, no, no, no, no," muttered Balud. "There's no article in front of it. It's just palladium. Like gold. Not The Gold. Or The Silver. Just silver. Just palladium. It's an element. Similar to platinum. According to my research, humans only discovered it a couple of hundred years ago. But here it says it was used back in the fifteenth century to destroy a necromancer who was wandering about the French countryside. Nowadays it gets used for jewellery, dentistry, catalytic converters for cars, that kind of thing."

"The English language is indeed a curious thing," I said, half to myself.

"You are a strange little girl."

"Do me a favour, Balud, call me Mack."

He shrugged. "You're correct that the English language is a curious thing. Why would your parents call you Mackintosh?"

I gave him a dirty look. "You know perfectly well that it's Mackenzie." I turned my attention back to the grubby piece of paper. "So you think this will work? That Endor will be vulnerable to a weapon made from palladium?"

"I need to do some more research to cross-check, but it does indeed appear as if we have a winner."

"Do you have any?"

"What?"

"Weapons made of palladium," I said impatiently. "The more we can spread around all of us, the better."

He laughed sharply. "Why would I have any weapons made of palladium? It's a soft metal. Unless you're apparently defending yourself against a necromancer, it would really be no good in any fight. And it's a very expensive metal anyway."

I took a deep breath, willing myself to stay calm. "Can you make some then?"

"Little girl, I'm a master artiste of weaponry. I can make anything."

"Great. Start with around fifty. Perhaps a mix of things. Some swords, daggers, and try some bullets and arrows as well. I imagine the guns and bows themselves wouldn't need to be made from palladium, just the actual pointy dangerous parts that stick in you."

Balud held up a single finger. "And where will I get all that palladium from? Shall I just nip down to my local palladium hardware store? Hmmm?"

I stared at him. "You just said it was used for jewellery and dentists and cars. It must be freely available. Order some online."

"Who'll pay for it?"

I gaped, nonplussed. "This is to save the fucking world! Who cares who pays for it?"

Balud shrugged. "Someone's got to. This stuff doesn't come cheap."

"Fine," I said, pissed off. "I'll get you some money. Raid my piggybank or whatever."

"Says the girl who couldn't afford to buy two silver daggers just last month."

"I'll get you the money, alright?"

Damn it. I'd just have to talk to the council and

get them to free up some funds from somewhere. How hard could it be? I knew the mages were pretty broke, but the shifters had plenty of spare cash hanging around, and I reckoned that the Fae had to be minted. It'd be easy. And if I spoke to the council then I could avoid having to deal directly with the Summer Queen or the Arch-Mage. Or Corrigan. He'd said he didn't want to ever see me again, and I was going to respect those wishes. For now. Once Endor was out of the way, however...I pressed my lips together.

"I'll sort it out and get back to you. Is there anything else?"

He craned his neck up at me. "I think your bruise is still growing."

I scowled. "Whatever. I'm going off to talk to Wold."

"Tell her to shut down her shop or else you'll turn into a dragon and breathe fire all over her!"

"That's meant to be a secret," I said petulantly.

"Not a very well kept one."

I growled and turned on my heel, showing myself out of the shop.

Chapter Three

It took me an hour or two to travel across the city via the Underground to where Wold's shop was located. I garnered more than a few odd looks, no doubt as a direct result of the large bruise that was beginning to throb across my cheek. My eye was continuing to swell up to the point where my vision was becoming limited. I'd have to hope that the loss of my periphery focus wouldn't allow anyone – or anything – untoward get the jump on me. At one point, a kindly looking woman, with laughter lines at the edges of her eyes which masked a deep pain from within, handed me a card for a women's shelter.

"It's never too late to ask for help," she said softly.

I just smiled slightly and said thank you. Getting into an explanation with a complete stranger about how I really had walked into a door seemed far too ridiculous, even for me. I hoped the bruising would subside enough before I had to venture back to Alcazon to meet the council again, or indeed any other Otherworlders. The last thing I needed was for my badass reputation to become even more inflated. I was aware the result would probably just be a bunch of irritating challengers trying to take me on to prove their own prowess. That was indeed a hassle I could do without.

I did need to contact the council about the

money to procure enough palladium to create an arsenal of devastating weaponry, however. A carefully worded email would probably do the trick. That way I wouldn't have to bother talking to any of them. I didn't think my head could cope with the onslaught of their complaints again today. Deciding that I'd sort out that little problem once I finally got home again, I focused on the matter in hand: getting the Batibat onside to help me with locating Endor. The success Alex had had with her the previous week seemed to suggest that he would be a good person to include so, as soon as I'd hopped off the train, I cast around for a phone. I really needed to get myself a bloody mobile.

Eventually finding a familiarly red phone box just outside the station gates, I dug inside my pocket for some change and inserted it into the machine. The customary beat of the Beach Boys thrummed from across the line, then the phone clicked into voicemail.

"Hey dude. I'm not available to take your call right now, but if you leave a message I'll get back to you before the surf is up."

Rolling my eyes, I left a quick message. "Alex, it's Mack. I need you to meet me at the Batibat's shop as soon as you can. Definitely sooner rather than later. I need to talk to her again about Endor and your expertise would be appreciated."

I hung up. It was less his expertise than the fact he was an apparently virile young man that had probably made the Batibat spill her secrets to him. It didn't really matter though. Anything extra I could glean from her about how to track down Endor would be good. And, let's face it, the faster I found the freaky necromancing serial killer, the faster I could get my life back on track. Or rather get Corrigan to forgive me so we could pick up from where we left off.

I set off in the direction of the shop. Fortunately, the flyer that Balud had waved so unceremoniously in front of my face had included an address, and the borough of London had thought to helpfully provide maps next to the station entrances to help lost souls like me find our way around. Wold's little empire was, naturally, down a quiet side street off the main tree-lined thoroughfare. The kind of quiet side street where creepy Otherworld nasties could hang around without fear of being bothered by pesky humans. As soon as I turned down into it, the distinct smell of rotting meat reached my nostrils and the shadows abruptly deepened. Jeez. It even appeared as if the sky had dramatically darkened, although I was sure that was just my own fanciful imagination.

"Bad guys 'r' us," I muttered to myself, then halted suddenly in my steps as I caught sight of a figure leaning up against a wall further along. Interesting. Was this a waiting customer or a guard? Carefully, I reached behind me and pulled out my daggers from my back sheath, before concealing them in the folds of my sleeves. It didn't hurt to be prepared.

I'd barely gone three more steps when the figure pushed off from the wall. The shadows still concealed their identity, but it was definitely someone male and large.

"Don't come any closer," a gruff voice called out.

The corners of my mouth lifted up. Excellent. Not a customer then, but someone who I could pump for information once I'd beaten the shit out of them. I'd been needing to release some tension all day long. It might even help get rid of my headache. Things were starting to look up.

I continued forward.

"You heard me," growled the voice again. "Turn around and go back the way you came."

Ooooh, scary. I tightened my grip on the daggers and shifted my weight as I carried on, my eyes gradually starting to adjust to the dim light. I wondered whether to see who it was first or just to let my silver fly and ask questions later. Prickles of heat danced merrily up and down my veins. It occurred to me that there was probably something wrong with me for being excited to see a bit of action. I shrugged inwardly. No-one's perfect.

Unfortunately, at that moment, the figure took a step forward into a patch of dull sunlight and I registered who it was. It was just a fucking shifter. Corrigan had probably sent him here to keep an eye on the shop. My good eye squinted at him. He looked like a wolf, all lean and muscly, but with a shaggy mane of hair on top of his head. I relaxed, although I was cursing slightly inside.

"It's alright," I shouted out, starting to re-sheathe my weapons. "It's me. Er, Mack. Mack Smith. I'm here on official business."

"Ma'am, I'm going to ask you again. Turn around and go back. This area is off limits."

My eyes narrowed. What the fuck? I was the

31

head of the sodding council investigating the Batibat's boss. No, this area most definitely was not off limits. And I was certainly not a 'ma'am'.

"Perhaps you didn't hear me the first time," I commented, aware that there was an edge of hot fury to my tone, "I'm Mack Smith. I have every right to be here. If you don't believe me then call your fucking boss and check."

"I know who you are, Ms. Smith, and I have strict instructions not to let you come any closer."

I stopped in mid-step, more out of shock than anything else. Seriously? I knew that Corrigan was beyond pissed off with me, but he couldn't stop me from doing my job. Who the hell did he think he was? I'd thought many things of the Lord Alpha in the past, but never that he was petty. And did he really believe that one pathetic wolf was going to make me turn around with my invisible dragon tail tucked between my legs? It looked like I was going to end up having a little fun after all.

I pulled out my daggers again, and began to move forward. "You're going to want to get out of my way."

"Ma'am…"

"Don't call me that."

I let one dagger fly, striking him in his shin. The werewolf screamed in agony and yanked at it, scrabbling at the hilt to pull it away from where it had embedded itself in his skin. To be fair, I hadn't put much force behind the throw, and it was really only the very tip of the weapon that he was howling about. I didn't actually want to hurt him badly; after all, he was only following orders – and stupid orders at that – and I knew silver was excruciatingly painful for shifters, even just to touch. But I also had a point to make to His High and Mightiness. Don't get in my fucking way.

I gently pried the dagger from the shifter's fingers, and stepped over his writhing body. "Sorry," I muttered. "Take it up with your boss."

Leaving him there, I returned both weapons to the halter at my back, and walked over to the shop's entrance, trying to keep my senses as alert as possible. There was no way Corrigan was idiotic enough to think that one measly little teen wolf could stop me, whether he was a member of the big scary Brethren or not. There had to be more shifters around here somewhere, and I was damned if I was going to let any of them even begin to get the better of me. Studying the splintered wood where Wold's front door had clearly been kicked in, I was starting to get an idea about where they actually were. And that made me royally pissed off.

I nudged the door open with the tip of my shoe, creating enough of a gap to slip through. Muffled angry voices floated over from deep within. Bingo. Taking care to stay as quiet as possible, so that I knew just exactly what I was dealing with, I edged forward. Despite the obvious signs of carnage that Corrigan's minions had left in their wake, it was clear the Batibat kept a considerably tidier and cleaner shop than Balud. Of course, Balud didn't live in daily fear of having his very life-force drained from him by a crazy necromancer. That in itself would probably provide incentive enough to do a daily dust.

The voices seemed to be coming from behind a half-open door at the far end of the corridor. I inched towards it, making sure I stayed planted against the far wall to avoid casting any telling shadows which might give my presence away before I wanted to advertise it. What I really wanted to know was what on earth Corrigan was actually up to. A few words were starting to drift over and it appeared that it was the shifters who were doing all the talking.

Moving close enough to catch more, I sidled up to the door, and cocked my head to the side to listen.

"You're going to tell us everything you know sooner or later," barked a steely voice.

Good grief. That line was straight out of a Hollywood movie. These guys weren't exactly subtle.

"Except I don't know anything."

Figuring that had to be Wold herself, I twisted around to peer through the crack in the hinges. The Batibat was cowering in a chair, and there were three other figures – shifters – all standing around her. At that point one of them, who had his back to me, reached round and smacked her on the face.

"Listen up, you ugly bitch. You're going to tell us where your slimy boss is cowering and you're going to do it now."

I recoiled. Brute sexist intimidation. Why they thought that would be successful in getting information, which the bloody Batibat probably didn't know in the first place, was beyond me. A tendril of bloodfire reached up and squeezed its way round my heart. Maybe Corrigan wasn't quite as nice and balanced as I'd come to think after all. Regardless, there was no way I was going to let this continue on any longer.

I thumped loudly on the wall, causing all four of them to jump, and then stepped out and slammed the door fully open with a sharp crack. The three shifters were already taking up attack positions, teeth bared. Wold, whose resemblance to the Haughmond Hill Batibat was really quite remarkable, was leaning back in her chair, eyes wide, as if in a bid to get herself as far away from this new threat as possible.

"He said she might show up," growled the shifter to the right.

"Well, I guess he was fucking right," I responded, then leapt up and scissor-kicked the offending shifter in the chest, knocking him backwards and onto the floor. He groaned, tried once to get up, and then fell back down again, clutching his chest.

The familiar prickle across my fingertips alerted me to the return of my green fire. Smiling humourlessly, I shot out a stream to the one on the left who was already in mid-shift. It instantly lit up the fur that was beginning to appear across his skin, and he shrieked in horror, falling to the ground and twisting this way and that in a vain attempt to put out the flames. That just left the bully boy. He threw himself at me, apparently realising the space was too small, and the time too short, for him to shift into what would be his most effective attack form. It wouldn't have mattered what he'd chosen to do, however. Using my energy in a manner that Thomas, my old teacher, would have been proud of,

I simply pushed out my hand and grabbed him by the throat.

"That was almost disappointingly easy," I commented, bringing his face close to mine. "Now tell me, what exactly are you trying to achieve by torturing one of Endor's victims?"

He choked, eyes bulging. I shook him slightly. "Sorry, I didn't quite catch that. You'll need to speak up."

A floorboard creaked behind me. Shit. There were more of them than I had thought. I was about to use my free hand to pull out one of the daggers again and throw it behind me when I heard a familiar, stomach churning voice speak up, dripping with hatred.

"Let go of my wolf, kitten." There was a pause. "Now."

Chapter Four

I turned around slowly, not relinquishing my grip on the squirming shifter. So much for keeping out of his way then.

"My Lord," I stated emphatically, injecting in as much venom towards Corrigan as he had managed for me.

For a moment, a flicker of surprise crossed the Lord Alpha's face, then his jade green eyes fixed on mine, turning flinty and emotionless. I felt a tiny measure of satisfaction that there were dark shadows underneath them, but was beyond irritated at the fact he still managed to look so good despite the apparent lack of sleep. Until ten minutes ago, I'd have been thrilled to bump into him; right now, after witnessing the Batibat's interrogation, my feelings weren't quite so clear cut.

"Release him," he repeated.

I raised my eyebrows. "Make me."

Corrigan sighed and ran a tanned hand through his jet black hair. "Mackenzie, don't complicate my life further. Let him go and get out. I will take things from here."

I growled. "Take things from here? Take things from fucking here? What does that mean? That you'll break out the hot irons to make sure you squeeze every single bit of information you can from her? She's as much a fucking victim here as we are! How dare you send your minions here to treat her like an enemy combatant? What gives you the fucking right? Oh, the majestic Brethren, sweeping in to save the day and torture innocents. Is that how you get your kicks?"

His eyes flashed pure fury before shutters came slamming down again, masking his thoughts. "So now you think we're monsters again, do you? It didn't take you long to change your mind." His voice was soft, but edged with steely menace.

"What else do you expect me to think? You can't go around acting as if you're the fucking Gestapo! You can't treat people like that, Corrigan!"

"As a Batibat, she's not technically a person," he said mildly.

"You know damn well what I mean when I say that. What Endor has done, what he is doing, it's not her fault!" I spat the words out, still appalled at what he'd sent his shifters here to do.

"She's not entirely innocent," he reminded me. "We know that he used this place to get the money he needed to begin his campaign. Right now she's the best lead that we've got."

"And beating that lead to a pulp is going to help?"

Wold let out a squeak from behind me. I didn't turn around; instead, in return, I tightened my grip infinitesimally around the shifter's neck. He gasped, but otherwise made no other sound, his eyes trained on his lord and master.

Corrigan took a step towards me and I caught the sudden scent of his aftershave. The familiar headiness of it momentarily made my senses reel. A swirl of heated bloodfire rose up from the pit of my belly. Damn him.

"I was unaware of what was happening."

"Bullshit!" I exploded. "Every single one of these shifters knew to watch out for me and not let me in. And they'd been told to do that by you. They wouldn't be here if it wasn't for you."

Corrigan's fists clenched. "Get out of here."

"I already told you I'm not going anywhere until I get fucking answers! You can't…"

I stopped mid-sentence as I realised he'd not been addressing me. The two shifters on the floor painfully pulled themselves up, eyes downcast, and scuttled out of the door. Corrigan raised his eyebrows at me. I sighed and loosened my grip on the wolf. He half fell down, letting out a small whine that belied his current human form, then bolted out on all fours.

Once he'd gone, Corrigan spoke again. "I didn't know what was happening until I got a call saying that they were here and under attack. I just happened to be in the vicinity anyway."

I should have aimed for the heart of the shifter hanging around outside. My face twisted. "Stop fucking lying. I thought better of you than that. At least be honest with me, Corrigan."

A tinge of red lit up across his cheekbones. "You mean like you were honest with me? Fucking me and leading me on one minute then discarding me the next?"

"I had my reasons!" I spat. "And stop changing the subject. Own up to what you've done and what you are. Coming here and doing this makes you almost as bad as sodding Endor himself."

For a moment I thought he was going to strike me, then his muscles relaxed slightly and he composed himself. "I had decided, in light of our," he paused for a heartbeat, "relationship with each other, that it would be wise to withdraw myself from this situation with the necromancer. I instructed Staines to take the lead. He has exceeded his authority and, believe me, will be dealt with."

The formality of Corrigan's words lanced through me. Then his green eyes softened for a moment and he looked over my shoulder at the Batibat. "Ma'am, you have my apologies, along with those of the entire Brethren. This will not happen again."

I opened my mouth, then snapped it shut, realising the shifters had only referred to 'he'. They hadn't mentioned Corrigan himself. He could very well be telling the truth. But Staines was still Corrigan's henchman. He wouldn't have done this if he'd thought that it would really piss his Lord Alpha off. My eyes narrowed slightly.

"Yes, but..."

Corrigan turned his attention back to me. "Not that I owe you any explanations."

"I'm the head of the council tasked to bring Endor down. You owe me every explanation."

A humourless smile crossed his face. "Ah, yes. Your new job." He leaned in closer. "Tell me, how does it feel having all that power and control? Is it everything you wished for?"

I snarled at him. "Fuck. Off."

He laughed sharply. "Why so moody about it? You got what you wanted."

"I didn't want this, Corrigan. I didn't ask for this. There wasn't a choice."

"There is always a choice." His eyes raked across my face. "So what happened? Was that one of my shifters?"

"Huh?" I asked, suddenly confused.

"Your face. There's a rather conspicuous bruise and it appears that you can only see out of one eye. What happened?"

"Nothing."

"Mackenzie..."

"I walked into a door."

A muscle throbbed in Corrigan's cheek. His voice deepened to a rumble. "What really happened?"

"I told you," I said, exasperated, "I walked into a door."

He leaned in towards me until I could feel his breath hot upon my cheek. My chest tightened. "Who's lying now?" he whispered.

Just then there was a crash from out in the corridor. Both Corrigan and I tensed immediately and my hands reached back for my daggers. He tilted his head up, nostrils flaring, then took hold of my arms to stop them in midair. An expression of irritation flickered across his eyes, and a nervous looking face peered round the gap in the door.

"Dude! Sheesh! What happened here? And what the bejesus happened to your face?" He sent an accusatory look in the Lord Alpha's direction.

"It's alright, Alex," I said, pulling away from Corrigan, and trying to ignore the burning imprint his hands left on my skin. "There's nothing to worry about."

"Are you sure? Because, man, it looks like a hurricane tore through this place." He rubbed at his cheek worriedly. "Was it that Endor dude? Was he here? Did he take Wold?"

I started. "What? No, Wold's here, she's just..."

I turned around to the chair where the Batibat had been sitting. It was empty. Fucking hell. Had I really been so engrossed in Corrigan that I'd not noticed a three ton naked woman get up and leave? A window towards the back of the room gaped open, as evidence of my own idiot culpability.

I swivelled back to Corrigan. "Didn't you see her get up and go?"

He growled at me, clearly pissed off. "Didn't you?"

I glared. "You were the one facing in her fucking direction!"

Alex held up his hands, palms facing outwards. "Whoa, should I go out and come back in again?"

"Set up a Divination spell, Alex," I snapped, looking away from the Brethren Lord in self-directed disgust.

He nodded, and half closed his eyes, starting to chant. A snake of blue inveniora light curled up from his hands and etched its way through the clammy air of the room. I moved out of its path as it veered over to the empty chair where it hovered for a second before screwing upwards and out of the window. Without pausing further, I followed it, leaping out of the window and landing with a heavy clatter on the ground three feet below. Corrigan, right at my heels, arched out and hit the ground while barely bending his knees. Stupid cat reflexes. Then the pair of us took off in pursuit.

Alex's blue tracking spell made a beeline for the end of the narrow street. Keeping up with the front of the trail, we followed it down.

"It's heading for the main street," I said, stating the obvious. "She can't go there. A huge naked female Batibat is hardly going to go unnoticed at three o'clock in the freaking afternoon."

Corrigan grunted his assent. As soon as we reached the sunlight of the crossroads that stretched back into the less shadowy manifestation of London, however, the blue inveniora arced upwards into the air and disappeared into one of the leafy green trees that edged the pavement. The light hung there for a second before it too vanished.

"Fuck." I slammed my hand into the trunk of the tree, ignoring the answering shot of pain that I received back. "We'll never catch her now."

Corrigan's eyes followed the street down, glancing from tree to tree. "She could jump from one to the other and we'll never know where she is," he agreed.

"This is your bloody shifters' fault."

"They might have a lot to answer for," he growled, "but they're not the ones who allowed her to disappear in front of their eyes."

I had no answer for that. My shoulders sagged in defeat.

"Screw this," I said. "I'm going to get Alex and go home."

"Corr? Is everything okay?"

I stiffened, and glanced over at the owner of the

voice. A pretty blonde was standing a few feet away, her perfectly manicured eyebrows raised in Corrigan's direction. I instantly hated her.

"Everything's fine." He didn't even look at me, but instead held out his arm for her. She took it and he smiled down at her. "Come on. Let's go and get that late lunch that I promised you."

Without so much as another glance, the pair of them walked off. I watched them go, mouth hanging open. Well, it didn't take him fucking long to get over me, I thought, brimming with unjust ire. "In the sodding vicinity, indeed," I muttered to myself. "In the sodding vicinity wining and dining so that he can get freaking laid later on. Prick."

Alex appeared by my shoulder. "Where's Wold?"

"Gone."

"His Lord Shiftiness?"

"He's gone too."

"Ah. What do we do now?"

I was still staring down the street in the direction of Corrigan and his new 'friend'.

"Mack Attack? What do we do now?"

I chewed my lip. Fine. Corrigan could go off and live his life how ever he saw fit. I was going to do my job, preferably without the interference from the furry ones this time. "We're going to see if we can't get hold of a lot of money so that we can get make some weapons of necromancing destruction."

Alex beamed. "Cool. You don't need him anyway, Mack Attack."

"Damn straight." A sudden rip of roaring bloodfire lit through my chest. I ignored it. At least my headache seemed to have finally dissipated.

"Let's go."

Chapter Five

On our return journey, I filled Alex in on what had transpired before he'd arrived. He was suitably appalled.

"Sheesh, Mack Attack. And they'd been told not to let you near the place? What in the Founder's name was the Lord Alpha doing?"

I desperately wanted to give Corrigan the benefit of the doubt, despite the fact I was still smarting from the revelation of his new lady friend. "He'd said that it was on Staines' orders, not his."

Alex sucked in air through his teeth. "Staines? The bear? Why would he do that though?"

I couldn't think of any reason that made any sense. I tried to rationalise it. "Maybe he was afraid I'd go in all guns blazing and temper flying, and scare her off."

"Except they were the ones trying to torture her."

"Yeah."

"Does he want the credit of hunting down the necromancer dude for himself?"

"I don't like the guy, but he's never struck me as a glory hound. I just don't get it," I said, frustratedly.

"You could call him and ask. He's on the council, isn't he?"

"I could but..." my voice trailed off.

"What?" prompted Alex.

"I'll lose my temper again. I need to try to act more responsibly if this council is ever going to work. I can't be the one flying off the handle at every moment."

A grin spread across Alex's face. "Is this the new improved Mack Attack that I'm seeing?"

I sighed deeply, the image of Corrigan and the blonde strolling off arm in arm still seared into my brain. "I gave up my shot at happiness when I took on this fucking job. The last thing I need to be doing now is screwing up the job itself."

He patted my shoulder. "You'll work it out."

I wished I had his confidence. Before I could mull it over further, however, a voice came over the train tannoy, announcing that we were pulling into the next station. I tugged at Alex's arm.

"Come on."

He looked confused. "This isn't your stop."

"We're taking a detour."

The train whined as it came to a halt, and the pair of us stepped off onto the platform.

"Dude, this isn't going to be, er..."

"Dangerous? " I smirked slightly at his predictability. "No."

We walked along, dodging the other commuters, and then emerging out into the late afternoon sun. Because we'd disembarked at King's Cross, the streets were predictably busy. I began to hum to myself, a particularly tuneless creation that matched my melancholy mood. Alex sent me a sidelong glance, then started to snap his fingers at various intervals, speeding up as he went along, and forcing me to change my beat.

"Woohoowooooooh," he sang, with even less musical dexterity than I was managing.

"Oh, oh, oh, oh, ohhhhh," I continued.

He injected a little skip into his step. "Beedebopdelooolah!"

A harried looking woman pushing a pram gave us a funny look. Alex beamed at her and linked my arm in his, pulling me along with him until the pair of us were both bounding down the pavement and singing at the top of our lungs. I directed him to the left and we continued down the street in the same manner, eventually coming to a halt in front of a large brown building that curved its way in both directions around the street corner.

I gave him a grateful look. "Thanks for that."

He reached over and gave me a wrist jolting high five, then looked at where we were, raising his eyebrows. "Great Ormond Street Children's Hospital?"

I nodded.

"I know that bruise on your face is looking kind of dodgy, Mack Attack, but you're not normally so keen to jump in to see a doctor." A furrow creased his brow. "You're not a child either."

I grinned, and pulled him over to the main entrance, veering to the left once we were inside and doing my best to ignore the clinical odour, which hung unpleasantly in the air. We weaved our way along the sterile white corridor, passing the full gamut of doctors, nurses and visitors. One couple in particular caught my eye: a slightly older man with his arm tightly round a woman who I presumed to be his wife. Both their eyes were red-rimmed. I swallowed, and my resolve strengthened further. Alex remained quiet, although I was very aware of the tension that he was exuding.

Before too long we ended up in a small waiting room. I gave both of our names to the receptionist, and she handed over two brightly coloured 'Welcome Packs'. I took both and then sat down, handing one to Alex.

"You may as well make yourself useful," I commented, "seeing as how you're here."

His face paled as he scanned the red and blue folder, realising the purpose of our visit. "Mack Attack," he whispered, "I hate needles."

"Shush," I said, flipping over the pages and starting to fill out the first form.

He watched me for a few moments, and then sighed and began to do the same. The first page was easy; just basic details of name, age, address, that type of thing. Opting for the safety of a lie, rather than the danger of the truth, I was about to write in an invented address, then, on the spur of the moment, changed my mind and scratched down the address for the Brethren's keep. I didn't want to use my real address on the off chance that something which hinted at my bloodfire emerged from whatever tests were undertaken before my blood was donated to a living patient. However, it amused me that the shifters would end up receiving no end of NHS leaflets; and they could easily disavow any knowledge of my existence if there were to be any problems. Besides, it would piss off Corrigan to get junk mail with my name on it. Petty, I knew, but he had been rubbing into my face the fact he'd already moved on. This would make sure he didn't forget that I existed. Yes, it was ridiculously childish behavior - but I couldn't be smart and responsible all the time, could I?

I hovered over blood type for a moment, finally ticking the box that stated 'unknown'. I really would have to hope that when the lab actually tested my type it came up as something vaguely normal and didn't spontaneously combust inside a test-tube, or anything weird like that. Thinking of the tragic couple we'd passed on the way here made it a danger I was pretty sure I could swallow.

"Is this really a very good idea?"

I ignored Alex's question, and flipped over to the next page, then ticked off the answers as I went. Have you ever had malaria? No. Have you tested positive for AIDS or HIV? No. Have you paid a prostitute for sex in the last twelve months? No. In the past 12 months, have you had an accidental needlestick or come into contact with someone else's blood? Er, I'd come into contact with quite a lot of blood, but not in the sense that I thought the questionnaire was focusing on. I ticked No.

Then there was a series of questions regarding my recent sexual partners. There had only been one since I'd left Cornwall and I had to admit I knew very little of the truth about who else Corrigan had been with before me. Doing what I could, I made educated guesses, assuming that The Lord Alpha didn't have HIV, hadn't recently slept with another man, and was free from hepatitis. Unfortunately, all the questions put me in mind of his perfectly presented blonde again - and just what he was doing with her right at this particular moment in time. A spark of bloodfire flared up, but I quickly dampened it. This was neither the time nor the place to allow that to happen.

There were some more pages of information following the forms. I scanned through them quickly, not paying a huge amount of attention. I skipped the long list of conditions that apparently precluded people from donating blood. I didn't think being able to transform into a dragon would have made it onto the NHS guidelines, so I reckoned I was probably safe.

As soon as I was done, I glanced over at Alex. He was signing his name at the bottom. Interestingly, there was a remarkably green tinge to his skin.

"You don't have to do this, you know," I said, suddenly feeling guilty for dragging him along.

"No, you're right, it's a good idea. Just," he leaned over so his voice wouldn't carry, "what exactly will your freaky Draco Wyr blood do to a patient?"

I shrugged. "It's meant to have healing properties. I don't know how far that carries. I don't know if donating blood this way will help anyone. But it's got to be worth a try. It healed a fucking vampire," I reminded him. "Why can't it heal some sick kid?"

He looked pensive. "It's addictive, though, isn't it? It made that dude in Cornwall, the one you didn't like, go all nutzoid."

"You mean Anton. And, yes, it did. Iabartu also said something similar about it. But Aubrey had no interest in drinking it once he'd turned human so it might just affect Otherworlders."

"And if it doesn't?"

"The addiction is temporary. And whoever ends up receiving my blood isn't going to know where it came from. Being cured of cancer is surely worth a couple of days of strange cravings." I gave the mage a serious look. "I've thought this through, Alex. And I've got a book that the Fae translated for me that gives lots of information about the Draco Wyr. It definitely said there are no adverse effects on humans if they come into contact with my blood. I'm going to take getting hooked as an adverse effect. I really don't think it'll be a problem."

He yelped slightly, drawing looks from the other would-be blood donors in the room. He lowered his voice again, but his tone remained urgent. "A book about the Draco Wyr? Why didn't you tell me before? What else does it say?"

I opened my mouth to speak again, but was interrupted as the figure of a smiling nurse appeared in front of us. "All done?"

I smiled back and handed over my forms. Alex did the same, but elbowed me sharply in the ribs as he did so, as if to remind me that this conversation was most definitely not over. I gave him a demure look of innocence and then we both followed the nurse into a larger room, which had various reclining beds set up. I continued forward, sitting down as the nurse bade me to do, then looked back at Alex. He had stopped at the entrance and was staring aghast at the set up. He still looked green. When he clocked me watching him, he swallowed, his Adam's apple violently bobbing up and down, and then came and sat on the bed next to me.

"I hate you for this," he murmured sickly to me.

"Is it your first time?" asked the nurse.

The pair of us nodded in agreement.

"Okay then," she said kindly, taking pains not to notice his trepidation. "I'm just going to prick the tip of your finger to test your haemoglobin levels, and then, if everything is okay, we'll get started."

She moved over to Alex first, using a small lancet. He withdrew his breath sharply, then the nurse moved over to a small table.

"All good," she called out cheerily, a moment later.

"Excellent," responded Alex, sounding as if it was anything but.

The nurse headed in my direction with a fresh lancet. I barely felt the prick, observing with interest as she collected the tiny sample. She returned to her table, and remained there, frowning slightly. Uh oh.

"Is something wrong?" I asked, suddenly feeling slightly nervous about what exactly my bloodfire might be doing.

"Oh no, not really," she flicked me a quick glance filled with reassurance. "It's just that your levels are slightly on the low side. Nothing to worry about, of course, you might just need some more iron in your diet that's all. It's completely normal for a woman of your age."

Disappointed, I watched her carefully for her reaction. "Does that mean I can't give blood?"

"No, I think you'll be alright. It's not so low as to prevent you from donating. We might send your blood in for a couple of extra tests though." She smiled at me. "Just in case."

"Um, what kind of tests?"

"Anaemia, sickle cell deficiency, that kind of thing. It's really nothing to worry about. If you're concerned in any way though, we can easily delay your actual donation for a few weeks."

I shook my head vigorously. I didn't really like the idea of my blood undergoing a battery of tests, but I figured it would be to look for specific known problems. Being a dragon probably wasn't something that even the helpful people at Great Ormond Street Hospital would think to look for. And, considering the situation with Endor, goodness knew where I'd be or what would be happening in a few weeks' time. I wanted to get this done now, while I still could. Even if my weird Draco Wyr blood only helped one person, that would be enough.

"Okay then. Who would like to go first?" she asked.

Sneaking a look at the pallor on Alex's face, I volunteered. The nurse took a band and fixed it tightly round my upper arm, then slowly inserted the needle. I watched, fascinated, as my blood began to snake its way out. It certainly didn't look any different to anyone's else's.

"I'm going to be sick," moaned Alex.

"It's fine," I reassured him. "You can hardly feel it."

"But it's so...so...*red*," he exclaimed. "Anyway, I thought we were going to be doing something about money, Mack Attack."

"All in good time."

The nurse moved over to Alex, instructing him to look away. He moaned again, and turned his face towards me, screwing his eyes tightly shut. I shook my head. Given all that we'd been through since we'd known each other, I'd have expected Alex to cope with this a little better. When she inserted the needle, he gave out a little shriek. The nurse patted him on the shoulder.

"There now, just ten minutes and you're all done."

He sniffed and nodded, keeping his eyes firmly closed. There was a clatter from behind, and the nurse looked up, holding her hand towards me to indicate she would be back in a few minutes. I gave her a nod of acknowledgement then, once she'd gone, turned back to Alex.

"You were asking about the money?"

He didn't respond.

"Alex! Hey! You were asking me about the money."

"Mmm."

I guessed that was the most I was going to get out of him for now. I continued. "Well, the thing is, I was round at Balud's this morning." I quickly outlined what the troll had told me, and that the expected cost of making a bunch of palladium based weapons was going to be high. "So my plan is to go home after this and send out an email to all the council members and get them to talk to their organisations for some cash."

Alex's eyes flew open. "What? No! You can't do that!"

Okaydokey. That wasn't quite the reaction I'd been hoping for. Apparently it was possible to bring him out of his needle-induced nausea, after all. I eyed him warily.

"Why not? We need the money to get the metal. We need the metal to make the weapons. We need the weapons to defeat fucking Endor."

"The Ministry doesn't have any money."

"I know they don't have much, but..."

"No, Mack Attack, they really don't have any money. Every missive I've been sent recently has been about how we can start to raise some funds. You have no idea how hard the recession has hit us."

"If there's no money, then the Arch-Mage can just decline. The Brethren and the Fae will step up. I wasn't expecting much from your lot's side anyway."

"You're forgetting the politics. The Arch-Mage can't be seen to be the only person not stepping up to the plate. If the faeries and the furries give money, then we have to as well. Otherwise the loss of face will be catastrophic. We'll have no choice but to match whatever the others put in, and that will completely bankrupt us."

"That's so fucking stupid!"

He shrugged expressively, a troubled look crossing his sun-kissed face. "You can't just avoid asking the Ministry to contribute either. If it got out that you, as the all-powerful dragon council leader, went to everyone else except us for money, then the result would be even worse. No-one likes being made to feel like an object of pity."

Outfuckingstanding. "I need to get hold of palladium, Alex."

He sighed. "Let me see what I can do first. There must be some other way to source it without having to pay for it."

That sounded a hell of a lot like stealing to me. I gave in for the time being, however, murmuring a reluctant assent. "Just don't take too fucking long. Goodness knows when Endor will decide to show up again."

The nurse bustled back in, removed the needles and swabbed over the small wounds on our arms, before covering them with a blob of cotton wool and some surgical tape.

"There now, that wasn't so bad, was it?"

Alex grunted weakly in return. At the very least, the colour was starting to return to his cheeks. She handed us both over a biscuit and cup of something luridly orange.

"Just lie back, and relax, and finish those off, then you'll be good to go."

"Thanks," I said, looking doubtfully down at the drink.

"Would you like me to take a look at your face while you're here?"

"No, it's alright. It looks worse than it is, honest. I just walked into a door this morning, that's all."

Both the nurse and Alex gazed at me with unmistakable skepticism. I gave a short laugh, more out of continued exasperation than humour. "No, really I did. But thanks again, anyway."

"Yeah, thanks," agreed Alex. He arched an eyebrow at me. "While we're waiting, Mackenzie, you can tell me all about that book you've been reading." He sent me a pointed look.

I took a sip, wincing at the rush of sugar that the juice provided, "Sure," I said, unenthusiastically. "I can't wait."

Chapter Six

Once the nurse had disappeared to deal with her next donors, Alex propped himself up on one elbow and fixed me with a serious look. He'd recovered so miraculously from his terror of giving blood that I was having doubts it had been anything other than a vaguely psychosomatic induced hysteria.

"So? Spill all the gory details, Mack Attack."

I sighed. "I have a book. Or rather the book has me; I'm not entirely sure which."

At Alex's quizzical look, I explained further. "I found it in Clava Books. The original Clava Books in Inverness. Then the shop burnt down and I thought it was lost forever. Until, that is, I was wandering along the shelves of the mages' library at the academy and it showed up again."

"Another edition?"

"No, I'm actually pretty sure it was the same book." I tucked a curl of hair behind my ear uncomfortably. "I know it sounds daft, but…"

"No, dude, not at all. There are more sentient books around than you'd think. It stands to reason, if there was one about the Draco Wyr, then it'd be one of those."

I was reminded for a moment that, despite Alex's apparent fear of confrontation and his surfer dude persona, he was still a remarkably competent mage and I didn't often give him the credit he was due. Shooting him a grateful look for not being more cynical about the book's origins, I continued on.

"Anyway, it was written in Fae runes so it was a fucking pain trying to work out what it all meant. I had a dictionary, and I know some of the more basic runes, but…"

Alex nodded vigorously. "Yeah, I never got much further than the faerie equivalent of Where The

Wild Things Are."

Slightly distracted at the idea the Fae's version of that famous kids' book probably had the humans as the 'wild things', I shook my head to clear away the peculiar vision and stuck to the subject.

"Well, to cut a long story short, I gave it to Solus and he got it translated for me. I've had it for a while, except every time I was going to read it, something came up."

"But you've read it now?" he prompted.

"Yes, Alex, I've read it now. I finished it yesterday."

"And?"

"And what?" I knew I was being deliberately obtuse, but for some reason I didn't really feel that comfortable talking about my heritage, even to Alex. There was a lot about it that was just too weird.

Alex pulled himself up to a sitting position then blinked several times. "Whoa, head rush." He looked directly into my eyes. "It's okay, Mack. You don't have to talk about it if you don't want to."

I felt a rush of warmth towards my magic mate, then stared down at my feet and came to a decision. "None of it is that surprising. There's stuff about where the Draco Wyr originally came from. We really are descended from honest to goodness dragons. Well," I paused, "one dragon, anyway. We pretty much always have red hair. We always have bad tempers. A lot of my ancestors apparently died young as a result of picking just one too many fights. There were vast amounts who where just hunted down though. You know," I said shifting, uncomfortably, "because of the crazy addictive blood with unbelievable healing properties."

Alex raised his eyebrows. "Yeah, I can see why it would be a good idea to keep it as secret as possible and not go giving away any of that blood. Especially not to knowledgeable medical personnel who are going to test it."

I waved him away. "They're testing it for human stuff, not Otherworld stuff. Nothing's going to show up."

"You hope," he returned grimly.

"It's a calculated risk. It's not like I'm handing it over to vampires or demi-goddesses or anyone like that."

"Hmmm," he murmured, in a non-committal manner.

"Besides, by the sounds of things, my bigger worry as a Draco Wyr should be ancestors of this warrior guy called Bolux. He killed the original Draco Wyr, but died of his injuries as a result. All his descendants have sworn through the centuries to make the Draco Wyr extinct, once and for all."

Alex whistled. "Sheeeeit. That's not great."

"No," I agreed. "In fact, it seems as if they were pretty much successful. By the time of the Great Fire of London back in 1666 –which was the result of a Draco Wyr inspired fight - they banded together to make a concerted effort to rid the Earth of my race. By all accounts, they succeeded. In theory, the knowledge and desire to slaughter as many Draco Wyr as possible died out because there were no more Draco Wyr to go after."

"But you're here," he pointed out.

"That I am. There were hints in the book that at

least one family had managed to escape the Bolux-inspired scourge, but there was nothing concrete."

"Of course, if they survived and, as a result, you are here now, it stands to reason that the same might be true of these warrior dudes."

"Yeah." I fell into silence for a moment, brooding over the other revelations the book had offered.

"Maybe that's the reason why your mother left you with the pack in Cornwall when you were just a kid. They were after her and you, and it was a good place to hide. She pretty much said so in the letter we found, which she had given to your old alpha, didn't she? That 'they' were getting closer and something terrible would happen if they caught you?"

I nodded. "She wasn't a Draco Wyr though."

"How do you know?"

"She was scared of me, Alex. In that same letter, she said how terrified she was of my power. If she was a Draco Wyr too, then she wouldn't have felt that way. She'd have known how to deal with it. She must have been human." A bitter note entered my voice. "She was fucking afraid of me, Alex. I was just a kid and she was scared of me. That's what kind of monster I am."

"Dude! You're not a monster! What the hell are you saying that for?"

I raised my eyes for a moment and stared at him balefully. "Maybe because it's true."

"No. No way, Mack," he said, vigorously shaking his head. "You're the most loyal, the most thoughtful, and the most heroic person I know. You are *not* a monster. " The corner of his mouth lifted up. "You have a shitty temper but, let's face it, you are a woman. It goes with the territory."

I leaned over to where he was sitting and thumped him on the arm. He let out a mock squeal of pain. "You're not a monster," he repeated fervently.

I gave him a half smile. "Thanks." Now if only I could believe that myself, I'd be set.

We were both silent for a few moments, then Alex spoke again. "So if your mum is human, then you must be a Draco Wyr because of your dad. What happened to him?"

"I don't know," I said quietly. "I don't remember anything about him. My mother never so much as mentioned him. The thing is," I swallowed and looked in Alex's eyes, "and you can't ever tell anyone this, but the book said that..." My voice drifted off for a moment. Alex just waited. I took a deep breath and tried again. "The book said that Draco Wyr are almost always born as twins. Something to do with fallopian tubes and dividing eggs. Biological stuff."

I tried to look nonchalant. Alex's mouth, however, dropped open. "There's another one of you? Nooooooo way."

"Yes way. Or probably yes way. I don't know."

"Wow. Another Mack Attack."

"It almost doesn't bear thinking about, does it?"

"Wow. I mean, wow. And you don't remember...?"

I shook my head. "Nope."

"Damn."

Alex absorbed that information for a little

longer, clearly as stunned as I had been when I'd read it only yesterday. "Who else knows this?"

"Solus definitely. I'm not sure if it was him who translated the book. Even if it wasn't, he's pretty loyal to the Summer Queen, so goodness knows how many Fae actually know."

"Do you think they'll blab?" His expression was serious.

"No. It'll suit them to know more than everyone else. I think the Fae, as a whole, enjoy feeling superior to everyone else."

Alex laughed slightly. "You're not wrong there. So, what did the book say about the magic stuff? You know, your spooky green fire?"

"Some Draco Wyr manifest it and some don't." I shrugged. "Apparently it's not much of a big deal."

"Are there any other powers that are likely to, um, manifest themselves?"

"Not unless I can get a grip on the whole transformation thing," I said. "If I can manage that without completely losing control of my senses, then I'll be able to theoretically fly, breathe fire and generally destroy anything that gets in my way." I smirked slightly, then started abruptly as I realised something.

"What?"

"When I was in Balud's shop earlier today, he made some weird comment about my eyes. I didn't get the chance to make him tell me what he meant but..."

"Yeah?"

"But according to the book, that's sometimes meant to be an indication a Draco Wyr is about to shift. If their eyes start glowing."

Alex looked suddenly alarmed. He jumped up, shoulders tense and looked around the room, then grabbed me by the shoulders and looked deep into my eyes. "Is it about to happen? Here? Can you stop it?"

I laughed. "Relax, I feel fine. It was probably nothing. I think being here in this hospital and being drained of a pint of blood has had a remarkably calming effect. I don't even feel that pissed off at Corrigan any more. I should definitely do this more often."

He raised his eyebrows. "You really like him, don't you? Corrigan?"

I stared down at my shoes again. "According to the book, he's my soul-mate."

Alex didn't immediately say anything. I sneaked a glance up at his face. His eyes were wide.

"It says that if I can initiate the Voice with someone, then it means they're my soul-mate," I explained.

He blinked, but still remained silent.

"And he hates me," I said simply. "I had to choose between him and the council, and for the sake of making everyone work together to bring down Endor, I chose the council. You saw him earlier. He not only hates me, but he's already moved on. I thought that if we could find Endor quickly and get rid of him then there might be a chance to make things up to him and get him back, but now I don't think that'll work." A ripple of fire ran up my spine and, despite its heat, I shivered.

"So let me get this straight," said Alex slowly,

"you have a secret hidden twin. You were abandoned as a child and you don't know who your father is. You're trying to manage a high-powered job in the middle of the worst recession the country has seen for decades. There's a super-villain with murderous tendencies and shadowy motives after you and many others. And you're in love with someone who hates you."

"Pretty much," I said sadly.

"Well, you know what this means," he said, in a particularly sombre tone.

"What?"

"We need to get working on a theme tune right away. Because if this isn't a soap opera, darling, then I don't know what is."

We looked at each other and simultaneously burst out laughing. I stood up, ignoring the slight wave of dizziness the action gave me, and grabbed Alex in a hug.

He squeezed me tightly back. "How about 'Beedebopdelooolah'?"

"Sounds great," I said into his shoulder. "Come on, let's get out of here."

"You got it, Mack Attack. But we should come up with a code word first, you know. In case your, no doubt, evil twin shows up and pretends to be you. Then you can warn me and I can run away in time."

I grinned. "Beedebopdelooolah."

Chapter Seven

Unburdening myself to Alex had a remarkably cathartic effect. Now that there was someone else who knew all the book's secrets, I no longer felt I was alone. I was nigglingly aware of Solus and the way he had repeatedly urged me to get around to reading the translation but, after his role in forcing me to become head of the council, I wasn't convinced that I wanted to sit around discussing my life and all its possibilities with him. I had to admit, even to myself, that the twin thing had me rather fazed. To quote the book directly, it had stated that the 'majority of Draco Wyr' were born as twins. So that didn't necessarily mean it was true in my case. The fact I had no knowledge or memory of anything even remotely sibling related made me think I could be one of the exceptions to the rule. Of course, I had no knowledge or memory of a father either. Let's face it, there definitely had to have been someone in that role at some point, no matter how fleeting their, er, physical presence had been. However, in the absence of anything or anyone to prove or disprove the twin theory, I had no option right now but to completely ignore it. Perhaps if there wasn't the increasingly frustrating case of Endor to deal with, then I might have considered devoting some time towards investigating it further. As it was, I really did have bigger fish to fry.

Leaving Alex at the gates of the hospital, with strict instructions to look into getting hold of large quantities of palladium as a matter of extreme urgency, I headed for home. I decided to check in briefly at Clava Books, then take a nap. Once darkness fell, I'd venture out on the streets when all the real nasties were around. Even if I didn't bump into anyone darkly evil enough to know where Endor might be, beating a few of the less desirable members of the Otherworld up would at least give me something to do, and feed my burgeoning desire for action. The pathetic fight with the shifters just hadn't cut it.

When I finally stepped off the train at my home station and trotted down the steps onto the busy little shopping thoroughfare, the light in the sky was already starting to dim. I wended my way towards the little bookshop, humming the same tune that Alex and I had created, then dodged out of the path of a small child clutching a melting ice-cream and staring up at me with huge shocked eyes. I grinned at him, trying to be friendly, but his face crumpled and he started to wail. His mother yanked his arm, pulling him away, and sent me a vicious look. Tingles of irritated bloodfire prickled at my skin. And then at the back of my neck. I almost stopped and turned around but managed to catch myself just in time. Someone, or something, was following me. Please let it be Endor, I silently prayed. The first time I'd ever met him had been around this area so it wasn't beyond the realms of possibility that he'd be stupid enough to come back. Please, please, please.

Without breaking my stride, I turned right rather than continuing forward. I needed to draw whoever it was away from the bookshop and instead to somewhere more secluded where I could confront them. If I'd been right about my eyes glowing earlier, then perhaps I was ripe to transform into a dragon again. I didn't want to; I was still terrified about what I could become inside when that happened - especially in this crowded little borough of London. Goodness only knew what the result might be. However, if I had no other choice...I set my mouth into a grim line. Bring it on.

I reached into my back pocket and brought out the letter from Alex, halting for a moment and pretending to study it. It was hardly a sophisticated move, but I'd have to hope that Endor had enough of a hard-on to come and attack me to not suspect anything untoward. I let it drop, exclaiming overtly loud irritation, then bent down to scoop it up, carefully watching the side mirror of a nearby parked car as I did so. I was completely baffled by what I saw. Apparently I was being tracked by a giant penguin. Okaydokey. Either it was some new kind of Otherworld creature that I'd not yet come across, or I was going completely crazy.

Abandoning my more cautious instincts, I glanced over my shoulder. The penguin, trying to conceal itself from my sight, immediately shoved its body in a particularly ungainly fashion into a doorway. Its beak and protruding stomach were still clearly visible. There was no way that this was going to end up being the elusive Endor. I turned my head to the front again, as if to continue my amble, and took a few steps. Then I pivoted around, just in time to see the penguin suddenly waddling in an alarmed fashion to the side of the pavement and ungracefully falling over onto its back.

I stalked over to it, and kicked its large soft stomach. "What's the fucking deal? Who are you and why are you following me?"

"Mmmmph," it said.

I kicked it again. The penguin rolled left and then right, in an apparent bid to try to get back up again. Its webbed orange feet flapped helplessly in the air.

"Mmmmph," it repeated.

I rolled my eyes and moved over to the thing's head, pulling it by the beak until the head came off and the face underneath was revealed. When I saw who it was, I stared down in exasperation.

"What the fuck are you doing, Aubrey?"

"Hi, Mack." The ex-vampire grinned up at me weakly.

I shook my head, placing my hands on my hips and watching him continue to twist around to try and get back onto his feet. Eventually I got bored of his attempts and stuck out a hand, pulling him up.

"Thanks," he chirped out.

"I'll say it again. What the fuck are you doing?"

He appeared momentarily nonplussed. "Well, following you, of course."

I frowned in annoyance. "That much I worked out. Why?"

"Because you're big and strong and can protect me. Well, you're not big, but you're strong. I thought that maybe if I just stuck close to you then no-one would attack me because they'd be too worried about you. I didn't think you'd notice me."

"You're a bloody idiot," I hissed. "You're dressed

like a giant furry cartoon character who'd be better handing out leaflets in the street. How the fuck could I not notice you?"

A hurt look crossed his face. "It protects me from the sun."

"The sun's not going to hurt you, Aubrey. Newsflash: you're not a vampire anymore."

"I needed a disguise," he whined. "They're trying to track me down, Mack." He clutched at my hand with his large fluffy wings. "You can't let them take me. You can't!" Clearly the past few days of alone time hadn't done much to rid him of his self-induced petulance.

I yanked my hand away. "You mean the vamps," I said flatly.

"Of course, the vamps! Who else?"

"I've got other things to worry about than a bunch of bloodsuckers, Aubrey. Besides, if you go to them then maybe you'll get your heart's desire and they'll change you back." I smiled at him predatorily. "That way I'll no longer have any compunction about staking you."

His bottom lip stuck out. "That's mean, Mack. If I go back to them, they'll probably take advantage of the fact that I'm now a human and just bleed me dry. They won't change me back, they'll leave me as some kind of dried out husk. Or," he shuddered, "they'll lock me away and feed on me whenever it suits them."

The tone in his voice made me suspect that this was something that had happened before to some poor unsuspecting victims. Probably on his orders. My eyes narrowed. "Perhaps they'll welcome you back with open arms. The prodigal vampire returns to the bosom of his loving family."

Aubrey wrapped his wings around himself. "I don't think they'll see it like that."

"Why not?" I was only vaguely curious.

He looked slightly embarrassed. "I wasn't always very nice."

I snorted. That was hardly headline material.

"Besides," he continued, "I thought you wanted me to be human. You know, new life, start afresh, that kind of thing."

"And I thought you couldn't think of anything worse and you were desperate to get some of your old buddies to bite you and turn you back."

"I'm not sure they're my buddies anymore," he said in a small voice. He shrugged. "Maybe being human isn't so bad either." A glint entered his eyes. "This morning, I had a burger. For breakfast! You wouldn't believe the taste! The gherkins were sharp but tasty. The patty was full of meaty goodness. The tomatoes were red and juicy..." A dreamy look came over his face. "Red and juicy..."

Okay, that was quite enough of that. Feeling faintly nauseated, I leaned into his face. "Why me, Aubrey? Why do you have to bother me?"

"I thought we were friends! I helped you. At Haughmond Hill. We kicked butt together."

"Actually, no, we didn't. Nobody kicked butt."

"I'm under oath to do whatever you say! I can't refuse, remember? I can't even leave your side."

"Except you've been away from my side for the last three days so clearly that particular side-effect has worn off," I pointed out.

He bounced around. "I got you pizza!"

"You are indispensable," I said sarcastically.

Aubrey's head drooped.

I watched him for a moment then, like a mug, I gave in. "Fine," I said. "But you have to take off that ridiculous outfit."

"I'll be recognised! They'll come and take me away!"

I was really going to regret this. Especially considering the offer I'd had from his old mate back in Alcazon. I imagined myself walking up to the nearest wall and slamming my head into it several times. I sighed deeply.

"Aubrey, if you don't want to go with them, then I won't let them take you. All right?"

He peeked up at me, a grin blossoming across his face. "Really?"

"Really." I cursed myself for being an idiot. I was going to have to make damn sure that nobody else discovered that the vamps would give us info about Endor's location in return for Aubrey or I'd be laughed out of the council. Sooner or later, his undead ex-friends would find out where he was - and what he was - and there would be shit to pay. It just didn't seem right though, cold-heartedly handing him over to them, no matter what he'd done to me and mine in the past. Yes, I was a total fuckwit.

"Come on then."

He jumped up in the air, penguin belly flopping up and down as he did so. "Yay!"

"Where did you get that costume from?"

"Do you really want to know?"

I considered. Actually… "No."

He bent over and picked the bird head up, and shoved it back on again. Then he hooked his wing around my shoulder and we began walking, very slowly, heading out onto the main street. A man in a penguin suit and a woman who looked as if she'd gone for five rounds with Mike Tyson. What could be less inconspicuous?

*

The tiny bell hanging above the door of Clava Books signaled our entry. Or rather it signaled my entry, anyway. Aubrey, still clad in full penguin gear as he was, managed to get stuck within the door frame. I had to grab both of his wings in order to squeeze him through and, when I finally did manage to yank him hard enough, he propelled through with such force that he knocked me off my feet and landed sprawled on top of me.

"Feck," cackled Slim from somewhere above, "and I thought that penguins were flightless."

My answering remark was lost within the soft downy fur of the costume. It was probably just as well.

"Goodness me!" I heard Mrs. Alcoon exclaim. "Is that you, Mackenzie dear?"

I lifted my knees up, managing to push the rather voluminous shape of Aubrey off, and clambered to my feet.

"Hi there," I said, somewhat anticlimactically.

"That's not your young man trying to go incognito, is it?"

I was pretty sure Aubrey wasn't the 'young man' Mrs. Alcoon meant when she said that. Not that the idea of Corrigan in a penguin suit didn't hold a certain kind of odd appeal, however.

"It's Aubrey," I answered shortly.

"Aubrey! How wonderful! Where have you been? Are you going to a fancy dress party?"

There was some kind of muffled response from within the confines of Aubrey's penguin head. I shook my head at the ridiculousness of the entire situation. "He's trying to hide out from the vampires who have decided that they want him back."

"Oh dear. They don't want him back in a good way, do they?"

I snorted. "No. I don't think they do."

"What the feck happened to your face then? Lose your temper and attack someone?"

I scowled at the little gargoyle. "I walked into a door."

He stared at me for a moment, eyes widening, and then his mouth opened in some kind of bizarre wheeze that just seemed to get louder and louder, until I was starting to think that he was choking to death.

"Walked into a door? Walked into a fecking door? The big scary Mack Smith is wandering around with a bruise the size of an elephant on her face because she walked into a door?" He wheezed again.

"Mr. Slim, you are not helping matters." Mrs. Alcoon peered at me. "Are you alright, dear? Does it hurt?" She reached out to pat me on the arm, and then noticed the cotton wool swab still attached to my skin. "Mackenzie, what is that?" Her voice sounded rather strange.

I raised my eyebrows. "What happened to your concern with my face?"

She jerked her hand in the air. "I was just being nice. Clearly it's a superficial mark that's a mere result of your clumsiness."

I opened my mouth to complain, but she continued on before I could speak. "That thing on your arm is something entirely different."

"Not really. I just stopped off at the hospital to donate some blood, that's all."

I could tell by the tightening around the older woman's mouth that she disapproved. "And they let you?"

Feeling rather irritated by now, I sounded sharper than I intended to. "Well, they didn't ask me if I was a dragon first, if that's what you mean."

Then I realised what I'd said and cast a quick worried glance down at Aubrey. I'd been trying to keep my Draco Wyr identity secret from him. Just in case he did indeed somehow end up back with the slimy vamps after all. Fortunately, however, he seemed more focused on still trying to push himself to an upright position and didn't appear to have heard. Although it was difficult to tell considering he still looked like a giant penguin.

"That's not what I meant at all. You shouldn't have done it, Mackenzie, you really shouldn't."

"Donating my blood might help people, Mrs. Alcoon. Really help them."

"It's not people that concern me, dear, it's you. You shouldn't be doing that kind of thing."

"Why not?" I put my hands on my hips. She actually seemed rather angry, for probably the first time since I'd ever known her.

"Feck's sake, girl," butted in Slim, "it doesn't take a genius to work out why."

"They're human," I said tiredly. "They're not going to be able to tell anything from my blood whatsoever. They'll give it to some sick kids who just might end up getting a hell of a lot better. What's wrong with that?"

Mrs. Alcoon didn't answer. There was a troubled expression in her eyes though. "Will you please not do that again, Mackenzie? At least until…well, just please don't do it again for a few months."

I looked at her suspiciously. "Is this some kind of precognition thing you've got going on?"

"Mackenzie, dear…"

I threw my hands up in the air. She could be a stubborn biddy when she wanted to be. "Fine! I can't donate blood again anyway for another four months even if I wanted to."

"Good." Satisfied, she turned away. "I'm going to make a cup of tea. Who wants one?"

Nobody answered. Even Aubrey seemed to have stopped his writhing on the floor for the time being. "Excellent," she said, more to herself than to any of us. "I'll brew a big pot for us all."

I rolled my eyes, and glanced over at Slim. He was hovering in the air, little wings flapping at his back, and watching the old lady go with a speculative look on his face.

"Slim?"

"Hmmm?"

"Have you found anything?"

"Eh?"

"Have you found anything out about Endor?"

Aubrey started making strange noises. He appeared to be rolling around on the floor with increased vigour. I ignored him.

"No."

I stared at him. "What? That's it? Just 'no'?"

He shrugged. "There's nothing. No books. Nothing that fecking gives any clue as to who he really is or where he's come from."

"What about necromancy in general?"

"It's a nasty business and you shouldn't do it."

"For fuck's sake, Slim…"

He scratched unhappily underneath the scarf concealing his nether regions from the delicate sensibilities of Mrs. Alcoon in a gesture that, while really rather off-putting, also hinted at the frustration he felt at uncovering absolutely nothing. "There's nothing new. I can't fecking help you."

"The mages' library at the academy…?"

"Exactly the same. Whoever your Endor is, he's managed to stay out of the Otherworld limelight."

Sodding hell. It was as if he was some kind of ghost. I rubbed my forehead tiredly and wondered when on earth we were going to get a break. Aubrey broke into my thoughts by moaning again from within his penguin suit. Tired of watching him flail around, I reached down and gave him a helping hand back to his feet. Using his two massive wings, he started pointing and jumping up and down. Maybe he had ants in his pants or something.

"Okay then," I said to Slim, all business-like and trying to find some way of getting hold of even a tiny scrap of useful information. "How about what he's planning to do? We know from the Batibat that he is going after the four elements. We just don't know which one he's going for next or how he's going to try and harness it. Can you look for anything to do with that?"

Slim nodded grudgingly. He seemed embarrassed that his beloved books had come up short thus far. At least it meant he had a strong impetus to keep attempting to discover something valid.

There was a sudden loud thump as Aubrey succeeded in pulling off the penguin head all by himself but, in doing so, fell clumsily against a nearby bookshelf. His cheeks were bright red and he was breathing with heavy exertion.

"You're not listening to me!"

The pair of us just looked at him. I gestured for him to speak.

"I said I know someone who knows Endor," he exclaimed.

My eyes widened. "What? Why the fuck didn't you say something before?"

He flapped his wings against his body. "I did! You weren't listening!"

I took a deep breath and forced myself to calm down. "Where is this person?"

"I've not just been hiding under a rock for the last four days, you know. I've been trying to help, Mack," he said, not answering the question.

"Aubrey," I started, the warning audible in my tone.

"I tried to see what I could find out about him. You know, talk to some of my old contacts, that kind of thing. At great personal risk to myself, I might add. I wore a wolf's head and told them I'd lost a bet with a shapeshifter. If they'd tried to make me take it off though..."

"Aubrey!"

"I mean, really, I was being incredibly brave. I found this one guy, a Fae, after days of hunting and managed to learn from him that there are people who know who Endor is and where he can be found. Just because they don't move in your circles, doesn't mean they don't exist, you know."

"AUBREY!"

He looked at me. "What?"

"Who?"

"Huh?"

I gritted my teeth. "Who is it? Who knows Endor? Tell me now or, so help me God, I will not be responsible for my actions!"

"Oh," he cocked his head to one side. "A Fae. An UnSeelie Fae by the name of Tarn. Runs a nightclub over in Soho called Circle. Poncey place, if you ask me."

I nodded. "Okay." I glanced at Slim. "Tell Mrs. Alcoon I'm sorry about the tea but that I have to go."

He grunted. Then a thought struck me and I turned back to Aubrey. "That's amazingly helpful information, you know. We've been trying to find something concrete about him since we got back to London. You're the only person who's managed to come up with anything. Well done."

Aubrey blinked several times. Then he started to sniff, and his eyes became visibly glassy. He let out a small hiccup. Before he descended into full blown hysterics, I wisely took my leave. I'd done enough crying of my own recently. I didn't need to watch anyone else do the same, even if it was for a happy reason.

Chapter Eight

I checked my watch as I barrelled out of Clava Books and sprinted back home, feeling a burst of sudden renewed energy from Aubrey's intelligence. It was still early evening so that meant that there was plenty of time to prepare myself. Nightclubs weren't generally my thing, and Unseelie Fae nightclubs even less. If I was going to inveigle my way inside and get hold of this Tarn, then I had to be ready for every eventuality. The promise of what could finally be a real lead on Endor's whereabouts had set my bloodfire tingling. I smiled to myself as I unlocked my shiny red front door. It was about time things started to go my way.

Once inside, I quickly plonked myself down at the kitchen table with my laptop, lifting the lid and logging on to the Othernet. As promised, as soon I was connected, huge warning signs and plaintives requesting information about Endor popped up. At least the other council members were doing something right. A photo and caption towards the bottom of the page caught my eye and I frowned, clicking on it. As soon as I did so, a vast photo of Corrigan flashed up. My eyes lingered on it. He was wearing dark trousers and a green shirt that highlighted the jade of his eyes. My stomach squirmed. Quashing down those feelings as best as I could, I scrolled down, staring in horror at what was written there.

Our very own Lord Alpha, pictured here at a local

fundraising event, seems to have gotten himself into a rather fiery situation. After disappearing for a few days, apparently into the wilds of rural Shropshire, he was spotted with an as yet unnamed redhead. Word is that the draconian Brethren leader was smitten. That is until she unceremoniously – and very publicly - gave him the old heave-ho. A lesser man may have burst into flames of eternal embarrassment at the snub. Not so our dark-haired were-panther, however, as the very day after he was spotted with a brand new squeeze. No doubt the mysterious redhead is spitting fire at his fast recovery.

Fucking hell. Seriously fucking hell. I let out an inarticulate yell into the screen and I could feel little explosions of heat flaring up through my intestines. This wasn't just some inane piece of gossip from a tawdry Otherworld blogger. It was effectively calling me out. 'Fiery situation'? 'Draconian brethren leader'? Oh, this self-styled journalist was going to see exactly just how much fire I really was capable of spitting out if I caught up to them. It now appeared that the whole fucking world was about to know about my Draco Wyr heritage. The only thing that this spelled was trouble. Why the fuck couldn't this have happened after Endor was taken care of? Not only was there the chance that the necromancer himself might read it and I'd lose any element of surprise I could have had when I finally tracked him down, transformed into a dragon and bit his sorry little head off, but now I'd have all manner of idiots wanting to know more about me. The way that even the Arch-Mage and the Summer Queen had behaved before the events at Haughmond Hill, with their determination to follow me around and encourage my allegiance to them, had been sickening. I didn't need it from every other Tom, Dick and Otherworld Harry at the same time. And that wasn't even to mention the mysterious 'they' who'd been after my mother, or rather me, in order to theoretically rid the world of the Draco Wyr line once and for all. I thought of Iabartu and what she had tried to do and thumped the table in bitter frustration. I did not fucking need this.

I searched the page for any signs as to who might have written it. They were going to feel my wrath. Except there was no hint anywhere of the author's name. My mouth twisted as I stared angrily at the article. Could it have been Corrigan himself? Was this his way of getting back at me? I shook my head. No. He might have been hurt to the core by what I'd done to him, but there was no way that he'd be this stupid. It had to be someone else. I took in a gulp of air and held it in my lungs, trying desperately to compose myself. I had to focus on the matter at hand – interrogating this Unseelie Fae about Endor – and not my own sorry state of affairs. I exhaled slowly, focusing on the calming techniques that I'd learnt at anger management. Eventually I managed to force my muscles back into a more relaxed position. I'd just have to worry about what the results of the apparent exposé would be later.

Typing in 'Circle nightclub' into the search engine, I took another deep breath. Focus, Mack. I clicked on the first result that came up and a sleekly designed website appeared. I made a note of the address, then searched the rest of the pages to see what else I could dig up. Other than promising an exclusive clientele, designer cocktails and heart-popping beats, there was little other information. Tarn, the nightclub's owner, was conspicuously absent. I'd have to hope that his lack of presence in the virtual world didn't translate into the real world as well. If he wasn't going to be at the club tonight then, in the mood I was in, I might not be responsible for my actions.

Switching quickly over to email, I sent the council members an update on what had happened with Wold. Or rather what hadn't happened with Wold. I included that Slim hadn't yet uncovered anything helpful, but left off the information about Tarn. I didn't want to get anyone's hopes up just yet. I instructed them to tell me what they were up to, and to forward on the list of other planes that they were going to start investigating, and finished with a curt demand for Staines to meet me the following afternoon. I hadn't forgotten about his alleged desire to keep me firmly out of the loop as far as Wold had been concerned, or his orders to do whatever was necessary to extract more information from her. Despite my words to Alex about not wanting to lose my temper, it was high time I put the werebear in his place. If Corrigan thought I was stepping on his toes by doing so, then tough.

I powered down the laptop and closed my eyes. I might not entirely trust him after the events at Alcazon, but I was going to need some help and guidance with this venture and Solus was going to be the best person to provide it. Without raising my voice, I softly called out his name. Nothing happened. I tried again. When all that resulted was the answering silence of my little flat, I peeled off the surgical tape and cotton wool from my arm and started to pick at the already forming scab. I knew that he'd have registered my call, wherever he happened to be, but I was also aware that unless he thought it was an emergency, he'd probably take his sweet time in getting around to showing up. I didn't want to wait.

A tiny drop of blood squeezed out. Using my index finger, I wiped it off then went to my front door and opened it, wandering down the corridor and back into the outside world. I smeared the fleck of blood onto the grey of the pavement, then stood up and leaned against the wall. It didn't take long. There was a buzz in the air behind me, as Solus winked into existence, clearly choosing to materialise himself from within the building so as to avoid any surprised human eyes catching sight of his ability to appear from nowhere. I turned to face him, noting the tentative smile on his handsome face. Without saying a word, I gestured him to my flat, then followed him inside and firmly closed the door behind us.

Solus scanned my face. He was quite obviously desperate to find out exactly what had transpired to cause me to have a huge bruise splashed across my cheekbone, and one very swollen and painful eye, but the air of awkwardness between us thankfully prevented him from doing so.

"What's up, dragonlette?"

"I need to get into the Circle nightclub tonight and talk to Tarn, its owner. Can you help?"

A shadow passed across his indigo eyes. "It's not a very friendly place."

I shrugged. "That's okay. I'm not a very friendly person."

His jaw clenched. "Are we still friends?" he asked softly.

"I understand what happened and why it happened, Solus. I signed on, remember? But I'm pissed off that you couldn't have spoken to me about it beforehand. I thought that I could trust you to have my back."

"I do have your back, dragonlette. I'll always have your back. I'd never do anything to intentionally hurt you, but..."

"But the Summer Queen demands your obeisance," I finished.

"She's only trying to do what's best for everyone."

I sighed heavily. "As are we all." I eyed the Fae. If I could forgive Aubrey for what he'd done in the past by being practically responsible for the deaths of two of my friends, then I guessed I could forgive Solus for not warning me beforehand about what was going to happen at Alcazon. "It's okay. I get it. And it's done now, let's just move on."

Solus' eyes searched mine, then he seemed to relax. "Did you read the book?"

I nodded mutely.

"He'll come around, dragonlette. Once all this is over, he'll realise the error of his ways and the two of you can live happily ever after."

I wasn't quite so sure about that. Before I could say anything, however, a mischievous gleam lit up his face. "And if Corrigan doesn't, I'm always here."

I shot him a look of exasperation. "Who translated the book, Solus?"

"Me." The surprise must have shown on my face because he elaborated further. "I didn't want everyone knowing what was in it. I love my extended Fae family but, well, they are Fae. They're not always known for their discretion."

"Does the Summer Queen know what's in it?"

"Only the bare bones." He turned serious again. "She doesn't know that there might be another, you know, another Draco Wyr hanging around somewhere."

I scanned his face, trying to ascertain whether he was telling the truth or not. Eventually satisfied, I shrugged. "It's not definite that there is. And even if I do have a twin, I think the best thing they could do is stay as far away from me as possible."

He looked confused, so I explained about the article I'd just read on the Othernet. A flicker of pure rage was momentarily visible in his eyes, before he quickly masked it. "Do you want me to try and find who wrote it?"

Focusing on more important things, I shook my head. "Not right now. I need to concentrate on Endor. Aubrey seems sure that this Tarn bloke might know something about him. I need to find out exactly what."

"I meant what I said before, dragonlette; it's really not a very nice place."

I raised my eyebrows slightly. "Are you suggesting that it's going to be too much for me to handle?"

"God forbid," said Solus in mock horror. He looked me over critically. "We will need to do something about your outfit first though."

I looked down at my jeans and t-shirt. "What's wrong with it?"

"Dragonlette, sometimes you are very sweet."

I growled at him. He laughed musically. "Give me half an hour. I'll sort you out."

The air began to shimmer with streaks of purple again. Before he could vanish, I called out. "Solus, my fucking name is Mack."

He winked at me, merriment dancing in his eyes. "'Course it is, dragonlette."

I rolled my eyes. Idiot.

Chapter Nine

Standing in the cool night air outside the nondescript door to Circle, I felt incredibly uncomfortable. I picked at my clothes, grumbling to Solus. "I can't believe I let you persuade me into this stupid get-up."

"Dragonlette, you look gorgeous. And besides, if you want to fit in, this is what you need to do. You won't have any hope of getting close to Tarn unless you pique his interest. This outfit will certainly do that."

I stared down at myself. I looked like some kind of S & M dominatrix, clad as I was in a shiny lacquered skin-tight jumpsuit. A studded belt was cinching in my waist, and the top half was designed to be like a corset, laced together and pushing up my breasts to create an alarmingly overt cleavage. To make matters even worse, I had on knee high stiletto boots. Given my predilection for being entirely unable to wear high heels of any kind and not fall over, it didn't bode well. The very snug fit of the outfit also meant that there was nowhere I could conceal a weapon. I tried to experiment with shoving the daggers into my boots, but the leather outlined them in such a way that their presence was too obviously advertised to get away with. Solus had convinced me that I wouldn't get inside if I had any form of weaponry on me, so I'd grudgingly left them behind, figuring that I had other tools at my disposal should they be so required.

The Fae had kindly ministered to my swollen

eye, helping along the healing process so that at least it was starting to re-open somewhat, improving my vision. He'd been able to do little about the bruise itself, however, so the overall effect when coupled with the outfit was, well, striking. Solus had insisted I leave my hair down and I kept fidgeting with it while we waited for the door to open.

"Stop that," he hissed at me, as a small section of the door was drawn back and the unmistakable features of an ogre scowled out at us.

"Whaddyawant?"

Solus swept a dramatic bow. "Lord Sol Apollinarius, and companion, requesting admission."

The ogre grimaced at him, then looked at me. "No humans allowed," he grunted.

"I'm not human," I said, calmly.

"She's a shifter," Solus interjected. "A were-hamster."

The ogre stared at me unfathomably, then snapped the little wooden portal shut. The sound of several locks being undone reached my ears, and the door swung open. Licking my lips somewhat nervously and concentrating on not falling over as a result of my ridiculous footwear, I stepped over the threshold. Almost immediately, loud thumping music filled the space at a level of decibels enough to make me frankly astonished the sound hadn't been audible on the street.

"It's a spell," Solus murmured.

"Huh?"

"Tarn has a few pet mages. He uses them to cast

useful spells. Such as masking the sounds of what goes in here to anyone outside."

"And the Ministry is okay with that?"

"They're not exactly Ministry mandated mages."

Interesting. This Unseelie Fae had more power than I thought if he kept a couple of rogue wizards in his back pocket. I had firsthand experience of how the Ministry felt about anyone using magic outside of their fold. I wondered just how much Solus had to do with members of the Winter King's court. It was a world I'd never really come into contact with, and I had to admit that my knowledge about it was rather scanty. But with the ogre continuing to hover next to us, this wasn't really the time to ask. Solus delved into his pocket and I heard the distinct chink of coins, which he then passed over to the bouncer before I could see just how much this little excursion was costing him.

"I've crossed your palm with gold," Solus commented cheerfully. "Now let us in."

The ogre grunted, then gestured Solus towards another closed door with a distinct curl to his rather large, wrinkled and protruding lip. The Fae led the way, opening the door with a flourishing sweep that was melodramatic even for him. Then we were in.

"He's a real charmer, isn't he?"

I barely heard Solus' words above the music. It reverberated loudly through my body, until it felt almost as if my heart was thumping to match the beat. The interior of the club was vast, deceptively so from the small entrance through which we'd just come. Blue strobe lights flashed through the darkened dance floor, highlighting shadowy figures of all shapes and sizes, and a murky looking balcony hung over the space from behind the glow of the circular bar in the middle. There was an odd smell in the air, almost like cloves interspersed with cinnamon, and small flying creatures balancing trays with elaborate looking drinks flapping by.

There was a moan to my left and, upon turning, my mouth dropped open to see a vamp with her head curved into the neck of an apparently very willing victim, whose eyes flickered open when he felt my gaze. He smiled at me dreamily, as a trickle of blood dribbled down his neck and onto his bared torso. The vamp's tongue followed it down, lapping at it with the delicacy of a small cat. Sickened, I looked away.

"Let's get a drink," said Solus into my ear.

Feeling faintly claustrophobic, despite the size of the club, I demurred. "I don't want a drink. I want to find Tarn then get the hell out of this place."

"You're not going to find Tarn," he replied, although I had to strain to catch all his words. "Tarn will find you." And with that, the Fae tugged at my arm and led me through the crowd to the bar.

He shouted something to the bartender, holding up two fingers and then turned to me with a dazzling smile. "I'd forgotten how much fun it is here."

I decided that Solus' idea of fun and my idea of fun were poles apart. The flashing lights and the thumping music were encouraging the violent return of my earlier headache. The bartender set two drinks down in front of us; strange rainbow coloured concoctions that appeared to be smoking. I hoped that it was purely as a result of a scoop of dry ice and not some mage-inspired spell. I really didn't want to have to cope with any bizarre magic related hangover tomorrow morning. He lifted up his drink and raised his eyebrows at me. Sighing, I did the same. He chinked our glasses together, then downed the entire thing in one fell swoop. I took a tiny sip and almost gagged. Hastily returning the drink to the bar-top, I eyed the Fae curiously.

"You've been here before?"

He shrugged. "I used to hang out from time to time. The nightlife in Tir-na-Nog isn't exactly thrilling." A half-naked woman, with what appeared to be writhing snakes for hair, wandered past us. His eyes followed her swaying waist. "And there are lots of opportunities for," he paused momentarily, licking his lips, "excitement."

I glared at him with distaste. "Assuming you don't get turned to stone in the pursuit of that excitement."

He laughed. "Relax, dragonlette. It's just an Illusion spell. I had no idea you were such a prude at heart."

I bristled. "I'm not a prude, I just..." My words fell away as I felt a heavy shove from behind, and went careening into Solus' arms.

I twirled around, green fire already lighting up at my fingertips. In front of me rocked a satyr, clearly heavily under the influence. He had a smarmy grin on his lips as he looked me up and down. "Fresh meat! How about you and I take this party somewhere else?"

He reached out for my arm, but instead I

extinguished my fire and grabbed his bicep, twisting it and bringing him to his knees. His yelp of pain was audible even above the music. Solus stepped over next to me. "You are a were-hamster, remember, dragonlette."

I doubted very much that by now there were many people left in the Otherworld, ogre-shaped bouncers aside, who were still going to believe that. Regardless, I released my captive.

Solus' eyes' sparkled. "Come on. Let's dance."

"I don't want to fucking dance," I began, but he took my hand anyway, threading his long fingers between mine, and led me off to the cavernous dance-floor.

"If you want Tarn to notice you, then you need to do something other than look like a fire-breathing dragon with homicidal tendencies," he murmured in my ear. "He's UnSeelie. That means he has some baser instincts that take little encouragement. And you are, as our satyric friend over there stated, 'fresh meat'. Dance with me and make it look good, and I will bet you that we are in."

"In where?" I shouted back, but it was too late. Solus was already spinning me round, then pulling my hips against his. I was beyond irritated, but if this is what it was going take to get an audience with Tarn, wherever the fuck he happened to be, then I was going to give it everything I had.

Trying to look considerably more confident and dance-proficient than I actually felt, I shook out my hair and began to grind, reaching behind for Solus' waist and half-closing my eyes. That was more out of sheer embarrassment than due to my suggested pleasure at being thrust up against the Fae; I just had to hope that it was the latter that was being conveyed. At least like this there was less chance that I'd topple over as a result of my stiletto heeled height.

I felt Solus' hands leave my waist and travel up my body. "This is more excitement than I had anticipated, dragonlette," he murmured in my ear.

"Don't get any fucking funny ideas, Fae," I snarled back, albeit keeping a happy half-smile on my face for the watching public.

He laughed and spun me round until we were facing each other, then pulled me close again. I flung out my arms to give some semblance of wild abandon and, as the music's tempo increased, allowed Solus to grab hold of my hands. Our bodies twisted around together as we danced, taking up more and more of the space, and forcing other couples and dancers out towards the periphery. The shiny catwoman inspired get-up I was wearing might look sexy, but it certainly wasn't designed for any kind of real physical exertion. Sweat was dribbling most uncomfortably down my chest and back but, due to the tight nature of the outfit, was merely pooling in a slick mess against my skin.

Solus said something that I didn't quite catch so I leaned in closer until our faces were almost touching. "What?"

"I said," he repeated, "that don't look now, but we're on candid camera."

Slightly puzzled, I maneuvered myself around to where his eyes were directed, while still keeping up with the beat of the music. I realised that large television screens were broadcasting our dance to the entire club, beaming down images of the pair of us writhing together. Okay, maybe I did look kind of hot, for once in a sexy way rather than a bloodfire way. Watching myself gave me the oddest sensation of hedonistic voyeurism. Enough was enough.

"That's got to do it," I shouted back. "Let's go and get a drink and see what happens."

"Aw, dragonlette," purred Solus in my ear, "we're only just getting started." He allowed me to lead him off the dance floor, however, and back towards the bar. More than a few eyes were transfixed in our direction as we sauntered off; I just had to hope they included Tarn's.

Fortunately, my expectations were realised as, just as I gestured towards the barman, another hulking ogre appeared. This one was wearing a bowtie round his thick neck and very little else, as if he were a member of the Chippendales. I found it hard to imagine screaming women thrusting money towards him, but, hey, who was I to judge? He bowed formally towards us, in a manner even more incongruous with his shape and size than his outfit was.

"The owner would like to meet you," he said gruffly.

Yes! Trying not to be appear to overly exultant, I glanced quickly at Solus. He nodded, returning my look with a wink, and then the pair of us followed the ogre. The speculative looks in the eyes watching us were narrowing into jealousy as we weaved our way through the crowds to an ornate door set in the side. It opened automatically and we were beckoned in. At last.

The ogre ushered us into a waiting lift. I had been starting to assume that Tarn would be up in the balcony area although the presence of a lift suggested that we were going higher up than that. Clearly this UnSeelie Fae wasn't much of one for exercise, however, as the journey took less than five seconds and it was obvious when the doors dinged open that we were only one floor up. The music seemed less intrusive up here, and the surroundings were considerably more plush: gilt mirrors, dramatic paintings that were akin to some Hieronymous Bosch visions of hell, and comfortable looking booths in which various Otherworlders were lounging. A few of them gave us curious glances but, for the most part, we were ignored. The ogre pointed us towards the back, and then we were on our own.

Feeling slightly unsteady on my feet, I grabbed Solus' arm. I ignored the tiny flicker of humiliation I felt at needing his support to do nothing more than walk, but figured it might make me appear less threatening towards the club's owner. If I could persuade him to tell me about Endor without having to resort to violence, then all to the good. As we approached his table, I realised that what must be Tarn himself was in the centre, arms akimbo while several scantily clad women leaned in towards him. With a jolt, I recognised one of them as a shifter. I didn't think, somehow, that fawning over a Fae was quite what Corrigan had in mind for his minions. Tarn brushed the girls off, and stood up with a remarkable amount of grace, considering he was probably the only overweight Fae I'd ever come across. He was still remarkably good-looking, making me wonder if it was a prerequisite for the Wee Ones to be genetically disposed to attractiveness, no matter which side of the Seelie-UnSeelie spectrum they landed on. His head was shaved, as were his eyebrows, and his dark eyes glittered. I'd mistaken Solus for an UnSeelie Fae when I'd first met him - now I realised just how wrong I'd been. There was something of the night about Tarn that clung to him in a manner unmistakably of the darker side of faery.

He inclined his head. "Lord Sol. It's been some time since you decided to grace us with your presence."

"Let's just say I've been busy doing other things," Solus returned with a smile, although I was aware there was a slight edge to his voice.

"Yes, I heard you were in the Summer Queen's pocket now. I do hope you are enjoying being so close to so much power." Tarn was obviously being deliberately ambiguous with his words, suggesting merely through his tone that Solus' proximity to power was more due to where we were currently standing than being in the confidence of the Seelie Queen. "And who is your lovely companion?"

I met his gaze directly. This guy was starting to irritate me already. "Mack," I answered. "I'm a were-hamster."

Tarn snorted. "Of course you are. That's why you have a rather arresting bruise across your beautiful face. Because were-hamsters often find themselves the unwitting targets of attackers."

"I walked into a door."

He eyed me. "You're telling the truth. Fascinating. Unsightly facial disfigurement aside, that's an interesting shade of red hair you are sporting. Funnily enough, I was just reading this afternoon about a redhead. Something to do with the Brethren's Lord Alpha and some curious allusions to fire."

I stiffened, as did the shifter on Tarn's right. I pasted a smile on my face. "I don't think the Lord Alpha would be interested in little old me," I said, trying to sound breathy and girlish.

Tarn raised his eyebrows. "Are you out of breath after your show on the dance floor?"

Fuck it. I gave up. We weren't fooling anyone, least of all the target of our attention. I leaned over and injected in as much menace as I could muster. "You have some information that I want. And you're going to fucking give it to me."

He looked amused. "Is that so?"

I didn't blink.

The UnSeelie Fae shrugged expansively, then looked down at his expensively draped companions, dismissing them with a wave. All of them quickly stood up and headed for the door, although the shifter gave me a particularly dirty look as she did so.

"You don't have many friends, do you, Mack?" commented Tarn, noting her reaction towards me.

I looked at Solus, then back at Tarn. "Oh, I think I do alright," I said coolly.

"Indeed." He sat back down, stretching his arms out again against the back of the sofa. "Well, then, let's play."

I remained standing, folding my arms. "You know where I might find Endor."

"Endor?" he asked innocently.

"The necromancer. Tell me where he is and I'll leave you alone."

Tarn laughed. "Now why would I want you to do that when we've only just met?"

I snarled. "Where the fuck is he?"

"Come on, Tarn," Solus chimed in, "you know you've got nothing to lose. Just tell us."

"I've got nothing to gain either," replied the UnSeelie Fae, with a mellifluous lilt that did nothing but grate. The frustrations of the day were starting to get to me, and I could feel little starburst explosions of heat zipping up through my chest.

"You'll gain your life," I spat.

He laughed again. "Take a look around. Do you really think that you'd have gained admittance up here if I wasn't absolutely sure I could defend myself?"

I twisted round, clocking the fact that there were now several ogre sized shapes dotted around the open balcony. "Don't count your chickens that they'll be enough," I said, with slightly more confidence than I felt. I could probably take them all. Probably.

"What? A little were-hamster like you?"

Solus interrupted. "Fine, Tarn. What do you want in return?"

"Nothing you can give, Sol," he answered, his eyes still trained on me.

I gritted my teeth. "What do you want?"

A small smile played around his lips. "Well, now that you come to mention it, there is just one little thing..."

"What?"

His eyes glittered. "Give me a pint of your blood."

Solus exploded. "No way!"

"Done," I said.

"Mack, this is a really bad idea," Solus began.

"Too late," Tarn trilled. He jerked his head over to one of the waiting ogres, who lumbered over with a blood bag and a needle. At my look, the Fae smirked. "Let's just say I had a funny feeling we might be meeting in person. Although I did enjoy watching you dance."

I scowled at him, then sat down on an empty chair and held out my arm.

"Mack," Solus said again.

"We've got no choice," I answered shortly.

"You can't do this, dragonlette. You don't know what he'll do with your blood. What trouble it might cause."

Solus was right. But I was right too. The only thing that mattered was finding Endor. If this was what it was going to take, then so be it. I'd have to worry about the consequences later. Besides, the UnSeelie Fae might be pretty sure he knew my real identity, but I reckoned that he wasn't aware of the full power that my blood contained. And at least only having one pint would somewhat limit his resources.

The ogre tied a band around my upper arm, then started flicking at my taut skin to find a vein.

Solus rubbed his face and sighed, then sat down next to me for support. Tarn watched as the needle entered, a lewdly lascivious look on his face. I turned away, disgusted, and caught sight of my face in one of the many mirrors. My skin was pale, the purple bruise across my cheek standing out in stark relief. That wasn't what made me start, however. It was the fact my eyes were glowing from deep within that suddenly twisted my stomach in fear.

Chapter Ten

I turned and looked at Solus, my eyes wide. He hissed through his teeth. "Has this happened before?"

My mouth dry, I nodded.

"When?

I stared at him.

He reached over and gripped my arm, shaking it. "When, Mack?"

"I think earlier today," I squeaked. "But nothing happened. I went to the hospital and I was fine."

His body was very still and his tone was quiet and even. That was good. If Solus wasn't panicking then I wasn't going to panic either. It was probably nothing. Surely, that book couldn't be right all the time? The ogre at my side seemed oblivious to the byplay going on right next to him, but Tarn was leaning forward, eyes fixed on mine, and his hands touching his lips as if he was in prayer.

"Why were you at the hospital?" Solus asked.

I thought of my earlier promise to Mrs. Alcoon. Shit. It hadn't taken me more than a few hours to break it. I wondered if she had foreseen this all along. I swallowed. "To donate blood."

Solus widened his eyes fractionally. "This is the second time today you've lost blood?"

"Well, I wouldn't call it 'losing' blood per se. I know where it is."

He gripped my arm tighter. "Don't be flippant." He switched his gaze to Tarn. "This might be a good time to evacuate the building."

"What? You don't really think I'm about to…that doesn't make sense! I lost blood before when Aubrey attacked me. More than this. I feel fine. Nothing's going to happen. I just need to stay calm." As soon as I finished my sentence, a hot trail of fire scorched through my body from one end to the other. Oh, that wasn't good.

"Your eyes weren't glowing then, though."

"Well, fucking do something and make them stop now!"

Solus, face pale, looked over at Tarn. He'd not moved a muscle. Then he fixed his gaze on the ogre who was pulling away the needle and wiping at my arm in a surprisingly delicate manner. I could tell that his mind was flipping over the options, but there just wasn't any time. I immediately stood up, rubbing at the spot, and feeling distinctly woozy and nauseous. There were hundreds of people in here. I had to get out right now.

"Where's the nearest exit?" I shouted at Tarn.

He blinked at me. I reached out and grabbed him by the lapels of his shiny designer suit and snarled, "Where's the nearest fucking exit?"

For the first time since we'd entered the balcony area, the UnSeelie Fae appeared shaken. He lifted up a finger and pointed out towards the way we'd entered. "You can go that way. Up to the roof, not down. There's a staircase to the right..."

I didn't listen to anything more, and instead bolted in that direction. Losing the second pint of blood had just been too much, however, and I felt shaky and weak. Streaks of red began to zip across my eyes and my body was tingling all over with painful pinpricks of heat. I barely made it to the door, then scrabbled forward with my fingers, smashing the protective glass of the fire alarm and thumping on the button within. All at once, a siren sounded but, with the loud thump of music below, it didn't seem as if any of the Circle customers had heard. It probably didn't matter now. It was already too late.

A searing pain shuddered through me and it felt as if I was being ripped asunder. My fingers seemed cramped and, when I looked down, they were already curving into long talons. The shiny jumpsuit was becoming more and more constricting and I was starting to feel like I couldn't breathe. I gasped and choked for air, then wave after wave of bloodfire rippled through my body like some unstoppable tsunami of flame. Scraps of shiny black from my jumpsuit spat out in all directions. I dimly registered screams from below, and a hundred faces turning up in my direction. My head scraped painfully against something and I tried to duck, but it didn't seem to help. Then I realised that it was the high ceiling. How fucking big was I as a dragon? What was clearly my tail spasmed uncontrollably, and lashed out, seemingly of its own volition, smacking against a table and what sounded like a considerable amount of glass. I could feel the essence that was me already slipping away into a chasm far below, and my baser dragon instincts taking over.

No, no, no, no, no, no, no. This couldn't happen. Not here. I wasn't going to let it. I chanted in my head, telling myself in a repetitive mantra to stop. I opened my mouth to scream at everyone to get out, to stop staring and to turn and run. Suddenly I was aware of nothing but heat and flames pulling up through my body from somewhere deep within the pit of my stomach, forcing themselves through my intestines and up past my heart and into my throat. Then, everything went dark.

*

When I came to, I was lying curled up in a foetal position. Someone had draped something over me, but I still felt cold, and there was an acrid taste of burnt cinders in my mouth. Angry voices floated from all around me. It felt oddly like someone had been calling my name, as if to get me to wake up or pay attention, but it must have been my imagination. I pulled myself up into a sitting position, clutching what I realised was actually some kind of velvet throw to my body and, terrified of what I might see, carefully opened my eyes.

The overhead lights were on, making the entire club seem less like an opulent den for Otherworld joy seekers and more like a garishly seedy dive. Solus and Tarn were arguing about something from just a few feet away, and it sounded as if there were some more people down below. A hand reached out to my face, smoothing away my hair, and I blinked my eyes into focus. Tom.

"Hey," he said, gently. "How are you feeling?"

Tears swam into my eyes. "How many people?"

He looked confused. "What do you mean?"

"How many people did I just kill, Tom?"

He smiled at me. "None."

"How many people are hurt?"

"None." His thumb carefully stroked over the bruise on my cheek. "Well," he amended, "I think the barman might be eyebrow-less for a few weeks, but other than that, everyone's fine." He gazed at me in all seriousness. "You brought it back, Red. You shifted and apparently breathed fire down at the bar, but you brought it back. You were in control."

Control? That's what he called control? I transformed myself into a dragon in a humiliatingly public manner. I couldn't have chosen a worst spot to lose all of my senses than if I'd stood in the middle of Piccadilly Circus. Despite my overwhelming relief that I had managed to avoid hurting anyone, all I could think about was how in the fuck it had happened in the first place.

I staggered to my feet, doing everything that I could to avoid the sickening lurch of lightheadedness. The two faeries immediately quieted, and Solus came running over.

"Why?" I croaked. "Why did I shift?"

Solus looked stricken. "I don't know, dragonlette. Maybe the loss of blood?"

"My eyes were doing the fucking spooky glowing thing before that. Why now? Why today?"

I turned to Tom for help. "You're a shifter. Help me out here."

My old friend looked worried. "I don't know, Red. It happens when it's a full moon, you know that. We can't control the urges and so we just spontaneously..." he shrugged, "shift."

"It's not a full moon. And that's never happened to me before anyway." I smiled sourly, hugging the soft throw tighter to me. "I don't think us Draco Wyr work like that."

"It can happen in times of huge stress. You know like when you were at the mages' academy and that wraith showed up."

"I'm not stressed." I ran my tongue over my lips. "Not like I was then anyway."

"Sometime younger girls can't control their shifts when they get their periods. Betsy was like that for a while. I don't know what else to tell you."

I vaguely remembered waking up in the middle of the night years ago in my old dormitory to the sound of snarls and Julia's soothing tones. I wasn't a young girl in the first bout of puberty though, and I didn't have my fucking period. A flash of heat flared up uncomfortably in my lower stomach, then settled there, like a hot boulder. Bloody hell, I felt awful.

"So, pretty much, you don't know. Nobody

knows. I don't know. Apparently now, not only is the whole world going to be in absolutely no doubt as to what I really am, but there's the chance I might just spontaneously combust when I'm strolling down the road. Outfuckingstanding."

I slammed my palm against the balcony railing, and stared down. There were a couple of ogres hovering around, and a few people mopping up the remnants of splashed drinks and broken glass. A vast scorch mark now travelled from one length of the bar to the other.

Tom touched my shoulder. "The Lord Alpha's on his way."

Brilliant. Just brilliant.

I turned to where Tarn was standing, another bout of dizziness attacking my senses. "You got what you wanted," I snarled at him. "Now give me what I asked."

"You destroyed my club," he commented.

"Your fucking club is fine. Tell me where Endor is, Tarn or, so help me God, I'll fry you on the spot."

He leaned down, scooping up a delicate champagne glass and taking a small sip. "I don't know where he is."

That's it. I was going to kill him. I took a step forward, then wavered slightly. Solus moved over, putting his arm round my body to steady me.

"Well," Tarn continued, eyeing me with the nervy enmity of an old street cat, "I don't know where he is right now. At this particular moment in time. But I do know where he'll be."

I watched him, unforgiving, waiting for something else. And because, right at this moment, I wasn't entirely sure I'd be able to take even a step without collapsing.

"In five days' time, it's Lughnasadh. The pagan first harvest of summer. He's going to use it do a little harvesting of his own. I think he enjoys the symmetry." Tarn shrugged.

Five days? Alex better damn well have found a way to get hold of some palladium before then.

I kept my eyes trained on the Fae. "Where?"

A shadow crossed his face. "In Scotland. Loch Ness."

"He's going after the kelpies," breathed Solus in dawning comprehension. "And the element of water."

Tarn nodded.

"And how the fuck do we know that you're telling the truth? Given that you effectively already lied about knowing his current whereabouts?"

"Sol knows."

I twisted my neck round to look at Solus, and he gave me a bob of unhappy affirmation.

"Endor was in here a couple of months ago," Tarn explained. "He looked interesting so I called him up and we got drunk over a bottle of Glen Ord whisky. It's distilled up in that area. He dropped enough hints to make it clear what he was intending."

"It could be a trap," murmured Tom.

"It's not." The Fae was adamant.

I knew that Tarn's nature meant he'd be well versed enough in the lines between truth and lies to be sure of his assertion. I nodded.

He turned to leave, but I called out first. "I might

not be able to stand up unassisted right now, but if you do anything with my blood that harms others, I will come after you." I stared hard at him. "You know the truth of my words."

He just looked at me, but there was a note of acknowledgement visible in his eyes, then he flicked his wrist, and two hulking bodyguards appeared out of nowhere to flank him. Together, they turned their backs on us and left.

Once I was sure that he'd gone, I spoke quietly to Solus. "I'd like to go home, now."

"Of course, dragonlette. We need to go to the entrance first though. I can't transport you from within here because Tarn has some kind of portal shield in place. It stops any riffraff from materialising in whenever they like."

"I'll carry you," Tom interjected.

"No. I can walk." I was damned if I was going to be treated like some kind of invalid.

Very, very carefully, with Tom and Solus on either side of me, I began to hobble forward. The heated lump inside my stomach didn't appear to be abating, and neither was the dizziness. I gritted my teeth though, and tightly curled my nails into my palms. Bit by bit, we slowly edged our way forward until we were in front of the lift. I'd been mocking Tarn earlier for not having stairs, but now I was beyond grateful that he was a lazy wanker. The velvet throw was starting to fall down my shoulders, but I managed to hike it up around me. With any luck we'd be able to get out of this place before Corrigan showed up.

Unfortunately for me, when the lift doors

opened smoothly back onto the ground floor, and the three of us stepped carefully out, the familiar figure of the Brethren Lord was already there, eyes examining the scar I'd left burned into the bar. He turned and watched our progress towards him, not offering any help. Thank fuck. He looked somewhat ruffled, as if he'd gotten dressed in a hurry. I tried very hard not to dwell on what he might have been doing when he'd received the midnight call about my latest shenanigans.

When we reached him, he ignored me and looked at Tom, who gave him a little dip of a bow. Fucking Brethren caste system.

"What happened?"

Tom began to outline what he'd learned upon his arrival. I'd have kept going, out towards the exit, but unfortunately I knew I wouldn't be able to make it without both Tom and Solus' shoulders to lean on. And there was no way I was going to let myself collapse. Not at this particular moment.

When Tom had finished, Corrigan turned towards me. "Did he leave anything out?"

I shook my head, pulling the throw further up around me as if for protection. A muscle jerked in the Lord Alpha's cheek.

"It looks like you've missed all the action," commented Solus merrily. "That's okay though. Us faeries and dragons can take care of everything."

"The council should have been informed before you came here," Corrigan growled.

"How do you know they weren't?" I shot back.

His green eyes flashed. "Because I'm taking Staines' place as the highest ranking shifter representative. If you'd told anyone, I would have known."

I raised my eyebrows, unable to help myself. "Oh yeah? Just like you'd have known if any of your little minions were off torturing any innocent victims?"

Tom sucked in his breath at my words.

Corrigan snarled at me. "Watch your place."

Oh, he so didn't say that, did he? "Actually, my Lord, now that you've rejoined the council – of which I believe I am the head – you're the one who'll have to watch your place." I smirked. "It's my orders you'll be following. Not the other way around." As soon as I'd said that, I regretted it. Shit. I didn't want to antagonise the Lord Alpha. I wanted him to like me. More than like me.

His face twisted and he began to speak again but, before any words could form, his attention was caught by a flickering screen from above our heads. His skin paled dramatically. Frowning, I half turned to see what he was looking at. My stomach dropped when I did. A video loop of Solus and me dancing was playing. Our bodies were pressed together and my eyes were half-closed as if in ecstasy, with my hands round his back, and what appeared to be his lips on my skin.

"We're thinking of trying out for *Strictly Come Dancing*," said Solus. "I'm not sure they'll be able to show us before the watershed though. There's just no stopping a passion as deep as ours, is there, dragonlette?"

Just when I thought I couldn't feel any worse.

Corrigan pulled his eyes away from the screen,

ignoring the Fae. "If you're really going to lead the council, then you're going to have to start acting a damn sight more responsibly. Especially now that the entire Otherworld clearly knows that you're a Draco Wyr. So much for all that effort you put into keeping it a secret. I guess you just wanted to make sure that everyone was fully aware of your power. Well, congratulations. Because now you can bet that it's all over the Othernet and that Endor knows too. Thanks to your stupidity, we've lost just about the only element of surprise and real advantage that we had."

I probably deserved that. It didn't stop me from rising to the challenge, however. I was pissed off he thought this was what I'd wanted. "Oh yeah? I think that thanks to your presence on the fucking gossip pages, he was probably pretty much already aware of that. So don't coming knocking on my door to lay the blame."

Corrigan took an angry step towards me. I did the same, then abruptly remembered that standing was a bit of an issue, and my knees gave way. All three of them jumped forward to grab me, but Corrigan was first to catch me. Despite his vaguely unkempt appearance, he still smelled as good as ever. I jerked away, cheeks burning.

"We need to go," I mumbled, avoiding meeting Corrigan in the eyes. "There'll be another council meeting tomorrow. I'll call everyone in the morning." Asserting my authority one final time, I added, "And tell Staines I still want to see him."

With that, I moved to my left, Tom and Solus carefully supporting me from either side. I didn't look back. I didn't dare.

Chapter Eleven

I woke up late the next morning, my head pounding incessantly. The heavy hot feeling in my stomach hadn't gone away and I generally felt as if I'd been driven over several times by a ten ton truck. It was an unusual sensation. I was no stranger to getting hurt or passing out, but I normally started to recover fairly quickly. Even the very first time after I'd inadvertently transformed myself into a dragon hadn't been quite so physically bad as this. The stress of the last week was clearly getting to me.

Dragging my protesting limbs out of bed, I lurched over to the small bathroom and splashed my face with cold water. Then I leaned against the sink and stared at my reflection in the mirror. I poked at the bruise across my cheekbone. At least it didn't hurt quite as much as it had the day before, although I reckoned it looked considerably worse. The purple was darkening and the shape now looked oddly similar to the outline of Africa, just a rather skewed version. My mouth felt dry and furry and, even though I'd brushed my teeth for at least ten minutes before I'd gone to sleep, I could still taste ash. I sighed deeply, then pulled myself together. A cup of the strongest coffee that I could muster, and I reckoned I'd start to feel more human. So to speak.

I pulled on an old t-shirt, and headed to the kitchen, then almost gave myself a heart attack when I realised someone was already there.

"Fucking hell, Tom!"

He gave me a wave and handed over an already steaming mug of dark, delicious caffeine.

"I could have freaking killed you! What are doing here?"

He grinned amiably. "You passed out pretty quickly before the faerie and I could leave last night. He was going to stay to check on you and make sure you were alright, but I managed to convince him that it'd probably be better if I did that."

I took a sip, closing my eyes momentarily in pleasure. "Why?"

Tom looked at me as if I was stupid. "The Lord Alpha wouldn't be best pleased if he found out that you spent the night with the Fae."

"Somehow I'm not convinced he'd care. Not any longer."

He shook his head, tutting. "The pair of you are as bad as each other."

"What the hell do you mean by that?"

"Never mind."

I eyed him suspiciously. Once upon a time I could have cajoled Tom into doing or saying pretty much anything. He'd been a member of the Brethren for almost a year now though, and the effects were starting to show. Not only did he have the obvious physical changes of more lean muscle and strength, but there was also an edge of steel to him personally that had been absent back in Cornwall. Part of me felt sad for the slight naivety and puppy dog enthusiasm that he'd once sported and that had now disappeared, and part of me admired what he was becoming. It made me wonder just what he'd been doing for the Brethren all this time.

"Why did you do it, Red?"

I knew what he was referring to. "Nobody else was going to be able to keep an inter-species council intact. I had to."

"I don't mean the council. I mean dumping him like that."

"The Arch-Mage and the Summer Queen told me…"

"Screw them!" shouted Tom. "Since when have you ever done what someone else has told you to? You let them walk all over you. That's not you. That's not the person I grew up with."

"They were right, Tom. If I stayed with Corrigan, then the Fae and the mages would never trust me because the balance I provide would be shifted in the Brethren's direction. And if the Fae and the mages don't trust me then it all falls apart, don't you see? Endor will win. We need to work together!"

"I still don't see how being with the Lord Alpha stops them from doing that."

"You need to see what I see," I pleaded with Tom. "I've had the lot of you tailing me since I got to London so I have first hand experience of exactly how terribly all the different species get on. To be frank, I'm amazed that none of you have killed each other yet. And I'm not trying to be bigheaded here, you great oaf. Even with those token Otherworld meetings that the bigwigs head off to every so often, the only time I've seen any real cooperation has been when I've been taking the lead. Not because I'm so fucking amazing or anything, but because I'm not a shifter or a mage or a faerie."

"You shift into a dragon," he said sullenly. "And

you grew up in a pack."

"Exactly. So your lot think I'm okay even though I'm not a shifter. Just like the mages think I'm okay because I can do magic. And the fucking Fae think I'm okay because I can resist their glamour stuff and break their spells, and I get on with them. Name me one other person who is balanced across all three groups and I will give them this fucking job right now."

I stared at him in obvious challenge from across the kitchen table. Tom stayed silent.

"Once we've dealt with Endor, I will step down. This is only temporary. I thought maybe once Corrigan got over his anger, he'd wait for me and everything would work out in the end." I sighed, and tugged at my hair. "Except he's not. He's already moved on and that's that."

Neither of us spoke for a few moments. Then Tom rubbed his forehead and looked me in the eyes. "It's not going to be temporary."

"What?"

"You know what I mean. We'll work together and bring down Endor, and everything will be all hunky-dory. And then something else will rise up and take his place and it will start all over again. You're going to be tied into this council for the rest of your life."

I looked away. "That's not going to happen."

"Sure."

"It's not!"

"Okay."

I toyed with the handle of my coffee mug. I couldn't deal with this topic of conversation any longer. "I'm impressed that you managed to get Solus to leave," I commented, changing the subject. "If he'd thought that he could piss off Corrigan by staying, then I don't think that wild unicorns would have dragged him away."

"Yes," frowned Tom, "your friend does seem to enjoy being antagonistic." He gave me a long, thoughtful look. "Is he in love with you?"

I laughed slightly. "Solus? No."

He gave me a skeptical look.

I took another gulp of coffee. "He's my friend, Tom. Just like you. He's just a bit of a flirt, that's all."

Tom still looked doubtful. He gave in for the time being, however, and changed the subject. "Anyway, I managed to encourage him to leave because the two of us need to get that training started."

"I thought we were going to meet on Thursday?"

"Don't you think we need to move that timetable up somewhat now?"

I eyed him with a mixture of hope and trepidation. It was obvious that I needed to bring my dragon side under control, and the sooner the fucking better before I really did end up hurting someone innocent. I was just terrified that I wouldn't be able to manage it.

"Don't you have other things to do? You're getting bloody married in less than a month, Tom."

"You do remember Betsy, right? Do you really think she'd let something as important as her wedding day be screwed up by my poor decision making?"

I raised my eyebrows. "Fair point. You'd

probably do something shocking like order freesias instead of magnolias for the table settings."

"Roses and baby's-breath, actually." He grinned ruefully, "I almost ended up having my eyeballs taken out by a fountain pen when I suggested that we should just get all the invitations typed out instead of personally writing them."

"You'd better hope the sun is shining on the day, or she'll postpone it for a year."

"Oh, she's already got about three contingency plans in place." He smiled fondly to himself, then glanced up at me. "Now quit trying to change the subject and sort yourself out so we can get started."

Shit. I swallowed. "Yeah. Okay."

"Finish your coffee first, then we'll begin." He gave me an arch look. "I know what you're like when you don't get your caffeine fix."

"I'll just check the Othernet headlines and my email first."

"No."

Er, what? "Yes."

"It's not a good idea, Red. I spoke to the Lord Alpha this morning already anyway. You don't need your email because he's arranged the council meeting for four pm."

"Oh, he has, has he?"

Tom shot me a warning look. "We didn't know how long you were going to be asleep for. It seemed prudent not to wait."

I subsided into a series of grumbles.

"Staines will be here after midday to talk to you," he continued, "and there's nothing on the Othernet that's a surprise."

"What does that mean?" My eyes narrowed.

"Just that. There's gossip about last night and a few pictures, but nothing you need to worry about now."

"Pictures?" My voice rose and I began to get out of my chair. "Bloody pictures? Of me?"

"Red," Tom began patiently.

"Let me see them," I growled.

"No."

"You can't tell me what to fucking do, Tom."

He laughed shortly. "Red, I need you to be focused right now. Take some of that newfound sense of responsibility and turn it on. We don't have a vast amount of time and there's a lot to cover." He gave me a hard look. "Focus the fire."

I wiped the frustration off my face at his last words. John, the old alpha in Cornwall and the only real father 'd ever known, had always used that phrase to get me to pay attention and knuckle down. He'd known more about me then than I'd known about myself. I'd never be sure whether he had ever planned to tell me the truth about my Draco Wyr side but, instead of feeling betrayed, all I felt now was fondness. He'd simultaneously protected me and encouraged me to protect myself. And clearly Tom knew exactly which of my buttons to press just like John had. Focus the fire indeed.

I picked up my coffee cup and drained it, then looked him in the eyes. "Well, let's get this party started."

*

Tom cleared away the coffee cups, dumping them in the sink, then turned to me. "Right, we're going to do this in stages."

I looked down at the old t-shirt I was wearing. "Let me go and get changed first."

"No need," he answered dismissively.

"Eh?"

"We're going to stay here. It's probably better if you're wearing something loose anyway."

"Stay here?" Was he mad? "Tom, this flat is kind of small. I don't think it's going to hold my dragon form."

He tutted. "Didn't you pay attention to anything in Cornwall?"

"If I wasn't going to be able to shift myself, why would I have?" I huffed. "Anyway, I was off hunting with John when you lot were doing the furry thing."

"The furry thing?" he raised his eyebrows.

I shrugged. "Hey, it's better than scaly."

"You don't know what you look like when you transform, do you?"

"Finding a mirror hadn't been first on my mind either time," I commented. "Nothing's really been on my mind, Tom, because the fucking dragon takes over."

He smiled benignly. "We'll sort that out."

"I'm not technically a shifter, you know. It might not work like it does for you."

"Let's just see, shall we? Stop being obstructive and sit on this chair."

I did as he instructed, huffing melodramatically. Tom completely ignored my sulky reaction.

"Now close your eyes," he said patiently. "Create a picture of yourself in your head. It doesn't need to be what you actually look like, just what you imagine yourself to look like."

A vision filled my head of a scowling me, gripping two long silver daggers. Excellent.

"Now, you need to take that picture and turn it into something. A symbol. Something a bit more tangible."

"It's in my fucking head, Tom, how tangible is it going to be?"

He didn't answer. I sighed and tried to think. Okay. I turned the image of angry Mack into a vast bonfire, adding in logs and licking flames of different hues for effect. For a bit of a flourish, I stuck a stuffed figure with a stovepipe hat on the top, in the manner of a Guy Fawkes' pyre. Deciding that some fireworks would be pretty, I allowed a Catherine Wheel to set off behind the flames, and included some blue and green exploding showers overhead.

"The more simple you can keep it, the better," Tom added.

My elaborate vision vanished in a puff of smoke. Oh, well. I replaced it with a single burning matchstick.

"Okay, done."

"Good. Now, smells are particularly evocative so you need to develop some kind of aroma to attach to your symbol. It'll make it more useful to call up when you need it."

I imagined burning sulphur and wrinkled my nose.

"Take that image and think of it as being the essence of you. It's inside you at all times. Lock it away somewhere inside so that it's safe."

I moved my fictitious match into a little box deep in my mind.

"Is it there?"

I nodded, still keeping my eyes firmly closed.

"Great. Now picture your dragon self."

"I don't know what I look like, remember? Maybe if you let me see those photos on the Othernet then..."

"Shut up, Red," said Tom, not unkindly. "Picture what you think your dragon self to be."

Mentally cursing him, I did just that. It filled my mind, snarling and fiery.

"Don't think of anything else other than that dragon."

As soon as he said that, it was impossible not to think of other things. I screwed up my face and concentrated harder. It seemed as if an age went by but, finally, all that remained was my nasty Draco Wyr alter ego.

"When I say so, you are going to open your eyes and look down at your right hand. You're going to think about it as if it was in dragon form, just as it is in your head. As you do this, you are going to keep that symbol of you at the forefront of your mind. It's always there. You're always there, no matter what else you see."

My hand began to prickle with heat, and tendrils of flame snaked away from my fingers and up my arm. I really hoped Tom knew what he was doing.

"Have you got your symbol?"

"Yes." My voice sounded as if it was far away.

"Okay, then. Open your eyes."

I lifted up one eyelid just a crack, and peeked

down at my hand. It looked normal. Relaxing slightly, I opened both my eyes and stared down. Nothing happened.

"Imagine the dragon." Tom said calmly.

My fiery self roared up in my mind and then, all of a sudden, I yelped loudly as my hand began to twist and cramp. My fingernails lengthened out into long curving talons and my skin shimmered deep red. I started to panic, feeling my heart thump deep within and bloodfire begin to roar. My left hand started to ache in equal measure. I couldn't breathe and...

"The symbol, Mack!"

I remembered my little burning match and imagined it hovering in front of my eyes. That was me. I was still there. I gulped in air and my heart rate started to slow. I stretched out my left hand, feeling each finger wiggle one by one, but continued looking at my right.

"Wow," I whispered.

It didn't really look like scales. It didn't really look like skin, either. And the colour – red didn't really do it justice. It was more of a glittering burgundy. I flexed out and watched the muscles ripple underneath.

"Now bring back your human hand."

I didn't want to. I wanted to keep looking at my dragon shape. Desire to fully transform filled me.

"Mack..."

The imaginary smell of burning sulphur filtered through my brain and the little match flickered. I watched as my hand returned to its normal shape then stretched it out wonderingly, then looked up at

Tom. He was pale and sweating. I realised that my own skin was clammy and damp.

"Blimey," I said. "It worked."

Chapter Twelve

I said goodbye to Tom at my door, with the sincere promise to continue practising with the partial shifting, then headed back inside to call Alex for an update on his palladium sourcing venture. His phone went straight to voice mail, so I left a quick message, telling him to meet me after the afternoon's council meeting at Alcazon, and checked my watch. I had just enough time to grab a hot shower and put on some real clothes before Staines showed up. I mulled over exactly just what I'd say to the were-bear. I vowed to myself to keep calm and gently point out to him the error of his ways. Surely I could manage that.

I was just pulling on my jeans, however, when the phone rang. Convinced that it would be the man himself, with some pathetic excuse as to why he couldn't make it after all, I snarled into the receiver.

"What?"

"Goodness me, dear, are you still in a bad mood?" Oops. It was Mrs. Alcoon.

"Hey," I said weakly. "No, I'm fine. I just thought you were someone else, that's all."

"You left before I could make you a proper cup of tea yesterday, you know. I have just the right selection of herbs to help your condition."

"My condition? You mean being a grouch?"

"Something like that, dear. Anyway, the reason I'm calling is that Mr. Slim thinks he may have found something to help you. An old document relating to the four elements. He rather thinks that you ought to see it straight away. I told him that the best thing we can do is to let you rest, but he insisted."

I pursed my mouth. "I'll be right over."

I scribbled out a note for Staines, telling him to wait, and that I'd be back shortly, and stuck it to the front door, then jogged out to Clava Books. When I got there, Aubrey was making himself useful with a broom, dancing around and humming what seemed to be My Chemical Romance's *Blood*. You can take the vampire out of the boy, but...

"So? What the feck happened last night? He's going after Water next, isn't he?" Slim appeared out of nowhere, fluttering at head height and fixing me with a beady stare.

Great. If this was where I found out I hadn't needed to deal with Tarn after all, I was going to be seriously pissed off.

"Do you happen to know where he's going as well?"

"How the feck would I know where he's going? There's water everywhere, in case you hadn't noticed. We don't live in a desert," he scoffed at me.

"Water, water, everywhere and nary a drop to drink," said Mrs. Alcoon, emerging out of the back room and handing me over a foul smelling cup. "Here. Drink this."

"Actually," I stalled, "I've got to get back home. I've got a meeting."

"You're not getting the document until you finish that cup, Mackenzie Smith," said Mrs. Alcoon sternly, waggling her finger at me.

Slim snatched back the piece of paper he'd been

holding out. When I gave him a look, he just shrugged. Yielding to what was clearly the inevitable, I took the cup and sipped it. Yes, it tasted just as bad as it smelled. I gulped the whole thing down as quickly as I could, then passed the cup back.

"Thank you. Look," I said, feeling slightly embarrassed, "I'm sorry if I was snippy yesterday."

Mrs. Alcoon patted me on the shoulder. "That's alright, dear. You couldn't help it. There'll be more days like that."

"Well, I think maybe I'm getting a handle on it. Tom came around this morning and we made some headway. I think I'm going to be able to rid myself of this burden more easily than I'd thought."

The old lady looked vaguely alarmed for a moment, then her face cleared. "Oh right, yes, I see. That's very good. Well done."

Hmm. Something was definitely up with her. I chewed the inside of my cheek, trying to decide whether it would be worth pursuing. I didn't really have the time right now, but I'd try and weasel it out of her at some later date. I looked back at Slim, and gestured pointedly at the now empty cup, and the document he was still clutching.

"Can I have it now?"

He held out the yellowing paper. Taking it, I scanned down, reading it quickly. It was complete gobbledegook.

"I don't get it," I said, thoroughly confused.

Slim exhaled melodramatically. "If you'd been educated properly, it would make total sense. Endor started with Earth, correct?"

I was absorbed in trying to make sense of the marks on the page.

"Correct?" repeated Slim, in a louder voice, obviously irritated with my multi-tasking shortcomings.

"Okay, yes, correct," I said, hastily, before he decided to give up on me entirely.

"And of course it stands to reason that he'd begin with Earth."

"Eh?"

"Good grief! Look at the fecking diagram on the paper! Earth binds all three other elements together. It has to be first."

"Okay, I see," I said, nodding. Sort of.

"Think of a tree as symbolising the Earth element."

A sour feeling hit my stomach. "That's certainly what Endor did."

"A tree takes in water through its roots. That water is necessary for growth. The tree then breathes out through its leaves, providing oxygen." He sent me a quick look. "Oxygen's an important part of air."

I scowled.

"And if you set that tree on fire, it provides energy and releases all the other elements back again to the earth."

"Right." I paused. "But the tree needs air and sunlight to grow. Not just water."

"Exactly! You're getting it now."

I really wasn't.

Slim stabbed at the piece of paper with his index finger. "It's in there. He's taking all the vital parts of life and the way they're linked together in order to create power."

"But he's taking those parts of life by introducing death," I pointed out.

"Death is equally a part of life."

My head hurt. "Slim, how is this knowledge actually going to help?"

"He's going from Earth to Water to Air to Fire. And when he has all four, he'll have the power of life."

"But he's a necromancer. Why would he want the power of life?"

Slim waited, blinking rapidly, while I tried to connect the dots.

"He's taking strength from the life of the four different elements by introducing death." I held up my palm to forestall the gargoyle. "Yes, yes, I get that death is a part of life, but the death he's bringing in is unnatural. It breaks the cycle that he's already drawing from. As a necromancer he's already in touch with the dead anyway - except they're always going to be dead. The best necromancer in the world isn't going to change that fact. Unless he has the power of life." I chewed on a fingernail. "Oh."

"It'll disrupt the balance of nature. Of life itself. The dead are not meant to rise again. The results could be catastrophic."

I looked at Aubrey, who was intently chasing one little ball of dust around one of the stacks of shelves. "You say the dead aren't meant to rise again..."

"Vampires walk the delicate balance between

both worlds, neither dead nor alive." Slim's face twisted. "They're a bit of an anomaly."

"How much of an anomaly is a vampire who by his nature used to be dead-but-not-dead and is now alive?"

"Well, I didn't say I fecking understood everything now, did I?"

I gazed at the little gargoyle with a mixture of amusement and exasperation. "I'm not sure that knowing Endor's motives for doing what he's doing will make me feel any better, but it really is useful information. Thank you, Slim."

He bowed in mid-air. Mrs. Alcoon smiled at him fondly. "Aye, he's a canny lad."

Two high points of colour lit up his cheeks. He muttered something inaudible in a gruff voice, then flapped away to scold Aubrey for not sweeping with enough finesse.

"Are you feeling better now, dear?" asked the older woman.

Actually, I was. I guessed the icky tea had done its job. The hot lump in my stomach was still there, but it wasn't entirely uncomfortable, and my general well-being seemed much improved.

"I really am. Your efforts have not gone in vain, Mrs. Alcoon."

Her eyes crinkled with pleasure. "Now, didn't you say something about a meeting?"

I checked my watch. Shit. I was more than late.

"I have to go." I leaned down and pecked her on the cheek then skedaddled out of the shop in double quick time and pelted down the street, rounding the corner into my flat as fast as I could. I hated being late and it would put the already prickly were-bear into a bad mood. Whether he was still on the council or not, I needed to make it clear to him just what the rules of engagement were.

When I got into the small corridor leading to my flat, the note I'd left had gone, and the door was lying slightly ajar. Seriously? Staines must have wandered into my flat to wait, even though I wasn't there. That was a move worthy of Corrigan. These fucking Brethren guys had no sense of boundaries. Irked beyond belief, I stomped up, and pushed the door fully open. Then I inhaled.

Blood. There was no mistaking the salty iron laden hit to the air. My stomach leapt up into my mouth and back down again. I was frozen for a heartbeat, listening for sounds of anything then, when it appeared that everything was as silent as when I'd left, I slammed open the kitchen door and sprang through, bloodfire flaring through every vein in my body.

I was greeted by a horror scene. Splashes of arterial red covered the entire room, more than I'd have thought possible. Staines was spread-eagled on my kitchen table, froth bubbling up at his mouth. No-one was visible. Fire sparked up at my fingers as I peered round into the bedroom, checking to see where the assailant was hiding himself. But it lay empty, the duvet cover in the same position it had been when I'd gotten out of bed. I pressed myself against the wall, shuffling along until I reached the bathroom. Then I twisted round to face the small room and shot in twin bolts of flame. They crackled and hissed, scorching the wall and causing the wallpaper to curl up at the edges. And yet nobody was there either.

The only place left was the living room. I scooped up both my daggers from where they lay on my dresser and gripped the handles tightly in my fists. Heart thudding, I barrelled back through the kitchen, past Staines' inert body, and into the living room with a warlike cry.

"Come out and fight, you fucker!"

I stopped abruptly. It was obviously empty. Whoever had been there had come and gone. I pivoted round and ran back to the kitchen.

Staines was still breathing, but only just. I leaned over him, hands and eyes searching for the wound. If I could staunch the bleeding then I might just be able to save him. But there were multiple injuries cutting deep into his large body. He moaned slightly. Thinking quickly, I took the dagger and cut into the palm of my hand. My blood would heal him. I moved over and raised it towards his mouth but, without warning, his hand shot out and took hold of my wrist in an iron-clad grip.

"I wanted him to realise that he didn't need you," he gasped.

I yanked my hand away and down towards his mouth. But it was too late. A spine-chilling rattle sounded from deep within his throat and his eyes rolled back into his head. Staines was dead.

I fell backwards, staring in horror at his corpse. How in the hell had this happened? I'd been gone barely twenty-five minutes. I hugged my arms round my body. I'd failed him. If I'd only gotten here just a few minutes earlier, I could have been in time to save him. This was my fucking fault.

Shakily, I opened up my mind to call Corrigan with my Voice.

Lord Alpha?

A heartbeat later he answered. *What the hell do you want?*

*I need…*I stopped, taking a deep breath, then began again. *You need to get round to my place.*

Just because I'm re-joining the council, does not mean you have carte-blanche to have me at your beck and call. I'll put up with you when I have to but the rest of the time, my previous wishes still stand. I do not want to see you or speak to you. I'd appreciate it if you could respect that.

I closed my eyes in pain. *Corrigan, you have to get here.*

If you've gotten yourself into trouble yet again, then get that bloody faerie to help you out.

Sensing he was about to cut off the connection, I blurted out. *It's not me, Corrigan, it's Staines. You need to get here. He's…*Oh shit. *He's dead.*

There was a heavy oppressive silence from the Brethren Lord's end. It seemed to go on forever. Finally, his Voice returned, a dull monotone bouncing around my skull.

I'll be there within the hour. Then he snapped off.

My phone started ringing. Initially I ignored it, remaining where I was by Staines' body. After several rings, I shook myself and gingerly tiptoed over to pick it up, trying not to step in the pools of blood that lay in sickening glossy puddles around the floor.

"Miss Smith, it's the Arch-Mage. I've just

received intelligence that the Divination spells we have set up for Endor have been set off. It appears he returned to this plane for around ten minutes, then disappeared again. We're tracking what his exact location was right now. I should have the information any moment now."

I didn't answer.

"Miss Smith?"

"Don't bother," I said. "I know where he was." I looked back over at Staines. He was clutching something in his left hand.

"What? What do you mean?"

I put the receiver down, hanging up even though the Arch-Mage continued talking, and walked back over to check it out. It was a piece of paper. Uncurling the already cooling fingers of the were-bear, I extricated it and carefully unfolded the corners. It was smeared with blood, but I still recognised it as the note I'd left on my front door. Underneath it, however, something had been added.

I've been reading about you. It appears that you're even more interesting than I realised. I dropped by to say hello, and came across your friend instead. Sorry about the mess.

E

I balled it up in my hand, then backed away into the corner, and huddled down to wait.

*

It wasn't long before Corrigan showed up. He must have broken the land speed records to get here so quickly, I thought dully, as I opened the front door to let him in. I knew his shifter sense of smell had registered the blood long before he'd stepped inside, but I gestured him towards the kitchen anyway, then moved out of his way. Silently, he brushed past me and went in. For a few moments there was nothing, then I heard a keening howl of pain and anguish that ripped right through me. I briefly closed my eyes, then trudged outside to give him some privacy.

Wishing for once that I smoked, I rested against the rough stone of the building's exterior. At least sucking on a cigarette would have given me something to do. I kicked my heels pointlessly against the wall instead, only looking up when a screech of tyres signalled the arrival of a vehicle. The Arch-Mage, Alex, Max and Larkin all stepped onto the pavement. Their faces were pale. Then three other cars pulled up, and several shifters piled out, overtaking the mages who remained standing in front of me. They barely glanced in my direction, heading immediately inside to join Corrigan.

The Arch-Mage stepped forward. "What happened?"

I explained in as frank a manner as I could, and passed him over the note. He stared down at it, then nodded grimly and entered, Max and Larkin at his heels. I stopped Alex before he could follow them.

"We need some fucking palladium and we need it now. I can't afford to tiptoe around the Ministry and their lack of finances any more, Alex. Either you've managed to get hold of some, or I'll need to get the money from the shifters and the Fae now."

"I don't have any," he said, "but I know where to

get it. And it'll be of a higher quality and more useful than anything you could pay for."

I waited.

"Russia." He licked his lips. "There's a mine about sixty miles east of Moscow."

"So all I need to do is waltz in with a pickax?"

"The mining company that runs it ships out what they collect at the end of every week. They won't miss a small amount."

"You're telling me to steal it?"

He shrugged helplessly. I lifted my eyes to the heavens. Breaking the law and getting on the bad side of a bunch of wealthy Russians didn't strike me as a particularly responsible thing to do.

"That's not going to work, Alex. I need an alternative that's going to let me source it legitimately."

"We don't have much time," he began.

I exploded. "I know we don't have much fucking time! But I'm not going to start causing more problems than I'm solving. Not this time. Find someone who can help."

The expression on his face was strained. "Okay. I'll go to the bookshop. Maybe they can suggest something."

"Go."

He nodded and took off down the street. I clenched my jaw. Helping the poverty-stricken mages avoid losing face almost seemed like a pointless task in the wake of Staines' bloody assassination. If we could get hold of some palladium, and if Balud's research was correct, then we might just have a shot at beating Endor. It was going to take all of us working as a team to manage it; I couldn't keep pulling the lone wolf stunts.

But a large part of my role was to keep the three groups happy so that they could actually collaborate effectively as equals. Revealing the mages' lack of money, inadvertently or otherwise, wouldn't do that. Assuming Alex found a way to obtain some palladium without breaking the law, I was in a position to travel to Russia straight away. A flight to Moscow wouldn't last more than a couple of hours. Even better, a portal would be instantaneous. Factor in the journey to the mines, and whatever it took to get someone to just give me some palladium for free, and it couldn't take more than twenty-four hours. If it did, then I'd just have to give in to what was probably inevitable and get the Fae and the Brethren to stump up the cash after all. I nodded to myself. It was a compromise. An image of Staines' battered body filled my head. I'd get vengeance for him one way or another. We might not have been friends, but that didn't mean he had deserved to end like that. Not on my watch and not in my home.

Several of the shifters came out just then, carefully carrying a thick roll of carpet. Max and Larkin were following. They must have cast an Illusion spell so they could get Staines' corpse out without any humans noticing. Then the Arch-Mage exited with Corrigan, who lifted his head and stared at me, anguish lining his face.

"Where were you?"

"At the bookshop. I was late getting here to meet him."

"Deliberately?" he snarled, with a sudden flash

of irate emotion.

"Um..." I was confused, but equally trying to tread gently.

"Because he pissed you off yesterday. Were you deliberately late?"

I shook my head, suddenly understanding. "No. Honestly, no. Slim found something important about Endor that he thought would help. I was only gone for twenty-five minutes. It must have happened so quickly."

Tension seeped out of every pore of Corrigan's body. "I'm going to kill him." He said it quietly. In a way, that was scarier than if he'd been shouting.

I thought of Staines' last words, about proving to Corrigan that he didn't need me and just nodded. It wasn't as if I'd been a hell of a lot of use up till now.

"We'll get some people to clean up your flat," the Arch-Mage said.

I didn't react. I wasn't going to live there ever again. "We've got four and a half days until he shows up at Loch Ness," I said instead. Deciding not to lie outright, I continued on. "I have a lead on something that might help us defeat him. Instead of meeting this afternoon, we should start working on getting as many people up there as possible. We'll need to make sure we don't scare him off, but have enough troops on the ground to take him on."

"Do you need some help? I can spare a few people."

I shook my head at the Arch-Mage. "No. I may be out of contact until later tomorrow though."

Thankfully he didn't probe any further. He still seemed dazed from the scene of carnage just a few feet away.

"Can you get in touch with the Summer Queen and let her know what's happened? And tell her to contact the kelpies?"

"I'll do that," he agreed.

Corrigan was watching me. "Where will you stay?"

I avoided looking him directly in the eyes. "I'll crash at the bookshop. There's already a camp bed set up there for Aubrey."

"What if he shows up again?"

There was no need to ask whom Corrigan was referring to. "Alex is there now. I'll get him to put a ward in place. That'll give me enough warning to prepare, even if he manages to break through it. I had quite a bit of success with Tom this morning."

Corrigan's face was emotionless. "I heard. We will have a service for Staines on Friday morning, then travel up to Scotland after that. It would be good if you were there."

"Of course I'll be there. I'll be ready and waiting by the water's edge for the fucker to show his face."

"I mean at the funeral. Come to the funeral."

I looked up at him. His expression remained blank, but there was an odd note of pleading in his eyes. I'd be back from Russia by Thursday night, one way or another. I would make it. I nodded.

"I'm so sorry, Corrigan."

There was a flicker of acknowledgement in his eyes, then he turned and started to walk towards his car, his normally perfect posture sagging ever so slightly. My heart ached.

"I should go too," said the Arch-Mage.

"Okay. You will contact the Fae, won't you?"

His eyes were flinty. "The faeries and we might not like each other, but we do all have the same goal here. Yes. I will talk to the Summer Queen as soon as I get back."

I guessed I had just laid doubt on his honour. He needed to get over himself. I watched as, one by one, the cars all drove away until I was all alone again. With a heavy heart, I then turned back towards Clava Books.

Chapter Thirteen

It had been barely any time since I'd been within the safe warmth of the bookshop, but it felt as if the world had been tipped upside down in the intervening minutes. The door jangled its familiar tune as I pushed it open. I looked at it lying open for a moment, not really in an entirely conscious fashion, and then slammed it shut with such force behind me that the glass inlaid into the centre cracked.

Slim came flapping around but, for once, kept his mouth shut and his expression serious. He watched me carefully, I guessed in case I decided to try setting the interior alight or something like that. Eventually, I spoke.

"Sorry."

He nodded, then turned around and flapped back to the counter where he busied himself with the till. "I always thought a glass door was a fecking stupid idea with you around anyway."

I smiled faintly.

"Mack Attack? I'm guessing the sound of destruction means that's you," Alex called out from behind one of the shelves, then craning his head around, he beckoned me over. "We've got something."

I walked around to join him, noting once I'd rounded the corner that both he and Aubrey were sat cross-legged on the floor with several books and an open laptop strewn around them. I had to admit that I was surprised. They'd only communicated by phone before, and Alex had most definitely not been a fan of the ex-vamp's. Perhaps they were bonding over the excitement of research. It didn't seem likely. Then I spotted two empty tea-cups on the floor next to them. Interesting. Had Mrs. Alcoon been giving the pair of them some kind of 'friendly' herb to drink? I wouldn't put it beyond her.

"So," Alex said, "we know where the mine is, and that it's an entirely human run organisation. It would be easier if we could find some Otherworld connections which we could put to use, because it's by far the closest mine to travel to, but no such luck. However, that doesn't mean we can't introduce some Otherworldly action of the sort that will help them rather than hinder them."

"How so?"

Aubrey tapped at the screen on the computer. "The Karzelek."

I must have looked blank because Alex jumped in to explain. "A breed of dwarves. They live in mines and act as guardians of gems, precious metals, that kind of thing. Traditionally, the Karzelek will protect miners and help them locate the most bountiful veins of ore. This mine doesn't have one. We find one Karzelek to help us out, and we're gold."

Aubrey's eyes were shining. "You see the company is looking for some mining experts to help them make sure they've completely plumbed the depths of this area."

"And I've already contacted them and offered our services." Alex beamed. "We use a Karzelek to find the best palladium ore in the entire mine and ask for a small amount of it as payment in return."

Aubrey jerked his head at the mage. "No-one will suspect anything."

"We have an appointment with the mine's manager dude at one o'clock tomorrow," said Alex. "I'm not much good with setting up portals, but I reckon I can probably manage it. We'll be there with hours to spare. And be back here with all the palladium we need by nightfall tomorrow."

Alex and Aubrey grinned at each other. The pair of them together were like some bizarre tagteam. Mrs. Alcoon, with concern written all over her face, bustled over and handed me another cup of tea. To reassure her, and make my life as simple as possible, I took the cup and murmured my thanks. I held my breath in the hope of avoiding the smell and, as a result, the taste of the drink, and took a large gulp. It didn't really help. I turned my attention back to Laurel and Hardy.

"Yeah, that's a great plan," I said slowly.

Alex looked at his new friend. "Surf's up!" he bellowed out, and held up his hand for a high five. Unfortunately for him, it was clearly a gesture that Aubrey was unfamiliar with because when tentatively raised his own palm up, and Alex slapped it, there was a look of hurt indignation on the ex-vamp's face.

"What did you do that for?" he whined, snatching his hand away. "I'm human now, you know, you can't just go around attacking me for no reason."

Alex put his arm around his shoulder. "Dude," he said, shaking his head, "there is so much about the real world that I need to teach you."

I dreaded to think. Forcing their attention back to me, I cleared my throat. "There is just one thing. Just one teeny tiny fly in the ointment."

The pair of them just looked at me.

I sighed. "Where the fuck do we find a Karzelek between now and 1pm tomorrow and, even if we do, how do we persuade them to work with us?"

Simultaneously, their faces dropped. "Oh."

"Yeah, oh."

"It can't be that hard," blustered Aubrey.

"Sure," I said sarcastically. "Mythological mining dwarves who are out of work are probably hanging around all over the place."

They just stared at me. I sighed. "This isn't going to work. I'll just have to get some money from the Summer Queen and the Brethren so we can pay for the sodding palladium."

"You can't!" protested Alex. "It'll put the Ministry in too weak a position."

"And how weak a position will we all be in if Endor shows up again and decides that slaughtering one were-bear just isn't enough to satisfy him? I'm sorry if the Arch-Mage's ego is going to get a little bruised, but enough is enough. The Ministry will just have to suck it up."

"Mack, please," pleaded Alex. "We need to at least try. There's bound to be some Otherworld hangout in Moscow where we can find a Karzelek. You know how many creatures there are mooching around London. There must be that many in Russia too."

I started to shake my head.

"Cherniy Volk."

I twisted around and looked at Slim, who'd decided to suddenly enter the fray.

"Eh?"

"Cherniy Volk," he repeated. "It's a bar in Presny, in Moscow. If you're looking for someone or looking to stay hidden, that's the place to be."

Alex crowed. "See! We go there and see if we can find a Karzelek."

We were just leaving too much to chance. "I don't see how it can work."

"Give us one night, Mack Attack," he pleaded. "Since when were you the type to shy away from a challenge?"

I flicked a glance at Slim. "How do you know this place?"

He shrugged. "I spent some time in Russia. I think this is a fecking stupid plan, but if you're going to find a Karzelek, then that is the place." He pointed at Alex. "And he's right about the Ministry. One of the few things that maintains the balance right now is the fact that everyone feels they're equal. You don't need the mages to start feeling as if they're inferior to everyone else. The cornered animal is much more dangerous than the one roaming free. And I know the mages and their delicate sensibilities pretty well, remember."

"Fine," I said, yielding. "But if we've not found one of these sodding dwarves to agree to help us by tomorrow morning, then we high-tail it back here and we go with my plan to just get the fucking money instead."

A spasm of relief crossed Alex's features. "Okay.

I'll get onto opening the portal. And Mack Attack?"

"Yes?"

"Thank you."

*

Mrs. Alcoon had changed the sign on the shop door to 'closed', and pulled down the blinds. Alex stood in the middle of the room, and began to chant. I had to admit I was slightly wary about whether he'd have the ability to pull off opening and maintaining a portal to Moscow. Ostensibly, a mage could create portals that led anywhere and everywhere, but I knew from my time at the mages' academy that it wasn't always as simple as that. Not every mage possessed the skill to open magical doorways. I tried not to think about the horror stories that I'd heard of involving inexperienced mages bringing up shimmering portals that they'd blithely step through – only to find themselves in the opposite place to where they'd intended to go and next to a very angry Otherworld nastie about to chomp off their head. Alex had certainly travelled through enough of them, but I'd never actually seen him spell one open. Still, before too long, the air was crackling and the shiny purple swirls indicated that he'd had at least some measure of success.

It was good we wouldn't have to travel by plane after all, I told myself. Aubrey certainly wouldn't have been able to come along for the ride as the last thing he was in possession of was a passport. Of course, that didn't really quell my trepidation at having to step through the bloody portal, however. I eyed it narrowly. I hated these fucking things.

"Right," Alex said cheerily, "let's go."

Aubrey had about the same expression on his face as I imagined I had on mine. "What time is it in Moscow?"

I checked my watch. "It's three hours ahead of here, so early evening."

He relaxed slightly. "So it's getting dark?"

"Well, it's summer so not quite yet, but it's not blazing sunshine."

He sighed in relief. I shook my head. "You'd think that having stayed out of the sun for two hundred years, you'd be happy to get to spend some time in it."

"Old habits die hard."

I thought of the crack in the glass that I'd managed to put into the bookshop's front door, and my perennially bad temper. "Yeah, I guess so."

"Who's going first?" Alex looked from one of us to the other.

Better get it over and done with, I figured. "Fine. I will."

"What's wrong with her?" asked Aubrey.

Alex smirked. "You'll see."

"I am still fucking here, you know."

"We'll see you on the other side."

"Can't wait," I grunted, then stepped through, feeling the familiar tug through my body and inevitable nausea rise up into my stomach.

Almost immediately, I fell forward onto my hands and knees and began retching. I knew I'd landed somewhere quiet and dark, but all I could really focus on was the continual lurching of my stomach as I heaved and heaved. There was a snap as Aubrey came through, and I heard him say something over me, but it barely registered. I retched again, feeling a cold sweat break out across my forehead. Vomit spewed out, then almost immediately another wave of nausea rippled through my entire body.

When I was finally done, I staggered to my feet. "Fucking hell," I swore. That was about the worst transition I'd ever experienced. Sodding Alex. We should have gotten a more experienced mage from somewhere to open the portal. Clearly it was his wavering skill that had caused me to be even more ill than I normally was.

"Damn," Aubrey commented. "Is that supposed to happen? Because I feel fine."

"Piss off."

I peered at him through the gloom, and realised Alex had also materialised through and was muttering something to himself.

"Where are we?"

"Something went wrong. This wasn't where I'd been planning to emerge," he said, distracted.

Great. "And where is here?"

"I can't tell. Some kind of..."

"Cupboard," Aubrey finished for him. "At least it's dark."

I reached out in both directions with my hands, unable to see much but feeling my fingers scraped against walls on either side. I traced my hand slong the rough surface, suddenly yelping as I touched something cold and clammy.

"What? What is it?" Panic was clearly starting to set in for the mage.

"It's okay. Aubrey's right, we're in some kind of

cupboard. I think I just touched a mop."

"This is exciting! We could be anywhere. The mystery of it all is thrilling."

I wasn't sure which irritated me more: Alex's fear, or Aubrey's enthusiasm. I decided that, either way, I had an intense dislike of small dark places. "Come on. Let's find the sodding door and get out of here."

All of us started fumbling around. It felt like an age before Alex suddenly called out that he'd found it. He rattled a doorknob.

"It's locked - we're trapped."

"Move out of the way," I instructed, then maneuvered myself around. I pulled on the knob then, realising he was right, backed away slightly and took a breath. Then I lunged forward with a high kick, and the door sprang open.

The three of us piled out, blinking. Soft music was playing, and there appeared to be an escalator leading down to somewhere just ahead of us. There was also a small raised area upon which stood three well-dressed mannequins. Before I could stop him, Aubrey had leapt forward and started attacking one of them, hitting it with his fists and knocking it to the ground. Then he spun around, apparently ready for the next one.

"Tell us who you are!" he shouted.

"Er, Aubrey?"

"What?" He looked down at his fallen 'victim'. "Oh. Sorry, I thought that was a person. It looked like they were holding a sword and were about to attack."

"That's an umbrella."

He coughed. "I see that now. Where are we?"

"It looks like some kind of department store, I think. Are we even in Russia, Alex?"

"We must be," he muttered.

I strode over to the escalator and stepped on. "Well, let's find out."

The pair of them followed me. As we travelled down to what was apparently the ground floor, filled as it was with all manner of perfumes and make-up accoutrements, I spotted an advertisement with Cyrillic lettering hanging over to the right and pointed it out.

"See? I knew I could do it," Alex said, suddenly filled with renewed confidence.

"Yeah, okay. Good work, Alex. The trouble is," I fretted, "Russia is big fucking country. We could really still be anywhere."

"Allow me," drawled Aubrey, as we reached the bottom of the escalator. I watched, rather impressed, as he stepped confidently over to a well-dressed woman and introduced himself. He took her hand and kissed it. The object of his attentions was obviously flustered, and remarkably flattered, judging by the way she smiled and giggled.

"You are simply beautiful, madam," he intoned. "As are all the women of this wonderful city. It is a true pleasure to make your acquaintance."

She bit her lip.

"Tell me, because I'm not from this country as you can probably tell, but how do you pronounce the name of this great town?"

"Moskva," she said breathlessly.

He dropped her hand as if it was a hot rock and

returned to us, leaving her staring after him, open-mouthed.

"Yeah, we're in Moscow. Let's get a taxi to this bar." He caught my look. "What? I was a vampire, remember? I did have some skills."

"That kind of thing really works?"

He gestured behind him. "As you see." Then he grinned.

"I think I just threw up in my mouth."

"I'm amazed you have anything left inside you to throw up. Just make sure you don't breathe on me." He wrinkled his nose.

Hmm. He seemed to be getting over his vampire-to-human adjustment period. He was certainly a lot less emotional than he used to be.

"Oh my God," he suddenly cried out.

Alarmed, I followed his gaze. "What?"

"Look at that scarf." He almost ran over and began stroking a silk black scrap of fabric. "Isn't it gorgeous?" His eyes welled up. "It's almost hard to believe that something this stunning could exist." He sniffed.

Okay. He still had some way to go yet. I rolled my eyes and walked out to hail a taxi.

Chapter Fourteen

The air felt different from London. It was about the same temperature, but there was a smoky quality to it, somehow making the atmosphere even more claustrophobic than normal. The road in front was remarkably wide with intricately designed buildings on either side that included uniformly arched windows and high rooftops. I felt a sudden longing for the clean crispness of the open countryside and wondered if I'd be doomed to spend the rest of my life in cities.

I couldn't see anything remotely resembling a taxi, despite the heavy traffic, and I realised also that our unconventional mode of travel had meant we'd not managed to come across any form of money-changers. With no rubles, there would be no way to pay.

A battered boxy car pulled up alongside the curb and the driver wound down the window with what seemed like extraordinary effort. His face peered out, lined and weathered.

"Taxi?"

Alex appeared by my shoulder. "How much?"

A wide grin spread across the driver's face. "Foreigner? Special price. Where you go?"

"We don't have any money," I hissed at the mage.

"Chillax," he drawled back. "I've got it covered."

I shot him a suspicious look. At least he had the grace to look slightly embarrassed. "I changed money this morning."

"What if I'd refused to come?"

He shrugged. "Then I'd have changed it back. Or come myself."

I raised my eyebrows slightly at that.

"What?" he said. "It's not like there'll be any fighting involved."

I hoped he was right. I grunted and turned my attention back to the driver. Aubrey, apparently managing to have torn himself away from the seductive delights of the department store, moved forward then abruptly stopped.

"I'm not getting in that. Look at it. It's covered in rust! It'll probably fall apart as soon as we get in. I've got to take care myself now that I'm human, you know."

"This car is good," insisted the driver, banging the side of it with his arm. "Russian make. Very safe. Where you go?"

"Presny," said Alex.

"It's not even a taxi!" Aubrey cried. "It's just a man with a car!"

"Your friend very scared," the driver interjected, with an air of what could only be described as glee. "Is okay. I am bombily." At our blank faces, he explained. "Private taxi driver. I take you to Presny for only thousand rubles."

I gazed doubtfully at him. I had no idea how much that actually was, but it sounded a lot.

"Done!"

"Alex, we're supposed to negotiate!"

"Who's doing the paying here?"

Grumbling, I walked over to the back door and jerked the handle to open it. It didn't budge so I tried again. Goddamnit. The driver opened his door and ambled around while I got out of his way. He used his left hand to pull down the handle while propping his right foot up on the side of the car for traction. The door fell open with an ominous creak. Flakes of paint flew off in every direction.

Smiling cheerily and holding the door open, the driver gestured inside. I sighed and clambered in, followed by Alex.

Aubrey put his hands on his hips. "I'm not doing it - it's a deathtrap. I'd rather walk."

I shrugged. "Okay, then."

He stared at me incredulously, huffed, and got in. The driver slammed the door shut and got back into his own seat in the front. I reached back for the seatbelt, then realised there wasn't one.

"Er…"

"Is okay, I am very safe driver!"

Without warning, the car lurched forward onto the road, as he put his foot down on the accelerator, revving the engine and speeding up alarmingly.

"What's your name?" asked Alex.

"Vasily."

"Okay, Vasily, we are going to Dobchek Road. Do you know where that is?"

"Of course, of course! No problem!" He reached over and turned a knob on the radio. Immediately, loud music with incomprehensible lyrics filled the space.

"I'm going to die," moaned Aubrey as we screeched around a corner.

I was beginning to agree. Vasily shouted something from the front.

I leaned forward. "Pardon?"

He twisted his head around and looked at all three of us. "Business or pleasure?"

A truck loomed up ahead. "Vasily!"

He turned back to the front and slammed on his horn. "Russian truck drivers very bad."

I breathed out. "Yes. Er, we're here for business."

"Good, good. You want I take you for sightsee first? Kremlin? Red Square?"

"No, thanks, Vasily, we must get on with our business. We don't have a lot of time."

"Sure, sure, I understand. I no want you get angry, breathe fire."

Alex and I stiffened. Vasily let out a hearty laugh and waggled his finger in the mirror at me. "I see your picture. On Othernet. You shift dragon, no?"

Fucking hell.

"What does he mean?" Aubrey asked. "Shift dragon? What is that?"

"How do you know that, Vasily?" I asked, ignoring Aubrey for the time being.

He laughed again. "I am Zduhàc."

"Joohatch?"

"Zduhàc!"

Of all the taxis in all the world. "What is a Zduhàc?"

"Supernatural man. Big power. I stop storms, help farmers..."

"Drive taxis?"

"Ah, no. I – how you say – give up Zduhàc to move to city. No money. Machinery help farms, no need me. Before I stop Ala, evil storm demon. Now I drive taxi like demon!" He thumped his steering wheel and chortled. "So you go Cherniy Volk?"

"How did you know?"

"Otherworld people always go Cherniy Volk. You know what means? Black Wolf. Many shifter at Cherniy Volk." He laughed. "Many black wolf."

"How about Karzelek? Any of them hang out there?"

"Dwarf? Little man? I never see." He shrugged. "Maybe. Maybe not."

I exchanged a look with Alex. I wasn't exactly brimming with confidence that we'd find who we were looking for.

The taxi pulled to a shuddering stop. Vasily scrabbled around in his glove compartment and took out a small grubby card. "Here is my number. You need me, you call. Okay? I tell my friends I get crazy dragon girl in my taxi. They very impressed."

"Actually, Vasily," I said, taking the card, "we're travelling incognito. In disguise. We'd really appreciate it if you didn't tell anyone about us."

"Ah, secret?" He nodded vigorously. "You can trust me. I no tell. Or maybe you come eat me, eh?" He burst into yet another round of laughter.

"Thanks, dude," said Alex, slapping him on the shoulder and handing over an array of crumpled notes to pay the fare.

Aubrey, face white as a sheet, rattled the door. "I can't get out." His voice started rising. "I can't get out! I can't get out! I'm going to be stuck here forever with this psycho demon hunting taxi driver and a dragon. Get me out! Get me out!"

"Aubrey, fucking calm down," I said, trying to

hush him.

Vasily clambered out and did his hand and foot trick again, and the door sprung open. Aubrey fell out, then half ran, half crawled to the pavement in his haste to get away. Alex shook the driver's hand, as did I. His grip was surprisingly strong, and he winked at me when I finally managed to extricate my throbbing fingers.

"You need help, you call me!" He kicked shut the door, got back into his seat then, with an engine that sounded like it was an ogre with a sore throat, revved back up and screeched off in a cloud of choking blue smoke.

We watched him go, then Alex turned to Aubrey who was sitting on the edge of the dirty pavement, hugging his knees. At least he'd calmed down.

"You alright, dude?"

"No."

"Excellent."

He pouted up at me. "You didn't tell me you were a dragon."

I felt a flicker of guilt. "I'm sorry. It was a secret."

"A secret? Even the crazy taxi driver knew! How could I not know? After everything we've been through, Mack." He sounded genuinely hurt.

"I'm sorry. If it helps, I didn't want anyone to know. And I'm not really a dragon. I'm what's called a Draco Wyr."

"That's why I'm like this, isn't it? Why I'm human. That's why your blood tasted funny when I drank you. Not because of that herbal stuff you said you'd had."

"Yeah."

He buried his head in his arms. Fuck. I didn't really know what to say.

"I didn't know if I could trust you, Aubrey. You were a vampire after all."

He didn't answer. Alex twisted uncomfortably and looked up at the sign hanging by the door in front of us, trying to change the subject.

"I guess this is it. Let's see what we can find."

I shook my head. "I can't."

"What?"

"Vasily knew who I was, Alex. My picture must be all over the freaking Othernet. If I go in there, it's not going to help us. Not only will it be all over the wires that we're here, but I'll spend the entire time being inundated with bloody dragon stuff. We can't afford that kind of distraction."

He swallowed, suddenly looking nervous. "Damn it. I don't even think my Illusion ability is strong enough to hold a glamour. You're right, Mack Attack. I can wait out here with you, and Aubrey can go in."

We both looked down at the ex-vamp who whimpered and drew his knees closer to his chest.

"Okay," backtracked Alex, "Aubrey and I will go in together. Alright, Aubs?"

He made a small sound of agreement and got to his feet. "I don't like this. My life was much simpler when I was dead. I don't know why you're sending me in anyway when you don't trust me."

"I trust you now. You can do it, Aubrey," I said, with much more conviction than I felt. "Be a man. Remember how you thought all this was exciting less than an hour ago."

He looked at me miserably. It would have been easier if he'd just been pissed off. The way he looked right now, like a puppy who had been abandoned, was almost too much to bear. He had a point; I should have told him when I'd realised that it was coming out all over the Othernet. He deserved that much. Not sure about what to say to make things better, I jerked my head across the street, where a suitably dark alley sat just waiting.

"I'll be in there. Try not to get yourselves into too much trouble."

The pair of them nodded, then pushed open the door to the bar. Sounds of chatter and a drifting cloud of smoke seeped out, then vanished as the door shut behind them. I remained standing there for a moment, just on the off-chance that they were immediately turfed out again on their arses. When nothing seemed to happen, I jogged over to the alley and hid myself amongst the shadows, settling in to wait.

*

The moon was high in the sky when they finally re-emerged. I'd been waiting for what had seemed like an eternity, shifting position, and watching the various patrons of the Cherniy Volk come in and out. There was indeed a motley crew of Otherworld creatures. Unfortunately, I'd not seen anything resembling a dwarf, let alone a mine-dwelling, palladium-finding Karzelek. The night air was considerably colder than it had been when we'd arrived in the early evening and I'd had to keep jumping around and running on the spot to keep my circulation going. I'd been pissing myself off with imagining the unlikely pair sitting propped up at the bar, drinking gallons of Russian vodka, and generally having a fantastic time. Then I had pissed myself off more by remembering the look on Aubrey's face before he'd gone in. Life had certainly been a lot easier when no-one had known who – or what – I was.

When Alex came out, he made some kind of quick surreptitious gesture over in my direction before he was joined by Aubrey and one other. I couldn't make out exactly who their new companion was, other than that she was female, with long white hair, and must have been at least six and a half feet tall. This was no dwarf. I hoped that the boys weren't just trying to take advantage of some of Moscow's less desirable nightlife offerings. The three of them set off down the street with purpose, however, as if they knew where they were going. I followed at a safely discreet distance, keeping my footsteps light and staying close to the shadows of the looming buildings, just in case the woman should decide to suddenly turn around. She seemed, for the most part, to be engaged in earnest conversation with both of them, however, at one point even linking her arms through theirs in a companionable fashion.

Turning left when they reached the end of the street, I lost sight of them for a few moments. I jogged to catch up, just to make sure I didn't lose them, but when I reached the edge of the last building and peered around, there was no sign of them. Cursing slightly under my breath, I picked up speed, running lightly and keeping my eyes peeled.

Thankfully, I soon heard their voices down a near side street.

"He's just down this way. It's fortunate really that I bumped into you. He's a good friend of mine so I'm sure he'll be happy to help two friendly strangers in a foreign land with a small favour," she was saying, with just the faintest hint of a Russian accent.

That sounded hopeful, as if she was leading them somewhere, and to someone, who might actually be a Karzelek. I'd believe it when I saw it though. I waited a moment or two until their voices were further away, before skirting round and pressing myself against the rough wall as I moved down in their direction. The three of them then stopped abruptly up ahead. I halted too, right across from a trio of metal dustbins, which were filled to overflowing. A fleabitten looking rat was perched on top of one, blinking at me. I gave it a half-smile, as if in greeting. It twitched its nose in return, then delved inside the rubbish with only its tail still visible.

I cocked my head, trying to hear what was going on up ahead. I could only make out snatches of words here and there though. Unfortunately, there was a streetlight illuminating the area they were in, so I couldn't move any nearer without potentially giving myself away. I leaned forward, straining my ears when suddenly, somewhere, a door banged and there was a long loud shout that sounded like 'booooka'. I jumped about half a foot in the air, then a huge shape that seemed to be of the stuff of nightmares emerged from one of the buildings. Shit.

Without any suggestion of preamble it reached out, picking Aubrey up by the scruff of his neck and threw him to one side as if he weighed next to nothing. Without waiting any longer, I pushed off from the wall and sprang forward, the familiar burn of bloodfire sparking up inside me. Yeah, this had just been too good to be true.

The woman half turned, realising that someone was coming. I yelled at Alex to get away, but he was trapped between the two of them. Pelting down the street, I sent down a plume of green fire. It caught on the woman's white hair, instantly setting it alight. She shrieked, hands grabbing at her long locks in a vain effort to put out the flames. In that instant, I reached her and grabbed her arms and pulled back on the collar of her jacket. Then, I thrust her forward again and her head bounced off the wall. She fell, dazed. One down.

Pushing Alex behind me, I turned to the second nastie, then blinked as its features became clearer. It had vast gnarled horns on top of its head and, what appeared to be, four...five... no, six fucking legs. How in the hell were they all attached? I craned my neck upwards. It was about two freaking storeys high. Well, the bigger they are, the harder they fall, I figured. I jetted out more flame towards it, aiming for what appeared to be a vulnerable section in its belly. The thing's eyes seemed to narrow for a moment, as if in thought, then it huffed out and launched a kick towards me.

I only just managed to jump out of the way in time, feeling the air whooshing past my head as the creature's leg almost connected. I crouched down, then sprang up with as much power and bounce as I could muster, kicking off the wall and reaching upwards. I'd been aiming to lock my hands around its neck, but unless I'd suddenly morphed into a red-headed version of Spiderman there was no way I was going to get up that high. Instead I managed to link one arm around its bicep. With the other, I lashed out and upwards trying to claw into its skin. What I hit was so leathery and hard, however, it was clear that was equally a non-starter. Pursing my lips slightly, I ran backwards to where the dustbins were and grabbed one of the metal lids. I snapped back my arm and then flung the lid out, just like a Frisbee. It soared into the air, heading straight for its target and caught the monster in between its nose and its lip. It snarled loudly. Finally.

Unfortunately for me, it was a fast learner. It picked up the dustbin lid where it had clattered on the ground and flung it back in my direction. The force and speed meant that, despite my best efforts to get out of the way, it still caught me on my upper arm. I yelled out at the burst of sudden pain. Okay. Now I was getting annoyed.

I twisted back round to face it. It really was a big bastard. I felt a ripple of trepidation, then made my decision. Picturing my little match in my head, I stared down at my hands, willing them to transform. My bones creaked and there was a snap of pain, and all of a sudden I looked like I had on two oversized red mittens. Well, red mittens with lethal talons at the end of them anyway. I lifted up my eyes to the creature and then leapt right at it, claws extended. I thrust into its flesh, gouging out a trail that ripped through its lower belly. It bellowed in pain and clumsily turned around, its legs getting tangled up before, somehow, untwisting itself and galloping away into the night.

I watched it go, wondering how this fight would have worked out had I been confident enough to fully transform. At least it meant I felt more in control of my Draco Wyr nature, if nothing else, and that I was more desperate to learn how to fully transform with that same control firmly in place. It was a relief to not feel terrified at the prospect of giving myself over to the dragon. I darted over to Aubrey and checked on him, although his groans had already indicated that he wasn't in any real danger, and helped him up to his feet.

"When I was a vampire, these kinds of things didn't happen," he grumbled, rubbing his head where it had smashed against the wall. He sent me a look filled with malevolence. "Being around you should carry a health warning."

I felt a wave of relief. I could deal with this kind of attitude much better than I could with abject sadness.

"Really? Because last time I checked you were begging to be allowed to stick around so that I could protect you," I scoffed. "And besides this one's all on you. I wasn't the one following strange women out of dodgy bars."

He glared at me. I grinned in return.

"You should have told me, Mack. I would have a kept it a secret."

"I know." I reached out and squeezed him on the shoulder.

He gave me a half smile in return. The lack of hysterics from him was reassuring. I held his eyes for a moment, then turned around to check to see whether Alex was anywhere within the vicinity. He was standing over the crumpled body of the woman, frowning. I strolled over and joined him.

"So what actually happened?" I asked. "You reek of alcohol."

"I spilled some vodka down my shirt," he commented. "I was trying to look as if I was drinking without really drinking, if you see what I mean."

"And her?" I jerked my head down.

He rubbed his forehead. "We asked around. Nobody knew of any Karzeleks, apart from her. She said she was mates with one and would take us to meet him."

"You know you just fell for the oldest trick in the book, right?"

"Why do you think I made sure you were following? It did occur to me that she might be leading us astray, Mack. I'm not a complete idiot." The stress in his voice was palpable, making me feel instantly guilty.

"I'm sorry it didn't work out, Alex. You knew it was always going to be a long shot though."

He looked at me dolefully for a moment, then back down at the woman. "The monster that jumped out. What kind of freaky Otherworld thing was that?"

I opened my mouth to tell him I had no idea, when a deep voice from within the shadows several feet away suddenly interrupted. "Buka. They normally hang around in lakes, waiting to drown unsuspecting victims. Goodness only knows what it's doing in the city. You did well to get rid of it."

The voice's owner stepped out into a patch of moonlight. Interesting. He was clearly a shifter, but he appeared unfeasibly large, even when compared to Corrigan. He had coarse dark hair and glittering black eyes, along with a moustache. Usually, I found facial hair a bit of a turn off but, somehow, on this guy, it was rather appealing. His whole image was rather debonair, in a swashbuckling kind of way. He kept his distance from us, sensing that I certainly wasn't in the mood for any surprises, and looked down at the woman.

"She's a Shishiga. Known for generally bringing misfortune to drunks. I have to apologise. If I'd been aware that she was in the bar, I'd have thrown her out long before. I was in the back, dealing with some business."

"Oh yeah?" blustered Aubrey, "and who the hell are you?"

It was a fucking good question.

The man smiled disarmingly. "I'm Cherniy Volk. The Black Wolf. I hear you're looking for a Karzelek and I think I may just be able to help."

Chapter Fifteen

Volk took us back to his bar, allowing us to enter through a discreet back entrance that led into a private area. Aubrey and Tom carried the woman between them, taking an arm each and looking for all the world as if they were merely helping out a friend who'd had one too many vodkas. At Volk's behest, they left her locked in the bar's small cellar area. I had to admit I was slightly suspicious as to his intentions with her. Not that I cared that much about the well-being of someone who preyed on vulnerable victims in order to strip them of their cash and valuables – or worse – but I wasn't quite prepared to leave her entirely to the wolves, so to speak. However, he dug out a mobile phone and spoke low guttural Russian into it, then hung up and grimaced at us.

"Bratstvo. I believe you would call them the Brethren? They will come and collect her and take her far out of the city where she will not bother anyone for a long time. Russia is a very large country. There are many places on the outer edges that are...difficult."

"They're going to take her to some kind of prison camp?" I asked, appalled.

He laughed. "Oh no. We may have done that in our past, but certainly not nowadays. They will simply leave her in a frozen wood somewhere. She won't die. She'll just be very cold. And very far away."

"What about the Buka?"

"They are simple minded creatures. Without her around to lead him, he will return to whichever lake he came from."

"You sound very confident about that."

"I know my country and my countrymen," he replied, simply.

Alex twitched, clearly wanting to cut to the chase. "So, dude, you can find us a Karzelek?"

"Of course." Volk smiled, baring his teeth. "I can even help you encourage her to do what it is that you want."

"Her?"

"Katya. She is a friend of the family." His eyes glinted. "In a way."

"And what do you want in return?"

"What makes you think I want anything?"

None of us bothered answering.

He thrust his arms up in the air in an expressive shrug. "You have seen through me."

I rolled my eyes. Imagine that. "There is something you can do for me," Volk continued. He looked at me. "I have seen on the Othernet that you have a relationship with Lord Corrigan."

I moved my weight uncomfortably from one foot to the other. "Not exactly."

"But you know him. Intimately."

Jeez. My cheeks flamed in embarrassment. If I ever came across the author of that fucking Othernet blog, I would make very sure that they died a long and painful death.

"I guess. We're not really on speaking terms

though, so if you want something from him, then I can't help."

"All I want is a bit of quid pro quo. Tit for tat. I will introduce you to Katya, and you will introduce me to Leah."

Leah? I frowned. I'd heard that name before.

"Lord Corrigan's sister," Volk supplied helpfully.

I started. Sister? Since when had Corrigan had a fucking sister? I knew who she was now that he'd mentioned it. She was the girl I'd seen going into Alcazon with him, just before the events with Endor at Haughmond Hill. I'd assumed she was his girlfriend, or consort, or something like that. I'd never heard anyone mention any family in relation to Corrigan. I realised that I didn't really know the Lord Alpha at all.

"You want to meet his sister?" I asked suspiciously. "Why?"

"Now it is my turn to blush," Volk said, without actually looking embarrassed in the slightest. "I have met her before. I like her. I would like to meet her again."

"Dude, why don't you just call her?" Alex was looking very puzzled.

I shot Aubrey a quick glance. He was eyeing Volk as if he was some strange new species that he'd just come across.

The Russian sucked in breath through his teeth. "We didn't really part on the best of terms. There's a chance she won't take my call. I think things will work better if we could 'accidentally' bump into each other."

Accidentally? This was all starting to sound

rather Machiavellian. Or, at the very least, like high school.

"How do we know she doesn't completely hate your guts and that seeing you will be traumatic and distressing for her?" I asked. "Maybe there's a very good reason for her not to want to talk to you."

He looked pained. "I am happy for you to be present. I would not dare risk the wrath of a dragon, after all. I just need to see her again face to face."

The dragon comment irked me. However, I had to admit he seemed genuine.

"I'm not sure how quickly I'll be able to manage it," I said finally. "It's not as if I actually know her. And there are other things going on with the Brethren and myself that may delay matters."

Alex was momentarily put out. "Not just with the Brethren and you."

"With a lot of the Otherworlders in the UK," I amended.

"If you give me your word that you will engineer a meeting as soon as you can, then that's good enough for me."

"You don't even know me."

"I'm a pretty good judge of character."

For a werewolf, he was remarkably earnest. I looked at Alex and Aubrey and they both gave me slight nods of agreement. I sighed.

"Okay, then. But if I get the slightest hint that she really doesn't want to see you because it'll upset her, or if you're going to do something that would harm her in any way, the whole deal is off."

"I would expect nothing else." Volk smiled, and this time I got the sense of genuine friendship from him.

I smiled back. "Now about that Karzelek? I'm afraid we're rather under the kibosh as far as time is concerned."

"She's already outside."

Alex beamed. "Bring her in!"

"As you wish." Volk left the room.

I turned to the other two. "I hope this guy is alright."

"Alright? Dude, he's amazeballs."

I threw Alex a droll look. "Did either of you two know that Corrigan had a sister?"

Alex shook his head. "I don't really spend all that much time thinking about the Brethren, Mack Attack."

Aubrey shrugged. "I knew."

"Why didn't you tell me?"

"Why would I? It's not like I thought it was a big deal. Not like, say, knowing that the person you've been hanging around with has a secret identity as a dragon."

I opened my mouth, then closed it again. Clearly he wasn't going to give that up for a while yet. And he did rather have a point. It occurred to me that, as far as the Lord Alpha was concerned, I was becoming a bit of stalker girl. Fortunately, Volk re-entered at that point, saving me from muddling my way through some babble about why I should have known Corrigan's family tree.

"Here she is," he said, gesturing behind him.

I did my best to appear friendly, and stuck out a hand towards the Karzelek. I was shocked at just how short she really was. That might prove problematic in getting her into the mine initially.

"Hi," I said. "I'm Mack."

She bobbed her head. "Katya."

Alex and Aubrey introduced themselves, then she looked back at me. "So you're the dragon." It wasn't a question.

Shit. Was there anyone anywhere who didn't know what I was? I coughed. "Not exactly."

Aubrey threw his hands up in the air. "Even the dwarf knows what you are!"

"I'm a Karzelek, not a dwarf." She laced her fingers primly in front of her. "So, dragon or not, I am told that you require some help."

Alex jiggled in excitement. "Yeah! If we could just borrow your time for a couple of hours tomorrow, then we'd be so grateful." He quickly outlined his plan to the little woman.

She shook her head. "Won't work."

He stopped bouncing around and stared at her. "Yes, it will."

"Look," she said patiently as if he were a very small child, "if there's one thing I know, it's mines. They're not going to let you waltz in and tell them that you can lead them to a new vein. They don't know you and there are serious health and safety considerations in place. It's not a tourist attraction."

"I spoke to the manager on the phone. When I told him we could help him with sourcing more palladium within the mine, he was thrilled."

"Sure. But it still doesn't mean he'll let you inside. If he's feeling generous, he'll show you some diagrams and maps, and perhaps some geological surveys and ask you to point out where you'd suggest they investigate. And in about six months' time, once they've exhausted their current avenues, then maybe they will."

Alex was completely deflated. "But..."

"There are no buts. It simply won't work. It's not the Otherworld, it's the human world. They do things differently."

"Why don't you just take some?" Volk asked curiously. "Just go there, grab some of it, then leave. They'll have security, but nothing I imagine you wouldn't be able to overcome."

"We're not stealing it," I said, firmly.

"Mack Attack..."

"We're not. It's wrong."

"It comes out of the ground. It belongs to the earth, not to some faceless corporation. You can't steal from Mother Nature." Alex paused. "Well, you can, but only if you're the freaking necromancer who we're trying to defeat anyway. Sheesh, our intentions at least are noble and heroic, even if our actions wouldn't be."

"Then let's just buy it, Alex."

He ran his hands through his hair. "There's got to be another way."

Katya, her head craned upwards, watching us with her eyes zipping from side to side as if she was at a tennis match, spoke up. "The dragon is right," she said sternly. "Those miners work hard for that metal. They risk their lives for it. You can't just steal it from them."

I looked at Alex, raising my eyebrows as if to emphasise her words.

"However," she continued, "there is maybe a

way you could get some."

Hope flared in Alex's eyes and he started jiggling again. "How?"

She shrugged. "I know the area. There's an abandoned mine shaft not too far away. The company which owns it is going to seal it over because they've stripped it of most of its resources. I've heard there is still some palladium ore left inside though. I don't imagine it'll be much, and I don't really understand what you need it for, but you might be able to get some from there."

"How would we, you know, get it out? Extract it?"

"You'd have to work that out yourselves. And you have to bear in mind that it's not just as easy as digging it out. Palladium is found inside nickel-copper deposits. It needs to be refined in order to become the element that you need."

I massaged my temples. "We can't do that."

"Actually, we can, Mack Attack." The enthusiasm had returned to Alex's voice. "It's basic mage science. I can probably even do it on site at the mine. If we can just find it, I can leach out the parts that we don't need with a basic spell."

I looked at Katya. She shrugged. "I've seen it done."

Aubrey clapped his hands together. "So what are we waiting for? Let's go!"

*

Unwilling to risk depleting his magical energy unnecessarily, we borrowed an incredibly flashy car from Volk rather than have Alex open another portal. We'd need him to set one up so we could return to London later on as it was, and at this time of night – or rather early morning – it would take us little more than an hour to reach the site of the mine-shaft anyway. Unfortunately, being sporty and flashy as it was, the car only had two seats: one for the driver and one for the passenger. Because Alex was driving, I ended up on top of Aubrey's lap on the passenger seat, with Katya on top of me. Sandwiched between the two of them as I was, my head kept bouncing off the car's ceiling, and I felt incredibly hot and uncomfortable. Things only got worse when we drove off the main road and onto an uneven, untarmacked side road.

"Fucking hell," I grumbled, as Aubrey's elbow somehow dug itself into my ribs while he changed his position and I got a mouthful of the Karzelek's hair.

"It's not my fault you're so heavy," he complained. "Maybe if you ate a little more salad and a little less junk food, then you wouldn't weigh so much."

"Are you suggesting that I'm fat?" I said, disbelievingly.

"Well, when I was a," he began, before the car jolted over a pothole and all three of us ended up squashed painfully against the window.

"You were saying?" I asked, once we'd vaguely righted ourselves. "When you were a vampire...?"

"He's a vampire?" Katya squeaked.

"Used to be. He's not anymore," I reassured her.

"You got something against vampires?" he demanded.

"Aubrey..."

"At least I'm not so short that the only ride I'd be allowed on at Disneyland is the merry-go-round!"

"Have you even been to Disneyland?"

"They do night shows and I like Minnie Mouse. What of it?" he asked, petulantly.

Good grief. "Alex, please tell me we are nearly there." I couldn't see a sodding thing out of the windscreen.

"Two more minutes, dude," he said. "Why? Aren't you enjoying the ride? This is a seriously cool car."

I tried very hard not to curse. At least we did, indeed, arrive two minutes later, all three of us piling out and gasping for relief in the open air. I'd almost prefer to have travelled via a portal. Almost. I grabbed a small pick-ax that Volk had given us from the car floor, and gripped it. I had no idea why a large werewolf would have had mining equipment lying around in a bar, and I'd decided at the time that it was probably safer not to ask.

Katya pointed us towards a dark square shaped hole that seemed to be cut into the side of a massive cliff. It yawned open, almost like the gates of hell themselves. A faint smell of sulphur combined with rock dust lingered in the air.

"We should have brought a bloody canary," I said.

"Or perhaps a torch at the very least," Aubrey commented.

"At least we have this," I said, swinging the small pick-ax in my hand, then passing it to Aubrey. I sparked up some green fire at my fingertips and shot out a bolt towards the entrance. The light it cast was eerie, but at least we could see where we were going.

"Okay, team," I murmured.

We set off together. When we actually stepped into the mine itself, I felt a sudden wave of claustrophobic hysteria building up inside me. In order to calm it down, I called up a swirl of bloodfire, enjoying the familiar heat rush through my body. Aubrey gripped my arm, and Alex remained close to my other side, while Katya trotted ahead, completely unconcerned.

"You don't think there'll be anything bad in here, do you?" Alex whispered.

"Like what?" I had no idea why I was whispering back.

"You know, like maybe an evil cave-dwelling monster who we have to fight to the death?"

"I'm sure Katya would have mentioned if there was likely to be anything lurking around."

"Either that or she's leading us into a deadly trap. Like flies into a creepy spider's web." He stopped for a moment. "Shit. You don't think there'll be any giant spiders, do you?"

I tugged on his arm. "Come on. You're the one who wanted to do things this way, remember?"

"You're right. Yes," he nodded. "Everything will be fine."

We continued on silently, following Katya, who proceeded forward at an impressive rate considering the length of her little legs. Every time we rounded a hewn out corner, I used my green fire to light up the way ahead. The corridors seemed to be getting narrower, however, and the air was definitely becoming less fresh and much more oppressive. I thought of people who worked in places like this for a living. Maybe my life wasn't so bad after all.

Katya finally stopped, waiting for us to catch up.

"It's been too long since I've felt the freedom of the underground," she said, with a happy sigh.

Each to their own. She pointed down to a small hole.

"We need to go through there."

I traced it with my finger, letting the fire highlight where she meant. It was going to be a tight fucking squeeze. Aubrey moaned faintly.

She got down on her hands and knees and began to crawl through. Jeez. If the Karzelek had to crawl through, then I dreaded to think what it was going to be like for the rest of us. Perhaps Aubrey had been right and I should lay off the junk food after all.

Alex nudged me. "You first."

I swallowed and bent down, peering through. It didn't seem as if there was any way I was possibly going to fit. Katya was already far ahead though. I stuck my head through, then hunched my shoulders together, and began to wiggle forward. I'd never thought about what it might be like to be a worm, but this must pretty much be it. Pulling my hips through was painful, and I could feel my skin scraping against the rock above and below as my t-shirt got pushed up. Inch by inch, I shoved myself forward. This was not fun.

After what seemed like an eternity, the tunnel began to widen. I breathed in relief as I could first get onto my hands and knees, and then half stand up and stoop as I continued forward. The blackness of the mine seemed to be starting to smother me, even with the green fire still flickering at my fingers. I was concentrating so hard on keeping myself calm and centred that I knocked into Katya, almost making her fall over.

"Sorry."

She tutted, and pointed through the gloom at something. "It's there. There really isn't very much though. Even less than I thought."

I stared at it. I couldn't see anything. Alex pulled himself out of the tunnel, followed by Aubrey. Both of them were breathing heavily.

"We've made it," I told them.

"Praise the Founder," Alex sighed. "Whose idea was this again?"

I gave him a dirty look. "The palladium is there. We need to work out how to get at it."

We all stood there in silence. Shit. Finally, Aubrey spoke up.

"Heat it."

"Eh?"

"You're a dragon, or so I'm told anyway. Get some dragon fire going and heat it up. It'll expand, and crack the rock, and we get it out with this." He swung the pick-ax up.

"Even if I was confident enough to transform into a dragon shape so I could breathe fire, it would be impossible in this tiny space," I pointed out.

"Yeah, dude, but you've got your green fire, I've got my blue fire," Alex interjected. "We can try both of them together. That might work."

I pursed my lips then bobbed my head in

agreement. "Let's give it a shot."

Katya pointed to one small spot. "The greatest concentration is there. Aim for that spot."

I nodded, then stepped back to where Alex was. We exchanged glances and, on a count of three, simultaneously sent out our colourful streams of fire. The tiny cavern flared into life, with beams of light from the flames bouncing off the walls, which glittered in return. Sparks flew off the spot where our magic struck, making both Katya and Aubrey back away and shade their eyes from the glare.

The entire wall of rock seemed to heave and creak.

"Quick, Aubrey," I said, "get down there and see what you can do."

He stepped forward, swinging the little axe and striking the rock. Chunks flew off.

"Again."

He continued, chipping away at it. He grunted. "I think I'm getting something."

Alex took over, grasping the tool and digging it into the wall. Every so often he stepped back, and the pair of us lit the spot up again. We took turns to attack until, eventually, the cavern floor was strewn with debris.

"I think that's about your lot," Katya said.

She began scooping the darker oxidized chunks of metal together.

"There's not very much," I said, doubtfully.

"It's only going to take one weapon to stab Endor and be done with him," Alex responded grimly.

I nodded, thinking of Staines' corpse lying on my

kitchen table. The necromancer wouldn't know what hit him. Alex hunkered down next to the small pile and began to mutter. The bits of metal started to glow. I wiped the sweat off my brow. It was getting fucking hot. Thankfully, it didn't seem to take too much effort before it began to separate. We all watched fascinated as Alex waved his hands over each segment and it split away into silvery parts. I picked one up and held it up to my face. It was kind of pretty.

Katya produced a small bag and shoved the pieces inside. I added the one I was holding then she shouldered the bag and jerked her head back at the tunnel. As much as I was dreading the squeeze back through, I couldn't wait to get out of this place. One by one we headed back out. It seemed even a tighter fit than before this time, and the scrapes that I had garnered on my first journey through were merely aggravated by having to force my body along again. By the time I made it out of the small space, I was smarting all over.

Once Alex and Aubrey caught up, we began to wend our way back out.

"We did it, Mack Attack. No need to go begging for money or upsetting the balance of power."

"I'd feel better if we had more of the stuff," I said, "but you're right. Now all we need is for the wanker to show up at Loch Ness."

The thought of what was going to happen to Endor filled my mind and, distracted, I stumbled, kicking a small stone to the side as I did so. It gleamed in the light of my green fire. I pulled myself back upright while Aubrey moved over and picked it up.

"Wow. This is beautiful. It's the same colour as that scarf we saw. Katya," he called out, "what is this?"

She came trotting back and peered at what Aubrey was holding out. The little Karzelek's face paled. I felt the tendrils of dread begin to curve up through my body and I held out my hand. Aubrey dropped it into my palm. Oh fuck. Gingerly pinching the small smooth stone, I lifted it to my ear and heard a faint chiming sound which made my stomach drop.

"Can I have it back? It's pretty," said Aubrey.

I stared at him.

"What? I found it. It's mine."

I licked my lips. "Actually, I'm the one who found it. I kicked it."

"But I picked it up. Finders keepers, losers weepers. Give it back," he insisted.

I closed my fingers tightly round it and squeezed my eyes shut.

"Is that...?"

I nodded at Alex.

"Oh shit," he said.

Oh, shit indeed.

"What? Give it back! This isn't fair."

"Who found it, Mack Attack?" Alex asked softly. "You or him?"

I shook my head. I didn't know.

"What the fuck is going on?" demanded Aubrey.

I uncurled my fingers and handed him the stone. "It's a wichtlein's stone."

Katya jerked her head towards me. "You know

what it is?"

I felt sick. "Yes. I've seen one before."

"What happened?"

I thought of John, my old alpha, and his intestines gleaming in the moonlight of the Cornish night. "What you'd expect."

Aubrey spoke again. "What the hell is going on? What's a wichtlein's stone?"

"It's a harbinger of doom," Alex answered. "If you find one, then it's been left for you by a wichtlein. It usually means death and destruction."

"At the very least, the person who found it is probably going to die," said Katya matter-of-factly.

Aubrey's eyes widened and he stared down at the shiny pebble. Then he threw it behind him with a huge amount of force. It skittered away into the darkness.

We looked at each other. "You or me, buddy," I said, trying to keep my tone light.

"Maybe it's a mistake," Alex said, sounding panicked. "This is an old mine. It could have belonged to someone else and they just left it here. It doesn't mean that it's for either of you."

"You're right," I said.

Everyone else made murmurs of agreement. None of them sounded very enthusiastic.

I took a deep breath. "We can't worry about it now. We have to get back to London and get the palladium to Balud."

I didn't say anything else, just began to stride away. It was time to get out of this fucking mine. The others did the same. We grimly marched on and upwards, not speaking. There wasn't really anything to say.

Before too long, the rough corridor seemed to start lightening. When we rounded the corner, right in front of the entrance, the bright sunlight forced us all to shade our eyes and blink away. The relief I felt at finally getting out was more than tempered by the heavy knowledge of what had just transpired. I took Aubrey's hand and squeezed it tightly, then we emerged back out into the sunlight of a brand new day.

Chapter Sixteen

We said very little on the journey back to Moscow to return Volk's car. By common consent, no-one mentioned the wichtlein stone or what it might forbode. It did mean that the thrill of actually finding some useable palladium was considerably muted. I was nervous about the amount we had managed to extract from the mine; it would hardly cover one weapon, let alone enough for the army that I hoped by now was preparing to meet at Loch Ness. As Alex had said, all it would take would be one lethal strike to end the necromancer's plans once and for all, but having so little of the metal would make it more difficult to get in a hit. Underneath me on the single narrow passenger seat, Aubrey was slumped down, trying to avoid the bright sunlight, and making the drive even more uncomfortable than it had been on the way there. I didn't say anything.

When we pulled up back at the bar, we said our goodbyes to Katya, thanking her for her invaluable help. She reached up and grabbed both Aubrey and my hands, gripping them with her tiny fingers.

"There's no such thing as a foregone conclusion," she said, not quite meeting either of us in the eye.

My mouth dry, I just nodded. The hot lump in my stomach was starting to feel uncomfortable again, and I was anxious to get the journey back over and done with as soon as possible.

"If the sun doesn't kill me, then you will," grunted Aubrey, making reference to the fact that the Karzelek was holding on to both our hands so tightly it felt as if all the circulation was being cut off.

She released us, shooting a look of pity in our direction, then turned and trotted away. For our part, we trooped into the bar, using the front entrance this time. At this time of the morning, the place was deserted. Volk was sitting in a corner with a large mug of coffee. For some reason, the thought of caffeine was turning my stomach.

"How did it go?" he asked, in a booming voice that suggested he expected nothing less than total success.

Alex held up the bag containing the palladium chunks.

"Excellent, excellent." Volk's eyes moved over each of us. "And yet you do not seem particularly happy."

I shrugged. "We were hoping to get a bit more. Hopefully this will be enough to serve our needs."

"And we're going to die horribly because she kicked a stone," Aubrey commented flatly, jabbing a finger in my direction.

At Volk's questioning look, I told him about the wichtlein's little omen of doom. He looked worried.

"Don't stress about it," I said. "I will make sure I find a way to arrange your meeting with Leah before I cork it."

"That was not my first thought," he said, a small furrow in his brow. "You have the combined might of the Otherworld behind you, Miss Smith. I am sure that someone can find a way to help you change the course of fate."

I thought about it. It seemed a ridiculous waste of resources considering what else we were trying to stop right now. I gave him an uncomfortable smile.

"I'll be in touch." I glanced at Alex. "We really need to get going."

He bobbed his head and began to mutter. We all watched as the purple shimmer of the portal began to appear.

"I've set it to go straight to Balud's shop," he said.

Aubrey eyed him doubtfully. "Are you sure? If you've got it wrong and we end up in the middle of the M25, then that could be how I end up dying."

"It was me who found the stone, Aubrey." I looked at the portal. "I'll go first again."

I walked forward, just as Alex began to protest loudly at our lack of faith in his skills. His voice was cut off as soon as I stepped through, recognising Balud's little street the second before the vomiting began again. I wasn't sure how or why it happened, but my reaction was even more violent than it had been on our outward journey. When Alex and Aubrey joined me, they kindly waited to the side for my retching to finish. I much preferred being left alone with my own misery.

Eventually, once the seizing passed, I staggered to my feet and wiped my mouth with the back of my hand. I motioned towards Balud's door and then moved over to it, lifting my hand to knock. It swung open before my fist could connect with it, and Balud peered out.

"You're going to drive away my business by spewing up all over the street," he grouched.

"You saw me?"

"I heard you. Sounded as if you were dying."

Hmm. Maybe I was. I declined to comment, however, and passed him over the bag.

"Here's some palladium. There's not much, but whatever you can make will help."

He opened it up and looked inside. "I'm not a

miracle worker, you know."

"As I said, whatever you can." I thought of Corrigan and his quietly spoken promise. "Start with something that the Lord Alpha would use."

Balud looked at me, surprised. I shrugged. I'd never seen him use a weapon so I had no idea what his preference would be. But after what had happened to Staines, he deserved the first shot at taking Endor down. As much I was itching to pulverise the fucking necromancer into dust, I owed Corrigan that much.

"If there's anything left over, then you can try to make some daggers. Small ones that perhaps we can pass around."

Balud gave me an incredulous look and shook the bag. The palladium clanged dully inside.

"I know, I know," I said tiredly. "There's not a lot to work with. Just see what you can do, Balud, please? By tomorrow?"

He grunted an affirmative, and I turned to go.

"Hey," he called out. "Thanks for what you did with that bitch of a Batibat. From what I hear, her shop's been abandoned since yesterday."

Hot angry guilt trickled through me. "Sure," I said over my shoulder, not trusting myself to say anything else.

Aubrey, Alex and I walked away.

"What now, dudes?"

"I need to sleep, even if only for a few hours." I rubbed my eyes. "Then get on to finding out what's happened since we've been gone, particularly with the kelpies." I looked at both of them. "Thank you for your help today. And last night."

Alex regarded me seriously. "We're in this together, Mack Attack. It's not all on you."

I smiled at him, then faced Aubrey. "Are we okay?" I asked softly.

He felt his own pulse. "I'm still alive at the moment if that's what you mean."

"No, I mean with the, um, dragon stuff."

He flattened his lips and nodded. "Yeah."

I was surprisingly relieved. "Look," I said uncomfortably. "It's probably best if we don't tell anyone about the stone. It'll just make things awkward and it will distract everyone. We need to focus on Endor. It was me who initially came into contact with it. It was probably for me." I scratched my head. "There are other things that need our attention right now."

I was expecting some resistance, but Aubrey surprised me. "You're right. I don't want to die. I've only just come alive. But getting this fucker is more important."

I smiled faintly. Alex drew a line across his lips to indicate his own silence. Then he grinned and held out his arms. "Group hug?"

I rolled my eyes, but submitted anyway, and the three of us remained there for one long, but comfortable, moment.

*

After declining Alex's offer of a portal, Aubrey and I travelled the long way back, taking the train. I stopped off at my flat to pick up some things, impressed at how it already seemed to have been cleaned of Staines' blood. I'd have to remember to thank the Arch-Mage. The stench of death, unfortunately, still lingered in the air, along with the horror of what had happened to Staines. I spent as little time as possible getting my things together then we headed straight to Clava Books, stopping only to say a quick hello to Mrs. Alcoon and Slim, before going to the small room at the back and passing out, Aubrey on the campbed and me on the floor on top of a sleeping bag.

When I came to, a few hours later, I felt groggy and very, very hungry. Aubrey was still fast asleep, snoring gently. I stumbled out to the front of the shop, hoping that I could scrounge something to eat. Solus was there, one elbow propped up on the till counter, chatting to Slim.

"Where have you been?" he exclaimed. "No-one's seen you since yesterday. You've been out all night, dragonlette."

I looked away. "I had a few things to do."

"Like what?"

I shifted uncomfortably. I didn't want to lie to Solus, but I didn't think Alex would be very happy about me spilling the reasons for us entirely circumnavigating the Fae in order to get a couple of pounds of palladium. I tried to appear nonchalant.

"I went with Alex and Aubrey to get hold of some metal that Balud reckons Endor will be vulnerable to. No biggie."

He gave me a suspicious look but, before he could question me further, I changed the subject. "What's going on with the preparations for Loch Ness?"

"Everyone's ready. Some Fae and some mages have travelled up there already to scout out the land. The shifters are waiting until after the bear's funeral."

"And the kelpies?"

He wrinkled his nose. "They are being...difficult."

"Fecking slimy buggers," spat Slim. "You should just let Endor kill the lot of them first."

I raised my eyebrows slightly. There was a tinge of venom to the little gargoyle's voice that I'd not previously heard.

"They lure people to their deaths. Even fecking children! Drowning them just for kicks. And the whole Loch Ness monster thing." He shook his head. "It's fecking barabaric."

Solus explained. "The kelpies created the legend."

"Of the Loch Ness monster? Why on earth would they do that? We're supposed to stay out of the way of humans, not advertise our existence."

Slim folded his chubby little arms. "Exactly."

"They started the legend by appearing to the odd human here and there. Letting them get away instead of just killing them. It was probably a mistake, but you can never be sure with the kelpies. When they realised that it meant more tourists – and therefore more victims – came to the area, they kept it up." Solus shrugged. "They're not the nicest of species."

"That doesn't mean that we should just let Endor slaughter them all to take their energy."

"No," Solus agreed. "They're so heavily tied in to the element of water that he'll easily be able to take what he needs to master it."

"And we're not in the business of encouraging genocide," I said pointedly.

The Fae shrugged. "Sure. That too."

Slim snorted and began to say something, then his eyes widened fractionally, and he flapped into the back room with more speed than I'd have thought he was capable of. The front door of the shop jangled, and a young woman walked in. I gave her a cursory glance, registering that she was human, and then turned back to Solus to ask him about what had been done to make sure that Endor didn't get wind of our intervention and end up being scared off. He, however, was watching the girl, an odd expression in his eyes.

Wondering whether I'd misjudged what she was, I looked back at her. She was browsing along one of the shelves, looking through the Myths and Legends section. Or at least the Myths and Legends section if you were human. To the rest of us, it was the Historical part of the bookshop. She definitely seemed human though.

Solus straightened up, then sauntered over to her with an overly pronounced swagger. Interesting. I watched him, utterly fascinated.

"Good afternoon," he said smoothly, holding out his hand.

She jumped slightly, looking up at him through a long messy fringe, then started to blush.

"Er, hi." She took his hand in return but, when he started to lift it to his lips to kiss it rather than shake it, she snatched it away. You go, girl.

Apparently unfazed, Solus just smiled. "Welcome to our little bookstore."

195

I tried not to laugh. 'Our' little bookstore?

She muttered thanks, then turned away, obviously wanting some peace and quiet to look around.

"Can I help you find anything?" he persisted.

Probably realising that she wasn't going to be left alone, she looked back. "I'm doing some research into Celtic mythology," she answered. "In particular, Dagda. Do you have any books that might help?"

"Lots," Solus purred.

There was a moment's silence while they stared at each other. Then she spoke up. "Can you show me where they are?"

"Of course," he said, not moving. "I'm Solus. You can call me Sol though if you want."

"Great." She took a step backwards. "The books?"

He shook himself slightly. "They're over here." He moved past her, brushing against her body ever so lightly, even though there was more than enough room for him to manoeuver around.

Solus looked up and down the shelves. I watched, amused. He was in completely the wrong place. The books on Dagda, an Irish fae from long ago, were on the other side.

"Ah," he said finally. "We appear to be out of stock. There was a Celtic scholar in here a few days ago who probably took them all. If you give me your details though, I can order some more in."

"Which scholar?" She seemed momentarily confused. "I know almost everyone else in my field, and there's no-one looking into Dagda at the moment."

He shrugged disarmingly. "I didn't catch his name."

The girl looked at him assessingly, then pushed up her glasses rather nervously. "It's okay. I'll order them off the internet instead."

"There's no need. Our suppliers are old-fashioned, so they're not online. They have by far the best and widest selection. Honestly," he said, "give me your name and address and I'll find everything you need."

She sighed. "Okay."

"Then please, mademoiselle, come this way." He swept out an arm in my direction.

She started, as if noticing me for the first time. I grinned at her. This was fun. She walked over, Solus at her heels. I pulled out a pen and piece of paper and handed it to her, and she scribbled down a few words, then passed them back to the Fae.

"Isabel? That's a beautiful name. You know it means 'God's Promise'?"

She eyed Solus as if he were slightly mad. "Yes."

"Would you like to go out for a drink?"

"No."

I waited to see whether he'd put some of his more persuasive skills into action, however he simply bowed. "As you wish."

Isabel's cheeks reddened again. She inclined her head in farewell, then left. I smirked at Solus, who was still staring after her.

"Dragonlette, I think I'm in love. I've never..." he blinked, and seemed slightly stunned.

"I'm not sure she felt the same way," I pointed

out.

He waved the scrap of paper with her name and address on it. "That's okay. I can bring her around."

"You didn't glamour her into going out with you."

He shook his head vehemently. "No, that would be rude."

Huh. He'd tried to glamour *me* when we'd just met.

"I have to go, dragonlette." He leaned over and pecked me on the cheek.

"Don't you want to know where the Dagda books actually are?"

He gave me a dismissive look. "I can get better ones in Tir-na-Nog. She should have the best."

The door jangled again, and Solus spun around. His shoulders sagged, however, when he saw it was Mrs. Alcoon with her little tartan shopping trolley trundling behind her.

"Hello!" she called out cheerily.

I gave her a wave. She peered at Solus. "Goodness. You are almost glowing, Lord Sol. You must be having a good day."

A small smile played around his lips. "Indeed I am."

He tipped an imaginary hat in both our directions, then snapped his fingers and vanished into the Otherworld ether.

"We had a customer wander in. Solus was rather taken with her - I think it's love at first sight," I said with a grin.

Her eyes crinkled. "He did appear rather thunderstruck. Good for him. Now, dear, are you happy to mind the shop while I prepare us something to eat? I've got lots of fruit and vegetables and healthy things to keep you on the right track."

I shrugged. It saved me from going out to grab a sandwich. "Sure. Thanks."

She patted me on the shoulder. "Good girl."

I watched her carefully for some kind of reaction now that she'd touched me. Mrs. Alcoon's precognition wasn't the strongest – it wasn't even enough for the Ministry of Mages to take notice – but she did occasionally catch glimpses and snippets of the future that were often made stronger through physical contact. And she had been acting oddly of late. If that behaviour was somehow tied into what the wichtlein stone was predicting then it would start to make more sense. Nothing flickered in her face, however.

I debated whether to ask her outright about it, but figured instead it would be easier not to know. Que sera sera. When the wichtlein stone had found John, it had been mere hours before his death. Aubrey was safely in the land of nod so I knew he was alright. If hours were all I personally had left, then there were worse ways to spend it than having dinner with my old friend. Corrigan's face floated momentarily into my head, but I pushed the image away. He'd made his feelings clear enough. I'd leave the Lord Alpha in peace.

Chapter Seventeen

Several hours later, long after Mrs. Alcoon had wandered off home, Slim had gone off to goodness knew where, and I'd done all the reading I could on kelpies, I sat myself down in a corner of the shop and opened my laptop. I had to admit that I was curious to see the photos of myself at Circle after I'd transformed. However, the machine was just whirring into action when there was a sharp knock at the door. I frowned. It was, after all, the middle of the sodding night. The wichtlein stone flashed into my mind and I considered, just for a moment, running away as fast as I could and hiding. Unfortunately I knew doom-laden prophecies would merely laugh in the face of such frivolous action. And I wasn't the running away type. Whoever was out there rattled the doorknob loudly and violently in a bid to enter. Initially, I ignored them, wondering what exactly would happen if I didn't acknowledge them, but they continued to knock incessantly so, eventually sighing loudly to myself, I got up and unlocked the door.

I stared out at the visitor. Sodding hell.

"Miss Smith, may I come in?" It was the vamp who'd stopped me at Alcazon.

"No," I said shortly, hoping that Aubrey was still fast asleep in the back room.

Her face remained expressionless, but somehow I got the sense from her flat red eyes that she was furious I was daring to refuse her entrance.

"I was in the neighbourhood and thought I

would drop by. I had been wondering whether you had considered my proposition," she said glacially.

Great. I was an outstandingly bad liar so how I'd extricate myself from this I had no idea.

"Look," I replied, "I don't have time to go traipsing around all over the country to find one misplaced bloodsucker who probably doesn't want to be found." That was true. I didn't have time, and he didn't want to be found.

"And yet, if you find him, you will only be helping yourself. I told you that we can help you locate your necromancer."

I waved an airy hand. "I already know where he is."

She looked momentarily amused. "You know where he'll be. Not where he is right now. I've seen all the preparations your little council have been doing. Are you really prepared to put their lives at risk by having them face Endor? He'll squash them like flies."

My face was stony. "They know what they're getting themselves into."

"Just like the bear did?"

Bloodfire boiled in the pit of my stomach. Don't do anything stupid, Mack, I told myself. I stepped back and started to close the door. The vamp snapped her hand out, stopping it. Her blood red fingernails curved round it like claws.

"Wouldn't it be better," she said softly, "to find out where the necromancer is and confront him on your own? I hear you're a Draco Wyr. I'm sure that means you're powerful enough to bring him down without anyone's help. That way there's no danger of anyone else getting hurt in the process."

It was a nice idea, and six months before I'd have jumped at it. I was learning the value of teamwork, however. And everyone knew what they were risking. As much as I wanted to make sure no-one was killed, I had to respect their democratic choice to involve themselves. It was a new feeling for me, I admitted to myself, but it felt right.

"How nice of you to be so considerate," I said, sarcastically, "however I think I'll pass. Let's face it, you're a bloodsucker and I don't like bloodsuckers. I regretfully decline your offer."

A dark shadow passed across her face. "Very well. If the carrot doesn't work then we shall merely try the stick."

There was a thump from the other room. Shit. That meant Aubrey was stirring. I pulled the door away from her hand, and stepped outside into the street, closing it behind me.

The vamp's eyes narrowed. "Do you have company?"

"Pet cat," I grunted, trying to offset the lie. "Bring on your stick. I'm not afraid of you."

She smiled. "Oh, it's not me you should be worried about." She raised her long white arm into the air, and snapped her fingers.

"I'm not afraid of the merengue either," I commented. "No matter how badly you manage to dance it. If you start singing though, then that'll be a different matter."

She snarled at me. "You won't be making jokes for much longer."

From the other side of the street, a car door

opened, and another vamp got out. I pasted a bored expression onto my face.

"You were only just now suggesting that I had enough strength to take on Endor by myself. Do you really think I can't take on two fucking vampires?"

She smirked. "Watch."

The other vamp reached back inside the car and grabbed hold of something – or rather, someone – and dragged them outside. Whoever their victim was, their arms were tied behind their back and their head was covered with a dark hood. Damn it. I tried to think about who they might have taken to force me into capitulating. It couldn't be a mage, a Fae or a shifter. Those respective organisations would rain so much hell down on the vamps in retribution that surely it wouldn't be worth it. So who the fuck could it be?

The vamp pushed his prisoner forward, causing him to stumble. He picked him up and continued, jabbing at him until the pair of them had crossed the street and were standing in front of me. Nervous flames uncurled themselves and starting licking at my insides. If this was some bloody innocent who they'd scooped up, then they were going to feel the full force of my wrath. No, screw it, whoever it was - innocent or otherwise - the vamps were going to pay. They couldn't go around acting like terrorists.

I sparked up the green fire at my fingertips. "You're going to regret this," I said.

"No, Miss Smith," she answered. "I don't think I will."

She flicked a nod at the other vamp who then pulled the hood off from the hapless prisoner. While the mystery man who'd had the unfortunate delight of crossing the bloodsuckers' path blinked under the street lamp to try and adjust his vision, I stared at him, then shrugged.

"I don't even know who this is." Unbelievable. They really had just picked up some random guy from the streets.

The female vamp tinkled out a small laugh. "Oh, Miss Smith, you are funny. I know that. The thing is," she leaned in towards me and licked her lips, "he knows who you are."

I turned back to the prisoner and watched in confusion as his vision apparently came into focus. He registered the two vamps first, hatred spitting out from him as he did so. Then his eyes travelled over to me. His pupils narrowed into tiny dots and, bizarrely, I thought I saw a flash of green in his enlarged irises. Before I had time to think about what that meant, however, he spoke.

"The Draco Wyr."

The tone of his voice was filled with malevolence, but there was also an odd hint of satisfaction.

"Indeed," smiled the vamp. "Undo his restraints."

I stood there watching, utterly baffled, as the henchman fiddled with the piece of plastic cord holding the guy's wrists together.

"Look," I began, "this is really…"

And then he flew into me. I was knocked off my feet, more in surprise than anything else, and landed backwards on the pavement.

"Hey!" I protested, starting to rise up on my

elbows. "What gives? It's not me you want to be attacking, it's them!"

He ignored my words, straddling my body with his legs and raised a hand, his fingers tightly curled into a fist. What the fuck? I brought my knees up, blocking the blow adequately, then twisted to the side pulling away from his legs, and got to my feet. All the guy did was come at me again. He shoved his shoulder into my chest, then looped round one arm and cuffed me on the side of my head. I jumped backwards, head ringing, and sent out a jet of flame to create a barrier between me and him.

"I don't want to hurt you, but you need to..."

He leaped over the flames, seemingly unbothered by them, still completely ignoring everything I was saying. Another fist shot out, this time connecting with my cheekbone in the exact spot where the bruise already lay. I hissed in sudden pain, and reacted, lashing out and hitting him back. He barely registered it, coming for me yet again.

"Stop!" I cried out.

He didn't. I only just managed to dodge out of his path. Okay, now I'd had enough. I flicked out flame towards him again, this time aiming at him rather than the ground. It reached his body, however, and fizzled out. I stared in surprise. That was new. Shrugging, I stared down at my hands and brought my little imaginary match back into my head. Try this for size then.

Nothing happened. I frowned, and shook each hand in the air, utterly confused as to why my hands weren't transforming into their dragon claws. Were the vamps using some kind of spell?

I looked up, just in time to see my assailant barrelling into me, headfirst. The pair of us fell to the ground. I rolled, managing to get on top of his body and gain the upper hand, but it was only a brief glimmer of success because his elbow went flying into my upper stomach, completely winding me. As I gasped for breath, he twisted so that we switched places again. Then his hands curved round my neck and began to squeeze.

I kicked upwards with my feet, although it was a futile gesture as I missed him entirely. My fingers clawed at his hands, but they were only getting tighter and tighter round my throat. My vision was starting to narrow while my lungs burned, and my bloodfire whimpered, as if it were trying to surge up through my body and take control, but failing completely. As a last ditch attempt, I closed my eyes and attempted to call up my full dragon self, danger be damned. Yet there was nothing there; it was as if I was suddenly empty, devoid of my Draco Wyr side. The wichtlein stone had been for me after all then, I thought dully. At least we'd managed to get the palladium. Balud would get the weapon to Corrigan and he would deal with Endor. I stared upwards at my killer, as his face swam and my head reeled. Then, abruptly, I was released, automatically gulping in fresh air and heaving and coughing.

There was a thud next to me. I twisted my head to the side, only just recognising my attacker's body. His neck was broken and his eyes were wide open in an unmistakable death stare, although there still seemed to be a mixture of surprise and hatred glaring out at me. Before I could even wonder what had happened, the vamp brought her head down towards my face.

"That worked even better than I thought," she said, with a bright smile. "An interesting nullifying effect on your skills."

"What...?" I croaked.

"You still don't get it, do you?" She laughed. "You should have done more to keep your identity secret, little dragon. He's part of an ancient order sworn to keep the world free from the scourge of the Draco Wyr. They thought they'd been successful until pictures of you started popping up all over the Othernet. Now they're galvanized into action, desperate to hunt you down."

My head swam. "Bolux," I whispered.

He was a descendant of the warrior who'd killed my great-great-great-whatever and who'd died in the process. The same group of people who had probably been after me when my mother had left me with the pack in Cornwall.

"Oh, I can assure you that it's not bollocks at all, Miss Smith. There are plenty more where he came from." She smiled, her sharp white teeth gleaming. "They don't know where you are just yet. But that doesn't mean that someone won't tell them."

Her face moved away, vanishing from my sight. "Bring Aubrey to us," her voice said, drifting over to me. "Sooner rather than later."

I heard the soft purr of an expensive car engine start up, then drive off. I rolled onto my side and stared at the corpse. Outfuckingstanding. One had to wonder where on earth the bloody vamps kept getting all their information from. They had more sodding connections than BT.

I pulled myself to my feet, every muscle in my body screaming in agony. The welcome warmth of my bloodfire signaled its return, flaming up through my veins and arteries. I sent a small prayer of gratitude to whoever might be listening. I may often curse my Draco Wyr heritage and the very many complications that it brought with it, but the idea that the fire within me had vanished for good had been surprisingly terrifying.

From somewhere down the street, a dog barked. I slowly turned, realising there was a figure off in the distance. Someone was taking advantage of the clear quiet night to walk their furry friend. Alarmed, I quickly crouched down, trying to ignore the pain the movement created, and began pushing the dead body to the side of the road. If I could just get it underneath the nearby parked car, then perhaps the night stroller wouldn't notice it. The dog would, but there was little I could do about that now. I'd just have to hope I could distract the animal somehow. The energy I expended in shifting the corpse, and shoving it under the vehicle, was tremendous. I staggered back up, casting a quick glance to make sure it was hidden, then realised with a lurch that the guy's feet were sticking out, visible between the two rear wheels. The dog walker was getting closer. Quickly, I kicked them, managing to move them out of the way just in the nick of time, and then leaned casually against the car.

The man, who looked fairly young even though he had greying hair, stared at me through horn-rimmed glasses with a look of frank curiosity. His dog began to pull at its leash, having clearly scented the corpse and wanting to investigate further. He swore, yanking the dog back, but it just started barking instead.

"Quiet, Baxter!" He shushed with a definite Scottish lilt to his voice.

The animal paid him no attention whatsoever. Fuck. I thought quickly. What could I do to get this bloke away from here as soon as possible?

I opened my mouth without thinking, placing one hand on my hip. "Feeling lonely?"

It felt like someone had shoved a kilo of ground glass down my throat. At least an expression of discomfort flashed across the man's face. He tugged nervously at his t-shirt, which proclaimed something about the wonders of the Burntisland Golf Club, and quickened his step, virtually dragging the dog behind him. I breathed out. Goodness only knew what I would have done if he'd decided he was actually 'feeling lonely'. Although I imagined that the bruise on my face, and what were now probably the marks of fingers round my throat had helped scare him off. Along with the fact that my voice had sounded rougher than even the Marlboro Man's could have.

Once I was sure he was out of sight, I considered my options. I had to get rid of the body and I had to do it quickly. I flipped over the possibilities in my mind, then decided on the fastest one.

"Solus," I whispered.

No answer. Fuck it, I didn't want to have to make myself bleed; I was already hurting enough as it was.

"Solus, bloody get here right now."

The air snapped and he suddenly appeared. "Dragonlette, are you really missing me already?"

Despite my condition, I blinked at him. He seemed to be wearing a three piece grey suit. There was even a purple cravat at his neck. Noticing my look, he gave me a twirl.

"What do you think? Is this a look that an academically inclined woman would go for?" Then, he wrinkled his nose before I could say anything, and his violet eyes clouded. "Is there by any chance a dead body underneath this car?"

"Bolux," I croaked.

Solus looked momentarily confused, then his expression was replaced with appalled comprehension. He noticed the marks on my throat.

"One of the descendants. What exactly did he do to you? I guess he didn't realise just how powerful you are, dragonlette. It's fortunate you managed to put him under because it looks like it was a hell of a fight."

I just stared at the Fae unhappily. He was right that it may have been a hell of a fight, but it certainly hadn't been me who'd killed him. I hadn't even managed to slow the guy down. I suddenly felt drained, and my knees began to give way. Solus caught me before I fell.

"Let's get you back inside."

I opened my mouth to speak, but he interrupted me, placing a finger on my lips. "It's okay. I'll dispose of the body." Distaste flickered across his eyes. "Somehow."

Unable to feel anything more than gratitude, I

nodded, and allowed him to help me back into the little shop. Aubrey was sitting on the counter, a mug cupped in his hands, and his legs swinging. He was humming away to himself as if he had no cares in the world. When he caught sight of us, however, he jumped off and ran over.

"What happened? Mack, are you alright? Was it Endor?"

I shook my head and pointed Solus towards the back room. We hobbled over together, then I lay myself carefully down on top of the sleeping bag in the corner before I completely collapsed. I could sense him exchanging worried looks with Aubrey, but I just closed my eyes and curled up my bruised and battered body.

Chapter Eighteen

I had thought I wouldn't be able to sleep, but it had taken me no time at all to drift into a deep and dreamless coma. I didn't wake up until Mrs. Alcoon was gently shaking my shoulder and saying my name.

"Mackenzie, dear, you need to get up."

I stretched out, almost without thinking, and then hissed in pain. I felt even worse than I had the night before.

She tutted loudly. "You can't be doing this, Mackenzie. You can't be getting into fights like this. The consequences could be disastrous."

I thought about how close I'd come to actually snuffing it the night before. She had no idea.

"I'm fine," I said, sitting up, and trying to look like I was. "Is it time for..." my voice trailed off.

She nodded. "I sent Aubrey round to pick up something appropriate for you to wear. I'm not sure it's wise for you to go though. Not with the way you are right now. I'm sure your young man will understand."

The idea of pulling my sleeping bag over my head and just wishing the entire world away was remarkably appealing. But then I thought of Endor. And the weapons (hopefully plural) that Balud was going to bring after Staines' funeral service. And the odd pleading look in Corrigan's eyes when he'd asked me to go. I didn't think about Aubrey, or the bloodsuckers, or the fact that I had a group of undefeatable warriors after me, even though I'd nothing to antagonise them other than being born. Life was just getting far too bloody complicated.

I got up, wavered slightly, then gave Mrs. Alcoon what I hoped was a reassuring glance. "I'll be fine," I repeated, more firmly than I felt.

She looked troubled, but left me in peace anyway to change into a depressing black dress. She'd left me a scarf out, either having noticed the marks on my throat while I was sleeping or having heard about them from Aubrey. Either way I was grateful for the thought, and wound it round my neck to cover up. At least the bruise on my face was starting to look a little better, I thought ruefully, as I stared at my reflection in the mirror.

From somewhere outside a car honked, making me jump. A few moments later, Mrs. Alcoon curved her head back round.

"There's a car waiting for you."

Evincing surprise, I followed her out. When I recognised the number-plate as belonging to the Brethren, my stomach gave a little flip. I quashed it back down, telling myself not to be so silly. It was probably there because Tom had been thoughtful enough to arrange it. Even if it had been Corrigan who'd sent it, it would merely be because he wanted to make sure that I didn't bail on my promise to attend the funeral. I clambered inside, my eyes inadvertently falling on the spot where I'd almost died just hours before. I quickly looked away, my gaze landing on Aubrey instead. He looked worried.

I reminded myself that I'd have to find somewhere for him to go that would be well out of his former foster family's reach. Then the car door closed automatically, and we drove off.

The service was being held at the Brethren's stronghold. I spent the entire journey there in silence and, upon arriving and walking inside, little else changed. I could feel the eyes of numerous shifters on me, accusatory glances that held so much meaning, from how I'd treated Corrigan to allowing Staines' death to occur. There was so much I was responsible for. I carefully took a seat at the back of the hall, which was clearly used for such occasions, and folded my hands in my lap, closing my eyes. I allowed a trickle of bloodfire to run through my body, enjoying its warmth and hoping it would in some way reinvigorate me. Lughnasadh was less than three days away and, as unlikely as it was starting to seem that I'd make it that far, I had to get myself ready just in case.

The chair next to me creaked as someone else sat down. Surprised, I opened my eyes. I'd rather imagined that being persona non-grata as far as the shifters were concerned, no-one would wish to come near me. When I saw who it was, however, I couldn't help but smile.

"Hi Betsy."

"You look like shit, Mack."

I snorted. "I feel a hell of a lot worse." My voice was still croaky from my near-strangulation. I lifted my hand to my throat for a moment, then dropped it.

Betsy reached over and squeezed my fingers.

"Things have been tough."

I nodded, suddenly not quite able to trust my voice.

"The Lord Alpha's been screwed up. I've never seen him in such a bad mood."

I swallowed down the lump rising in my throat. "He's lost his right hand man, hasn't he?" Because I hadn't fucking been at home.

"It started before then." She watched me carefully.

I didn't want to go there. I couldn't go there. I gave her a watery smile instead. "I hear the wedding preparations are going well."

"Going well?" She shook her head. "You have no idea. Trying to get Tom to even begin to show enthusiasm is a nightmare. I was talking to him yesterday about cake, and he just shrugged and said I could choose whatever I wanted. Except I don't like fruit cake, he's allergic to chocolate, and you know what sugar does to shifters."

"Johannes isn't doing the catering, is he?" I asked in mock horror. Johannes, the designated chef of the Cornish pack, possessed a lack of culinary skill that was legendary.

She giggled. "No chance. He offered, but I told him I wanted him to enjoy the day, not be rushed off his feet cooking."

"Did he buy it?"

"Who knows?" A shadow crossed her face. "You are still coming?"

I thought about the upcoming battle with Endor, and my own apparent impending doom, and hoped the scratch in my voice would mask the lie. "I wouldn't miss it for anything."

Betsy beamed. "I think we could all do with a bit of celebration."

She wasn't wrong there.

"Is it bad talking about a wedding when we're at a funeral?"

"Life goes on, Bets. It has to. What are we all fighting for if not the chance to have weddings and celebrations and happiness?" I smiled sadly to myself.

Funereal music kicked in at that point, and a procession with Corrigan at the helm trooped in solemnly. As well as several highly placed shifters, both the Arch-Mage and the Summer Queen followed them in, their heads bowed. Tom came and sat down on the opposite side of Betsy, although I barely registered him, fixed as I was on Corrigan. The Lord Alpha's ramrod straight spine indicated just how hard this was for him. The hue of his suit seemed to match his jet black hair perfectly. He'd obviously taken a lot of care in getting dressed today, in order to show his respect for the one person he'd trusted above all others. I closed my eyes again and clenched my teeth together until my jaw ached.

It wasn't a long service, but it served the werebear well. He had clearly been well thought of across the Brethren, and they were going to miss his presence dearly. Once it was over, and everyone scattered off to get some food and drinks, I hung back. It didn't seem appropriate for me to join in the wake, even though Corrigan had asked me to be here. Staines and I hadn't exactly ever seen eye to eye, and I felt very much like an interloper amongst all his grieving friends. I promised Tom that as soon as we were both up at Loch Ness, I'd meet him for some more transformation training, then said my goodbyes to both him and Betsy. Once the room was cleared, I stiffly stood up and moved towards the door.

I was only a few feet away when a shadow fell across my path. I'd been staring somewhat dejectedly at my feet, concentrating on walking slowly forward in order to not cause myself too much more pain, so I was jolted to see Corrigan there, staring at me fathomlessly with his green eyes.

"Hey," I said softly.

He didn't say anything, just continued watching me. I didn't think he so much as blinked.

"I'm really sorry about Staines. I know how much he meant to you." My voice still sounded strange, as if I had a very bad cold. And it fucking hurt to speak.

"Are you?" Corrigan finally said. There was an antagonistic edge to his tone, as if he was hoping he could goad me into a fight.

"Am I what?"

"Sorry. Are you actually sorry?" He took a step closer, looming over me with his muscles bunched tightly inside his suit.

I nodded. "We didn't get on, but..." I swallowed, "But he didn't deserve that. I should have been there to help him."

Corrigan looked even more upset at my words and I felt my failure to save Staines' life even more keenly than before. He opened his mouth to say something, then just closed it again, his hands bunching into fists by his sides. I felt a tightness in my chest, and the awkwardness of the moment was excruciating.

"He didn't like you."

"No."

"He was a good man."

"I know," I said quietly.

"There's not anything he wouldn't have done to help defeat Endor. His methods might have been unsavoury to some but he knew how to get a job done."

I wisely kept my mouth shut.

"Did he say anything before he died?"

When I didn't immediately answer, Corrigan took yet another step in my direction, his face now only inches from mine. I gave him a small nod.

He grabbed me by the shoulders. "What?" he snarled. "What did he say?"

"That he was trying to prove to you that you didn't need me. I guess that's why he, you know, went to go see the Batibat."

"I don't fucking need you," he said, his fingers digging into my skin.

I nodded again. "I know." Boy, did I know.

He stared at me. I stared back at him. I couldn't work out for the life of me what he was thinking. If he wanted to use me as a punching bag to make himself feel better, then that was fine. I wasn't sure my body would be able to take much more abuse, but if it would help him...

"Fuck it," he said in a low voice, and through

obviously gritted teeth, then-pulled me towards him and kissed me hard, almost painfully.

My bloodfire immediately, and involuntarily, roared into life. I was so surprised, however, I didn't even have time to react before he was pushing himself backwards and glaring at me with loathing and disgust. Then he spun on his heel and left.

"Shit," I cursed aloud.

I'd thought he was going to punch me, not kiss me. I lifted my fingers up to lips. They felt bruised and sore. There was meant to be nothing between us any more; I'd promised the Arch-Mage and the Summer Queen there wouldn't be in order to maintain the shaky interspecies equilibrium on the council. So I shouldn't have let him do that. I should have walked away the instant he even came into the room. It was just too dangerous to be alone with him, especially when emotions were flying as high as they were. But I couldn't quash the little thrill I'd felt – I still was feeling – at the knowledge that at least a small part of him still wanted me. Damn me for a lovesick fool. I sat heavily down on a nearby chair.

But it was three days. Only three days until Endor was going to show up at Loch Ness. We had the palladium, which meant we could defeat him. Then there'd be no need for a council so I would be free of my promise. For the first time since that awful afternoon at Alcazon when I'd dumped him, I felt hope. We could still make it together.

Then the shiny little black stone – the unwanted gift from the unnamed wichtlein – popped into my head, along with the vamps and Bolux's bloodthirsty descendants. All the optimism drained away, and the remaining flickers of heat seeped out from my blood.

*

When I finally emerged out from the keep, with a heavier heart than it seemed I'd had even upon entering, a nearby car with tinted windows honked its horn making me jump. Scowling, I flicked up my middle finger. I wasn't in the mood to deal with idiots.

The car window rolled down and a little face appeared. "Really? You're going to treat me like that after I stayed up all night making your bloody steel?"

Oh. I walked over. "Sorry, Balud," I said, not actually feeling all that sorry at all. "I didn't realise it was you."

The troll harrumphed loudly. "I've got half a mind to just drive off. You can sort out your own necromancer-killing weapons."

I sighed. "I said I was sorry, didn't I?"

He tutted. "Well, do you want them or not? Get in."

I moved round to the passenger side and wrenched open the door, then got in. "A sports car? As a troll, shouldn't you be trying to stay under the radar?"

"People see the car. They're not interested in who's driving it. Besides," he gestured, "you can't see through the windows, girl."

"Oh yeah?" I snapped. "And I thought that times were tough? That with Wold as competition you were practically going under? It looks like you're fucking doing all right to me."

Balud's face screwed up. "Well, someone got out of the wrong side of bed this morning."

His flippant words and tone got to me. Ire rose up in my chest, almost choking me. I'd just about had enough of everything. I curled my fingers into my palms. Get a grip, Mack, I told myself. This isn't helping.

I took a deep breath, and looked at the troll. "What do you have to show me?"

He gazed at me for a moment, as if pondering whether I'd pissed him off too much to bother with me any more. Then he gave in to the greater good. "There's a box in the trunk. One sword, three daggers."

I jerked in surprised. "Three?" I hadn't expected he'd manage to create that many.

Balud looked smug. "I took existing weapons – my best ones, mind you, and I won't even charge you for them because that's the kind of nice guy that I am – and edged them with the palladium. They're not pure, but they'll do the trick."

Huh. That was kind of smart, actually.

"Okay, well, good," I muttered. "Thank you."

"What the hell is wrong with you? You're normally a grumpy bitch, but this is even worse than usual."

For some reason, the floodgates opened. "I can't have the guy I'm in love with, okay? He hates me. Or maybe he doesn't hate me, I don't know. Even if he doesn't hate me, I'm going to die because a stupid wichtlein left a stone for me in a stupid Russian mine. If the necromancer doesn't kill me, then the vamps will tell this crazy bunch of fuckwits where I am unless I give them Aubrey. But Aubrey's not a vamp any more, he's human. Not to mention that the crazy bunch of fuckwits, who think they need to kill me because a thousand fucking years ago my ancestor killed their ancestor and vice-sodding-versa, do something weird and stop me from being able to fight back in any fucking way. So generally, everything is shit!" I yelled.

Balud blinked at me. "You realise that was total babble and you're not making any sense?"

I slumped in my seat. "What. Ever."

He reached out and gingerly patted me on the shoulder in the same manner that you might try and comfort a rabid dog dying at the side of the road. "Now you have my weapons, you can kill Endor. He's not a problem." He shrugged. "And neither are the bloodsuckers. Just get them off your back by giving them this Aubrey fellow."

"I can't do that."

"Why the hell not? From what I heard, he's responsible for the deaths of a bunch of others. Others who you cared about. It's no skin off your nose if they do something to him. They'll probably just turn him back into a vamp."

I frowned. "It would just be wrong."

Balud shook his head. "You're crazy."

"I guess I am," I sighed. "But he's turned into a good guy." I looked at the troll. "I have no idea why I just told you all this. Please don't pass it on to anyone else."

"Girlie, if I tried to tell anyone, they would think I'm just as crazy as you. You're a Draco Wyr. One of the most potentially powerful creatures the Otherworld has ever seen. Pull yourself together and stop acting like a baby."

My mouth dropped open.

"You heard me. Honestly," he said, his eyes rolling heavenwards, "Women and their bloody hormones."

My eyes narrowed. "Hey!" I protested.

"Get over yourself, get out, get those weapons and get on with what you should be doing."

For once I had no reply.

He reached over me and opened the passenger door. "Go on."

Still slightly stunned, I got out and walked round to the back of the car and opened the boot, pulling out a long wooden box.

"Is this it?" I called out.

He revved the engine loudly. What the fuck? I slammed the boot shut, and the car immediately careened off, with the tyres actually smoking. I stared after it. Hormones? Fucking troll. I jutted out my bottom lip - and then realised how ridiculous I was being. He was right. I needed to get with the program and act like the council head I was supposed to be.

I hefted the box, feeling its reassuring weight, and glanced back at the keep. I could do this. I marched across the road and thumped back on the large door. After a minute or two, it creaked open, and a shifter stared at me. I pushed past him and stalked inside, following the hum of voices from beyond to get my bearings. Finding what seemed to be the right room, I banged open the door and stepped inside.

Three hundred pairs of eyes swivelled in my direction and the room hushed into silence. Spotting Corrigan at the far end, I strode over. He watched my approach, eyeing me as if I was about to completely flip out. I'd already done that in Balud's car though. Now it was time to get down to business.

There was a table next to him, covered with white china and the remnants of finger food. Seriously? Delicately painted tea-cups and cucumber sandwiches for a bunch of shapeshifters? Give me a break. I swept one arm across the entire table, and sent it crashing to the floor. No-one in the room moved a muscle.

I shoved Balud's box onto the table and undid the clasps, flipping open the lid. I had to admit that the troll had really outdone himself. The sword gleamed from within the purple lining of the box. It looked very heavy, and very lethal. I pulled it out, then offered it to Corrigan, hilt first. There was no indication on his face of his previous feelings of disgust, but he still didn't look very friendly.

"Staines is dead," I said, making sure my voice was loud and clear so that everyone could hear me. "And we know exactly who killed him. You've had your service and had your mourning. Now it's time to get your revenge."

A swell of hushed muttering rose up and died again.

"This sword is edged with palladium." I smiled thinly. "This is a necromancer's kryptonite. Your Lord Alpha is going to plunge this into Endor's fucking heart, and we are going to be rid of him forever."

I stared into Corrigan's eyes. Something flickered within their depths and he took hold of the sword, his hands curving round the ornate hilt. Thank fuck. It was so heavy, I'd been about to drop it. He cut it through the air, first one way, and then the other and nodded at me.

I spoke again. "He gets the sword because it was his right-hand man who died. But there are also three daggers. One for the mages, one for the faeries and one for me. We are going to end this week victorious. We are going to make sure that this bastard dies a thousand deaths. We are going to win. And the reason we're going to win is because we're going to work together as a team to do it." I paused, feeling momentarily carried away by my own sudden energy. Then I shouted. "What are we going to do?"

For a heartbeat there was absolute silence, then one lone voice called out from somewhere at the back, "We're going to win!"

I shouted again. 'What are we going to do?"

More people joined in. "We're going to win!"

"What?"

"We're going to win! We're going to win! We're going to win!" The voice of the crowd swelled until even the rafters were shaking with the tumult. I turned to Corrigan and smiled grimly.

He raised an eyebrow at me with an odd mixture of surprise and approval. There was something else too, which looked a little bit like respect.

"We'll fight him on the beaches," he said.

Hearing the conversation, the Arch-Mage stepped up. "We'll fight him on the landing grounds."

I looked at the Summer Queen. She rolled her eyes, patently exasperated. "Yes, yes, we'll fight him in the fields and in the streets."

I grinned. "I can't remember the rest. But you know what?"

They all looked at me.

"We'll never fucking surrender."

Chapter Nineteen

The trouble with Loch Ness is that, despite its obvious natural beauty, there's a distinct lack of cover. I'd been fortunate enough to find myself a tree next to the water's edge to sit myself behind, but I knew that some of us had ended up a few hundred feet away simply because there wasn't anywhere to hide. We couldn't afford to let Endor know that we were here. In that scenario no doubt he'd adjust his plans, and we'd be scuppered.

It was satisfying to know that since my impromptu speech, the mages, faeries and shifters had actually, honest-to-goodness and no-holds-barred, managed to set aside their differences and work together. I'd seen them discussing plans, considering strategies and even, once, a shifter asking a mage for advice about whether it would be better to combine their attacks or to separate out their ethereal magic and their physical brawn. Both the Summer Queen and the Arch-Mage had elected to stay away from the action, although they were still monitoring everything closely from a distance. I had to admit that it was a good idea. Their presence only caused more friction – not just amongst the other groups, but from within their own ranks also. Wild horses wouldn't have kept Corrigan away, however.

The Lord Alpha was positioned on the north edge of the loch, closest to where the kelpies' habitat was and therefore where we thought Endor would be most likely to attack. I was on the more westerly side, some considerable distance away. It was impressive, really, just how cordial we'd managed to keep our relations with each other over the past two days since we'd all arrived. Neither of us made any mention or even subtle reference to the kiss – instead we were entirely businesslike and focused on our goal. He'd even listened to me when I'd outlined my plans for communication, agreeing that it made the most sense to have everyone in groups of three: one shifter, one Fae and one mage in each. When Endor showed his face, whoever saw him first would use the Fae to transport straight to Corrigan no matter what was happening. That way Corrigan could then use his Voice to tell all the shifters where to vamoose their arses. Only alphas could initiate Voice contact, a fact that often made life difficult for the shifters. In this instance, however, it worked, because it meant that each and every one of us was crystal clear on just how vital it was to collaborate and communicate.

I was the only exception to the group of three rule. This was because I was the only one other than the Brethren Lord who could use the Voice to start a telepathic conversation. Admittedly, it was only Corrigan himself I could talk to, but I was just glad that no-one had questioned the reasons as to why that might be the case. According to the Fae book on my heritage, Draco Wyr could initiate Voice conversations with their soul-mate alone. As far as I was aware, only Solus and Alex knew that teeny little inconsequential fact. What Corrigan would think of it if he found out, I had no idea. It didn't really matter because he never would. Bearing in mind the wichtlein prophecy, it was unlikely that I'd make it to the end of this day alive... and I'd decided I was okay with that. It hurt like hell to imagine him with someone else – like that blonde he'd been with in London – but there was frankly not a damn thing I could do about it. As long as Endor was dead and Corrigan was safe, along with everyone else, then I could ask for nothing more.

Fortunately, the vamps had stayed out of my way for the time being. I'd convinced Aubrey to hole up in a nearby B&B and avoid coming to the loch itself. I'd also wrenched a promise out of him that in the unsurprising event of my death, he would never ever return to London again. Instead he was to find a small little country town somewhere to settle down happily for the rest of his days. It was the best I could do.

I stretched out my legs and yawned. The majority of my bruises were already considerably subsiding, and my body was in full healing mode. I had a funny feeling that the transformation exercises I'd been doing with Tom had helped. I was still a long way off being sure that I could fully shift into my Draco Wyr form and retain my own consciousness, but there was definite progress being made. If I had to become a dragon to defeat Endor, then I would. I wouldn't be happy about it, but I was more confident that I'd manage it without killing everyone else in the process. I'd not healed completely as the heavy ball of flame in my stomach was still making its presence known, but I actually felt rather glad about it. It meant that my bloodfire was simmering away, ready to spring into action as soon as it was required.

The sound of approaching voices caused me to suddenly tense. I pulled out the palladium tipped dagger, and heat rippled through me in a burgeoning flame. Twisting around, I remained crouched and camouflaged by the tree, craning my neck to see who it was. From around the curving path, a family appeared, each one wearing matching hiking boots with brightly coloured knee length socks. They were talking and laughing. I watched as the small boy with them stumbled and tripped, landing on his hands and knees. He looked surprised for a second, then his face screwed up ready to begin bawling. The father was already there, however, scooping him up and planting him on his shoulders, distracting him from the impending tears. I turned away.

There were just too many fucking tourists around. It was inevitable: it was the height of summer after all, but I was nervous that they'd end up getting in the way. Between the luxury cruises chugging up and down the loch with regular intervals, the cyclists and the walkers, it was going to be difficult for the mages to mask the signs of the upcoming battle. I chewed on my lip. I just had to trust that they'd manage it.

The glittering water in front of me rippled slightly, and a sleek dark head appeared. Kelpie. Its liquid brown eyes regarded me seriously, its almost impossibly long lashes blinking away the droplets of water. I scowled at it. Fucking thing. All of them gave me the creeps. They finally seemed to have come around to the idea that their entire existence was under threat, and agreed to do what we said, but it had been a struggle. And they were supposed to be keeping to Corrigan's end of the sodding loch.

I opened my mind, ready to tell the Lord Alpha to make sure that the bloody water creatures stayed in one place, but he was already there, the familiar growl of his Voice echoing in my head.

Something's happening.

My body froze. *What? Is he there?*

Corrigan's Voice sounded strained. *No, it's the kelpies. They're all coming up to the surface. They're…*

He broke off. I stared back at the water but the kelpie that had been there had vanished. Shit. It was starting. I sprang into action, grabbing the bike I'd hidden in a clump of bushes in case I needed to travel a long way, and tearing the leaves away from it with as much haste as I could manage. I pulled it away and jerked it up the small hill and onto the path, leaping on top of it and pedalling as fast as I could. As my legs pumped, I was aware of others emerging from their hiding places around me and doing the same. I cursed. No, that wasn't right.

Corrigan! I yelled with my Voice. *You have to get the faeries to stay where they are. If you don't have eyeballs on Endor, then they need to be there in case he shows up somewhere else.*

I threw my hands out as I whizzed past three of them. "The Fae!" I shouted. "She has to stay there!"

I didn't look back to see whether they'd heard me or not, instead I threw even more energy into getting the bike to move faster. Screw this bloody loch for being so big. I'd practised getting from different spots around it as quickly as I could over the last two days, but somehow this time Corrigan's position seemed much farther than had before. Air whipped past my cheeks and my palms felt sweaty and slippery on the handle bars. Fuck it, come on!

I swerved round a small boulder lying in the middle of the path, only just managing to keep the bike upright and myself on it. Flying over the handle bars at this speed would probably send me into a coma. I had to be careful. My heart was pounding in my ears, and adrenaline and bloodfire were zipping through every part of my body. Finally, I curved around and spotted Corrigan and several mages, faeries and shifters all at the water's edge. More were arriving every second. Even from this distance the water seemed to be churning. The daylight was already draining from the sky, making the blue bolts of magic the mages were zipping out into the water appear bright and unmistakable. I hoped again that they were still holding the concealing glamour in place. I screeched up, slamming on the brakes, and jumping off the bike, then sprinted to join them.

"What's happening?"

"The kelpies!" a young mage next to me gasped. "It's as if they're drowning."

I watched, panicked. It did indeed seem as if that was the case. There were at least twenty of them, all thrashing about at the water's surface. I went to run in, but Corrigan grabbed my arm and stopped me.

"Don't," he growled. "Any time we try that, it just seems to make them worse. It's as if there's some kind of barrier around them." He stared at my face, and somehow I knew without asking that my eyes were glowing.

Barrier shmarrier. I yanked out the dagger again and drew it against the palm of my hand. Beads of blood sprang up. I ran into the water, palm outstretched. I'd broken through one of Endor's wards before. I knew my blood could do it again.

As soon as the water was around my ankles, however, the kelpies began shrieking. One seemed to be being dragged under as if by some kind of mysterious force. I couldn't feel anything though. Usually when I connected with a ward, it was obvious. This time, it was as if there was nothing. I flicked out my hand, sending a spray of blood out in front of me. Nothing. That didn't make sense.

I looked up towards the darkening horizon, as if searching for something. Some inspiration from the gods or some kind of help. A tourist cruise ship off in the distance suddenly lit up, brightly coloured lights illuminating it from bow to stern. I glanced at the kelpies then at the boat. The creatures continued to pitch and turn, sending water in all directions, forcing every eye onto their plight. Oh shit. I knew where Endor was and it wasn't here.

"It's a diversion," I shouted back to Corrigan.

"What?"

"It's a fucking diversion! He's on the boat. He's not after the kelpies – they're probably working with him. He's going after the tourists!"

Blood drained from his face. "We need to get there."

I nodded, staring at the distance between us and the boat, which was getting further away by the second. I knew what I had to do. I closed my eyes, and inhaled deeply, feeling the fire rip through me,

233

coursing through my system with the rage of a thousand furnaces. I concentrated on my little match, standing it up straight in my mind's eye. I could do this. I had to.

Then pain scorched my skin, and I heard my bones creak and snap, and the fabric of my clothes tear and split. I pitched forward slightly at the unfamiliar weight of my tail, then managed to re-balance myself. I opened my eyes, my vision scored entirely through with a dull red haze. Clouds of boiling hot anger seethed through. Kill.

I whipped around and gazed at the group assembled on the shore. Kill. Many of them began to back away, eyes wide and fearful. A splashing side to the side of me caught my attention. My neck stretched out so I could see better. Kelpies. Kill. I opened up my mouth and a bellowing roar came out. Then I inhaled and breathed. In a sudden epileptic fit of movement, the water creatures ducked underneath the surface. No matter. I focused back on the others. Kill.

One figure was standing in front of all the others, dark and muscular. His lips were moving but all I could hear was the bloodfire pounding through me at the same rate as my heart. I opened my mouth again. He lifted his head and stared right at me, emerald green eyes searing into mine. I blinked as a small flame flickered in my mind. The figure took a step towards me. I flexed my foot and began to raise it, ready to lash out. Then an odd smell reached my nostrils, something like...sulphur. I blinked again. Mack. I was Mack.

I lowered my foot. Corrigan took another step

forward and I nodded, lightly flicking the tip of my tail. He relaxed. I bent my neck down and he leapt towards me, arms curving around and gripping. The weight was strange but not uncomfortable. I turned back to the loch, took a deep breath and jumped up into the air.

Then I smashed back down again, water spraying everywhere. Damn it. I was supposed to be able to fucking fly. I tried again, tucking my feet under me and throwing myself up and out. I bellyflopped back down yet again, Corrigan's body slapping against mine with a painful jolt. Okay.

The boat was starting to disappear from view. There was no more time. I took a deep breath instead and ran forward, pushing against the resistance of the water then, as soon as the loch floor deepened and widened out, I dived down, and began to swim.

About three seconds later, it occurred to me to wonder whether dragons actually could swim or not. It appeared that they could, however, and in a remarkably streamlined fashion, because I was pulling through the water at a rate that even Michael Phelps would admire. I lifted my head out of the water, allowing Corrigan to take a breath of air, and realised we were already gaining on the boat. Ducking under again, even though I could barely see anything through the murky depths of Loch Ness, I continued to push forward with great sweeping strokes that cut through the water. Then I looked up once more, and saw the boat had stopped and was lurching alarmingly to one side. I thrust forward until we came up on its left side, and felt

Corrigan's weight leave me as he stretched up and grabbed hold of a ladder dangling over the edge. There were several terrified screams as the vessel tilted again, this time in my direction. Enough.

I concentrated on my little matchstick flame, bringing my entire self back as much as I was able. My body changed with another streak of pain, and then I was floating in the water with the sudden sensation of feeling small and vulnerable. I hooked one elbow around the rope ladder and pulled myself out of the loch, shivering as the cold air hit my naked skin. Scrambling upwards, I yanked myself over the side of the boat and stood upright, bare feet feeling the wooden boards underneath. I grabbed a nearby life-vest, which was thankfully oversized enough to cover the majority of my modesty, and ran forward and around the front to where the tourists, Corrigan – and Endor – were.

The necromancer was standing amongst a group of cowering people, with Corrigan facing him. When he caught sight of me, he grinned.

"Miss Smith is joining us as well. What a joy!"

I moved up and stood shoulder to shoulder with the Lord Alpha. He had the palladium sword in front of him, its silvered length glinting even in the darkness. I realised that in the wake of my transformation, I'd somehow lost my little dagger. It didn't matter. Corrigan would stake the fucker with the sword and we would be done.

"It's the end of the line, Endor," I called out.

He laughed. "Is it? How terribly distressing for you."

He's going to sink the fucking boat, Corrigan

growled in my head.

I nodded. He'd drown everyone on board, leeching their life-force from them as he did so, and use the fact of their watery deaths to get the power he needed from the element of Water. He probably had some kind of deal going with the kelpies for the help of their acting skills set up to distract us. Maybe he'd let them play with a couple of the victims themselves.

The boat swayed alarmingly and several of the humans clutched each other and cried out. We had to get them out of the way.

"Everyone needs to come over here." I stretched out my hands, beckoning them forward. A few got up and ran towards us, but the rest stayed where they were, frozen in their seats.

"There's nowhere for them to go, you know," said Endor chillingly. "There's water everywhere. Even if they jump in to get away, it won't work. You know that."

I glanced over the side and spotted several dark bobbing heads. Fucking kelpies.

"I can see why they'd want to get near you, though," he smiled through his teeth, "charmingly attired as you are."

I hissed. "Let them move to the front of the boat."

A woman was at the back, sobbing loudly. Endor cocked his head for a second as if thinking, then shrugged. "Okay. They are rather distracting." He slapped a man on the back. "Go on then. Up to prow with you. You can take photos of each other shouting 'I'm the King of the World' if you want.

Your family will appreciate having something to remember you by." He frowned. "Well, if your cameras are waterproof that is. Otherwise I wouldn't really bother."

One by one, the tourists got up and began to move towards us. Several had taken out mobile phones and were clearly trying to frantically text or call someone for help. I had no doubt that Endor had already covered that angle and they'd find they couldn't get a signal. When the last one – the sobbing woman – was just about to pass us, Endor flicked his wrist and there was a loud splitting sound, as if the very fabric of the vessel was being torn asunder. She shrieked and ran forward, shoving past me. Then she jumped into the water with a cry that was abruptly cut off. My mouth went dry.

The necromancer looked amused. 'So," he said to Corrigan, "you were saying?"

A predatorily lethal look lit Corrigan's eyes. He hefted the weight of the sword and took a step forward.

"You've decided to forego the were-panther look then? I can understand that. I hear cats don't like water very much." Endor closed his eyes for a moment and audibly sucked in a breath. A dark swirl rose up from beyond the edge of the boat and drifted towards him. Then he opened his eyes and smiled again. "That woman may have been annoying, but she felt good."

Rage roared up inside me, and I sent two fiery bolts of green towards him. I should have known better, however, as they just bounced harmlessly off him. I stared down at my hand. Transforming into a dragon meant the cut on my palm was already healed. Fuck. I reached out and ran my index finger along Corrigan's blade then sprang forward and smeared my blood against Endor's ward. It crackled and smoked, then vanished. For the first time, his smile wavered.

""I'm getting annoyed that you keep doing that, Miss Smith. Of course I know now what the reason is. A Draco Wyr, here in the twenty-first century." He whistled. "Imagine that."

And if I wasn't sure that my dragon shape was so large it'd sink this boat, then you'd really know what it's like to face me, I thought.

It's time to end this, Corrigan snarled.

Oh, yes it is.

I took one last look at the Lord Alpha. Standing there, sword in hand, black hair sleeked back from the water, and his clothes sculpted to his skin, every muscle delineated, he looked like the epitome of every girl's hero. I didn't think he'd miss me too much.

Then I leapt forward towards Endor, scissor kicking in the air and connecting with his head. He reeled back with a spasm and pushed out his palms in my direction, black bolts springing forth from them and landing square in my chest. I gasped in pain and collapsed to my knees. Damn that hurt.

Mack! Corrigan yelled in my head.

I'm fine. I really wasn't. *I'm going to pitch left and catch him on his side. As soon as I do, you need to shove that sword and skewer this prick.*

There wasn't an answer.

Corrigan...

Okay.

I stumbled back up to my feet and then immediately ran forward again, this time lashing out with my fists, pushing out my energy into attacking. Endor defended himself against me with one hand, zapping me in the face with another deadly black stream of magic so that I fell backwards with a thump. He wasn't stupid, however, and he kept his other hand free to deal with Corrigan. I lifted my head and saw him about to strike. No way. I launched myself up just as Corrigan began to cut forward with the sword and grabbed Endor's other hand forcing it in my direction. The black magic spewed out of his fingers and into my chest, and I could feel myself falling and my own energy draining away. Corrigan, however, slammed the tip of the palladium sword into Endor's stomach.

The answering howl of pain from the necromancer proved that the Lord Alpha had found his mark. My vision darkening, I watched as he grabbed at the hilt and began to pull it out, snarling as he did so. The sword clattered onto the deck.

But instead of falling and dying, Endor raised up his hands and muttered something. A wall of water began to rise up on either side of the boat. It climbed higher and higher and higher, until it was towering up into the sky. Then it slammed back down, curving inwards and down upon us, while people screamed and the vessel began to break apart. Sharp splinters scraped against my skin as I struggled to stay conscious. I didn't understand. We'd used the palladium. Corrigan couldn't have thrust that blade into Endor's flesh with any more power than he had. Why hadn't he died?

I could feel myself falling backwards and smacking into the cold water of the loch. I couldn't hang on any longer. As I looked up into the sky, I saw streaks of blue mage magic zip over and converge on the sinking ship. Something brushed against my leg and began pulling me under. My life-belt resisted, determined to retain buoyancy. It was fighting a losing battle, however, as the tug on my legs was just too strong. A kelpie, I thought dully. Not Endor then. Or a vamp. Or a bloodlust crazed revenge seeker. Just a small seal-like creature. What a way to go. Then the water closed over my head and everything went dark.

Chapter Twenty

I felt very cold and very wet. Not in hell then. I shivered involuntarily and doubted very much that heaven felt like this either. Or indeed any form of the afterlife. Something was scratching painfully at my bare arms and legs, and the chafing and sensation around my torso felt very much like some synthetic plastic material – of the sort, say, that a deflated life-belt might be made out of. I wasn't dead after all then. How many freaking times was I going to almost – but not quite - shuffle off this mortal coil? It was starting to become tiresome, all these near-death experiences.

I opened my eyes and looked around, vaguely irritated to find myself on the shore of Loch Ness. With the amount of sodding times I found myself passed out, you'd think that I could at least, for once, wake up in a small thatched cottage with a roaring fire at the side and a kindly person handing me some chicken soup. But no, that would be too easy.

I pulled myself up to a sitting position. Corrigan was by the water's edge, sitting down and staring out over the darkened vista. Twinkling lights at the far end indicated where the small town of Fort Augustus and the others no doubt were. I knew Corrigan would have heard me stir, so I didn't bother saying anything, just stood up and walked over to him, wrapping my arms around myself to keep warm. I sat down next to him, resisting the urge to lean my head against his broad shoulder.

"It didn't work, did it?" I said finally.

He shook his head. It was a tiny movement, barely even perceptible.

I gritted my teeth. All that fucking trouble to get hold of a stupid metal that didn't even work. What a waste.

"How many?" I asked. "How many people died?"

He took a moment before answering. "Six at least."

I closed my eyes in pain. Then I opened them again. This was the shit we had to deal with. I wasn't going to get sucked under into a pit of useless depression again. It was time to re-group and fight back, not be defeated.

"If we weren't there, more would have died." It was cold-hearted, but it was also a matter of fact.

A muscle jerked in his cheek. "If you hadn't had a fucking death wish, then more would have died."

He turned and looked at me, green eyes blazing. "Do you have a total fucking disregard for your own safety?"

I stared at him. "You just said more would have died if I'd not done what I did. What other choice was there?"

He snarled, patches of black fur momentarily rising up on his skin. "You can't die."

"Last time I checked, my Lord, Draco Wyr weren't cursed with immortality," I said, trying to keep my tone light.

He brought his face close to mine. "What am I supposed to do if you die? What am I...?" His voice trailed off, and he pulled away.

My mouth was dry, and I felt a traitorous zip of happy bloodfire blossom up through me.

243

"When Staines died, all I could think was that thank God it wasn't you. That he'd been there and you hadn't." He pushed a hand through his hair. "I'm a fucking idiot."

He slammed his other hand into the ground with such force I was amazed it didn't embed itself into the dirt.

"If we'd beaten Endor, then I could have let the council go. I'd be free from," I licked my lips, "the constraints."

His face twisted, and he stood up and walked away, turning just once to stare at me, his eyes searing into my soul. Then his clothes ripped off and, in a heartbeat, he shifted into his werepanther form and bound away into the darkness.

I watched the spot where he'd disappeared. Fuck. Could things be any more messed up? I raised my eyes heavenward for just one breath, then stood up myself and limped painfully off.

*

It seemed to take forever to get back to the B&B where Aubrey was staying. By the time I finally reached it, my bare feet were very bruised and very sore. I passed clumps of Otherworlders on my way, but carefully avoided them. The last thing I needed was to speak to any of them right now.

The town was busier now at the dead of night than it had been the last time I was here during the day. Emergency service vehicles stood around, silently attesting to the tragedy that had taken place out on the water. There were also lots of press.

"It's not known what exactly had made *The Light of the Loch* sink," a reporter was saying into a camera as I passed, making sure I kept to the shadows to avoid any undue attention considering my practically naked form, "but the reports we are getting from eyewitnesses suggest that perhaps, just perhaps, it was a massive creature that swam up behind it. If those statements turn out to be true, then the Loch Ness Monster is indeed real, and is indeed a monster."

Jesus.

I picked up my speed and swerved right, then quietly opened the front door to the small guesthouse, and ran up the stairs. Without even bothering to get changed first, I went straight to Aubrey's room and knocked on the door. He opened it almost immediately, his face white. When he saw it was me, unashamed relief sprang into his face, and he reached over to pull me into a hug. If he thought it was strange that I was only wearing a fluorescent orange life-vest and was patently naked underneath, he didn't pass comment.

"I thought you were dead," he said.

I stepped backwards and looked at him. His eyes were glassy with unspent tears. Not the hysterical tears I'd come to expect from him, but a more deep-seated emotion. I was sorry for what I was about to do.

"Aubrey," I said, "a few days ago one of your friends sought me out."

He started, and looked even paler than before.

"She said that she could tell me where Endor was. The terms of the potential agreement were unacceptable, however."

I didn't spell out what her demands had been. I

didn't think I needed to. The former vamp just stared at me, waiting to hear what else I was going to say.

"How would she have known how to find him? His leak to Tarn notwithstanding, I don't get the impression that Endor is the sharing caring type, even with the undead, so how would a bloodsucker know where he is?"

Aubrey licked his lips. "Because we're – they're - undead," he said quietly. "Vampires have the ability to walk the line between the living and the dead, just like a necromancer would. They have a foot in both worlds, and can visit both worlds. We know Endor had close ties to the dead. They must know what he's doing."

A thought tugged at me. "So by going to the, er, dead world, they can talk to the dead?"

"Some of them. It's a very dark place, Mack. Even most vampires don't spend much time there." He smiled humourlessly. "This is one of the many reasons they're so keen to find me. Nobody is meant to know we have the ability to talk to the dead. They'll be concerned that I'll go blabbing all their secrets."

"They know you're alive now?"

He snorted. "No. That's meant to be impossible. But I imagine they think I'm working for you. Although why I'd do that if I was still a vampire would be a complete mystery."

I raised my eyebrows. "Indeed."

"You don't completely get it, Mack," he said earnestly. "You think you do, but you don't. When you're a vampire, nothing else matters beyond power. Power from blood, power from wealth, power from whatever. There aren't any emotions. To be a vampire is to be the ultimate sociopath. Taking orders from someone else, dragon or otherwise, is not power." He gazed at me seriously. "Do it."

I gave him a questioning look.

"Don't play dumb," he said softly. "Do it. Hand me over. They're not going to quit trying to get me back because having me loose in the world diminishes their power." A faint smile crossed his face. "Maybe you're right and they'll just turn me back."

"Is that what you want?"

He shook his head. "But if that's what happens, then I fully expect you to come after me and drive a stake through my heart. I've wronged you enough to deserve it."

I frowned. "You're on my fucking team now, Aubrey. I've got my dragon claws into you and I'm not going to let go. I need you to do one thing though."

"Anything." His eyes seemed lit up from deep within.

"You need to take me there."

He looked puzzled.

"To the dead," I explained.

"I can't. I'm not a vamp any more, remember? I can't get there."

I grinned. "I can. Well," I amended, "with a little help, I can. I just need you to point the way somewhat."

"It's dangerous, Mack."

"I know." I held his gaze. "We're out of choices though."

Aubrey took a deep breath. "Okay. Now?"

"We'll leave in fifteen minutes."

I quickly nipped to my own room, and yanked off the life-belt so I could finally put on some proper clothes. As I was shoving my feet into my trainers, I picked up the phone and dialed Alex.

"Hey. I guess you've heard what happened?"

"Yeah." His voice was was dull. "So much for the palladium."

I didn't bother dwelling on our failure. We needed to act now, not prevaricate. "I need you to get to Balud ASAP and find out why it didn't work. Maybe it was because the weapons were only lined with it and weren't one hundred percent pure palladium. Maybe it was something to do with the way we extracted it. I don't know, Alex. But you need to find out. And find out fuckng quickly."

"Do you think it was my fault? If we'd gone with the pure palladium and just paid for it, then do you think those people would still be alive?"

"Shut the fuck up. It was no-one's fault. It was shitty and it happened, but we need to stop worrying about what we can't change and find out how to fix it to make sure we get him next time."

"Okay, dude."

"Alex," I said warningly, "I mean it. If there's blame to be had, it lies with me. It was my plan. And I'm not sitting around crying about it, not any more. We're going to beat this bastard one way or another. Maybe not today, but we fucking will get him."

"Okay." His voice sounded firmer this time.

"Great."

I hung up and took a quick look around the room to make sure I'd not left anything behind. It would have been nice to enjoy a hot shower first, but I wanted to get moving straight away. I picked up my bag and jogged downstairs. In the small garden, sat on a picnic table, was a faerie. I didn't really recognise her, but it didn't matter. I walked right up to her.

"I need you to find Solus."

She blinked at me slowly. Our defeat was hitting everyone hard.

"Hey," I said, "go and get Solus and bring him here right now. And when I say right now, I mean right now."

She screwed up her face as if annoyed at being told what to do, but clicked her fingers anyway and vanished. I hoped she was actually going to do what I'd told her. Ordering people around was harder than I had ever imagined it to be. I was starting to feel a glimmer of sympathy for other people during all those times when I'd kicked back against authority. I was a fucking pain in the arse sometimes.

Fortunately, the Fae had been paying attention because just as Aubrey emerged from the front door, Solus appeared.

He bowed dramatically. "My lady. Are you all right? I tried to find you, but Lord Furry seemed to have things covered." He patted me on the shoulder. "We'll get him next time, dragonlette."

"I know," I replied grimly, then moved onto more pressing matters. "Do you realise where we are?"

"I believe we're in the poorly tended garden of a ridiculously small and quaint bed and breakfast." He wrinkled his nose. "It's not exactly the Ritz."

I gave him an exasperated look. "We're only about fifty kilometres away from Inverness."

"Where we first met. Happy times, dragonlette, happy times."

I kicked him. "Focus, please, Solus. What I mean is we are only fifty kilometres away from the Clava Cairns. The gateway to the in-between place."

It may have been over half a year, but I had very distinct memories of what it had been like in there – and how thankful I was that the Fae had come to find me and help me get out. I'd not had much choice at the time; I'd needed to get away from the mages and the police, and the portal at the Cairns had been about my only option. I'd been able to open it myself thanks to the fact it had been the Winter Solstice. This time I'd need more help.

He looked troubled."Yes, it's not far away. Why?"

"Because Aubrey and I are going to go in. Further in. I just need you to open it up for me."

"Dragonlette…"

I gave him my 'don't fuck with me' look. He sighed.

"Okay, then. I'm guessing by its proximity, you don't want to use a portal."

My stomach heaved at the mere thought. "There are enough shifter and mage cars around. We'll be there within the hour if we drive."

Solus gave me a half smile. "Then let's do this."

Chapter Twenty One

The Clava Cairns looked much as I remembered. Of course the smatterings of long-haired hippy types were absent, given that it wasn't the Solstice, so the entire area was as silent as the grave. Which in effect it actually was anyway. I took a moment to pause and drink in the night air. The darkness was comforting, rather than frightening, and the sky was perfectly clear. I traced the shape of the Milky Way out with my index finger. Those stars would be shining long after any of us were still around, even Solus. Even Endor. It was a nice thought that sooner or later the natural world would assert its authority regardless of my own actions. It somehow made the cloud of death that was following me around feel less intimidating and more just the way things should be.

"Dragonlette, what are you doing?"

I smiled at Solus. "Nothing. Just pondering the meaning of life."

He gave me a look. "Is something going on that I should know about?"

"No." My cheeks reddened involuntarily. Damn it.

"Dragonlette..." He switched tactics. "Mack, what is it?"

I felt a rush of warmth towards the Fae and leaned over and hugged him. "Thanks," I whispered in his ear. "For being such a great friend."

"Why does this sound a lot like goodbye?"

I shrugged and decided the best form of defense

was most definitely attack.

"I'm about to walk into the freaking Underworld! Is it too much to ask for a cheesy moment beforehand?" I gave him a glare. "It is kind of scary, you know."

"Sure." He didn't seem convinced. "And you're so often quaking in your knee high boots at any sign of trouble."

"Sarcasm is the lowest form of wit." Which was probably why I used it so often myself. "Now, please, can you open up the portal?"

He didn't look happy, but he jerked his head in agreement and walked past me, and through the narrow corridor of stones, stopping at the end. Aubrey and I were close behind him. The ex-vamp was, for once, staying remarkably quiet.

Solus placed his hands out in front of him, lightly touching the stones. He closed his eyes for a moment and muttered something. Nothing happened. Aubrey coughed. I gave him a quick look and realised amusement was brimming in his eyes. He saw me watching him, and a stifled giggle escaped his mouth. I gestured at him to stop. What the hell was so funny?

His shoulders began to shake. He clamped both hands around his mouth, but it didn't do any good. More snorts of laughter leaked out. Solus opened his eyes and turned around.

"Are you making fun of me?" He demanded.

Aubrey shook his head as he continued to giggle. Tears began to run down his face, and he eventually gave in, taking his hands away and collapsing in a fit of almost girlish titters.

"I'm sorry," he gasped. "I don't know why I'm laughing. It's not funny. I just..." he snorted again, chest heaving.

I rolled my eyes. "Just get on with it please, Solus."

His violet gaze was dark and troubled.

"Please."

He sighed. "How did you get in before?"

"It was the Winter Solstice. The gateway was weakened so I was able to get through."

"But you couldn't have just walked in."

"Oh, no, I said a Gaelic word. Oscail, I think. It means..."

"Open," Solus finished.

Aubrey began another round of uncontrollable laughing. Both of us ignored him. Solus turned back to the stones and muttered again. This time, there was a crack, and he stepped to the side, then motioned towards the uneven wall. I pulled Aubrey up by his shoulders and looked at him.

"Are you up for this?"

He nodded, wiping away the tears from his cheeks. "Yes, yes. I don't know what's come over me, really." He giggled. "I'm good."

I shook my head. I'd just have to work it out on my own. "Solus, make sure he gets back to the B&B."

"No!" Aubrey clutched my arm, suddenly and abruptly sober. "I can do this, Mack. I'm fine, really fine. You need me to come along."

I chewed my lip and watched him carefully, before finally nodding. 'Okay. But you need to get a grip of yourself."

He closed his lips and mimed zipping them up

then, without warning, stepped in front of me and vanished into the stones.

I looked at Solus. "Be seeing you." I hope.

I started to follow Aubrey inside. Solus said something behind me but his words were drowned out in the sudden engulfing silence.

"Well," said Aubrey, as I began to vomit copiously in a corner. "This IS fun."

*

When I eventually managed to stand shakily back up, I peered at Aubrey through the gloom.

"Let's get a move on," I said briskly, trying to downplay the fact that my reaction to magic portals was continuing to deteriorate.

"Okay. I think it's this way," he said pointing to his left.

"You mean you're not sure?"

"Every entry point is different. I only ever did this twice before anyway. I told you, it's not the most pleasant of places, even for a vampire." He gave me a quick smile. "I'll find the right path eventually."

He walked off ahead of me. My eyes narrowed after him. At least he'd stopped bloody laughing, even if it seemed we might be wandering around here for days. I sighed and began to trudge after him, trying to ignore the fact that I was actually feeling a teeny tiny bit scared, despite my brave words to Solus. We were so completely into the unknown that it felt as if almost anything might happen. Although I'd been here before, I was pretty sure I hadn't gone very far at all before Solus had found me and taken me out. This time I was going straight into the heart of darkness, and a darkness that even Joseph Conrad couldn't have envisaged. Aubrey began humming to himself again. I smiled slightly. At least I wasn't alone.

The pair of us continued walking for what seemed like some time. Nothing appeared to change. This wasn't like the mine where the air had gotten denser and the claustrophobic feeling of being underground had deepened with every step that we took. Instead it almost felt as if we were simply walking around in circles. It was dark and gloomy; not the comforting fresh darkness of outside or the oppressive eternal night of the mine, just dark and gloomy forever and ever. My fingertips prickled with heat, but I wasn't tempted to light the area to see more clearly. I kind of had the feeling that I wouldn't enjoy the sight. Some things were better left unseen and unknown. At one point, my entire body shuddered when a cold gust of air from goodness knows where brushed by, but Aubrey didn't comment on it, so neither did I. He just stopped humming for half a beat, then picked up again where he'd left off – only louder. I thought about injecting in a bit of humour and doing what Alex had done for me by adding in a beat. It didn't seem very appropriate though.

Eventually, Aubrey came to a halt. I'd been so lost in my own thoughts that I walked straight into the back of him. He turned around and hissed at me.

"Shhh!"

"I didn't say anything!" I protested.

He glared and motioned at me to keep quiet. I opened my mouth to tell him to piss off, when all of a sudden there was a distant rumble. I snapped my mouth shut. The noise seemed to get louder, trundling towards us as if it were a train. I felt as if my heart was in my mouth. The whole space was filled with it. I put my hands over my ears, trying to somehow muffle the sound. Then the ground underneath me started shaking, and I could feel my whole body reverberate with it. My eardrums thrummed and pressure built up inside my head – and then suddenly it disappeared.

I carefully removed my hands from my ears, and listened. There was nothing again. Just the silence.

"What the fuck was that?" I whispered.

Aubrey just shook his head. "We're getting close."

A wall of panicked terror hit me then that was so unexpected it almost knocked me for six. I swallowed several times, trying desperately to regain my equilibrium. Getting close was a good thing, not a bad thing. I should be happy. I concentrated on my bloodfire, allowing its warmth to rise up and comfort me. After a few moments, my body started to relax, and my breathing evened out.

"It's going to be alright, Mack," Aubrey said. "You'll see."

"Says the person who found this place scary even when they were fucking undead," I grumbled.

I let him lead me on, however, twisting left. Unfortunately this was in the direction the sound had come from. It's okay, Mack, I told myself. It's okay. It's...

"It's okay, Mack."

I let out a small shriek. That had not been

Aubrey.

My eyes wide, I searched the darkness frantically. There was something there. Someone there. I took a step towards the outline of the figure, and then Aubrey pulled me back by the scruff of my t-shirt.

"Don't," he hissed.

"But..."

The look in his eyes stilled me. I nodded. I'd probably just been hearing things. And seeing things. Aubrey took my hand in his and squeezed it. Then we continued on.

"I can feel the fire from here," a female voice murmured.

I jumped about five feet in the air. Fucking hell. Iabartu had said those very words to me when I'd confronted her, half an eternity ago. But it couldn't be her – she was very, very dead.

"Ignore it." Aubrey tightened his grip on my hand.

"What is it? Who is it?"

"They're drawn to you," he said. "I don't hear what you hear. The ones who passed this way before who have a connection with you are drawn to you. Only you can hear them."

My chest tightened. He was talking about fucking ghosts. But that meant...

"Don't get any ideas, Mack," Aubrey said dully. "They're not what you think."

I was about to ask him what he meant when another voice spoke. "What do you call a human with half a brain?"

My heart rate increased. The human hating

Brethren shifter who'd died on the beach in Cornwall. I swallowed and focused my attention on the real person in front of me.

"What are they then?"

"Not even what you would call souls. They're just," he paused, as if searching for the right word, "echoes. Reminders of what once was and is no more."

"So where are the souls?"

"Deeper."

We continued walking. I concentrated on putting one foot in front of another. I wasn't sure if I should be trying to listen out or trying to block out the voices. I caught myself straining my ears into the silence. What if I heard John? Or Thomas?

"Giiiiiiiiive meeeeeeeee it!"

Jesus. That was the wraith, Tryll. I should definitely be trying to block out the sounds. Aubrey tugged at my hand, pulling me along, attempting to get me to move faster.

"Aubrey?"

"Yeah?"

"What do you hear?"

He sighed heavily. "You don't want to know."

I bit my lip. He'd been a vamp. He was right – considering what I was hearing, I definitely didn't want to know what terrors Aubrey was being forced to listen to right now. I increased the pressure of my grip on his hand for just a second. I was still here and I was still with him.

The familiar voice of the painfully young Brock filled my ears. "You know Baldilocksh, you're okay."

I gritted my teeth and tried to stop the tears

from welling up. Oh God. I couldn't deal with this. To know that they were here but not here. I didn't want to hear them. Any of them.

"You know what it'll be like, Mack, more than anyone. I'll always be labelled as the crazy one who might fly off the handle at any moment. It doesn't matter whether I'm here or somewhere else. I thought I'd put all those troubles behind me, but I suppose I was wrong."

Thomas. I squeezed my eyes shut. Make it stop. Make it stop. Make it stop.

Then there was the most familiar voice of all. "It's a wichtlein's stone. Wichtleins do sometimes hang around old mines and tease the men that work there, but more often than not they are true harbingers of evil."

I cried out in involuntary pain, stumbling and crashing down to my knees, my hand wrenching away from Aubrey's. He pulled me back up to my feet.

"John," I gasped. "That was John."

"It's okay," Aubrey said softly. "We're here."

I gulped in air and looked around. It was still the same darkness, still the same place.

"Are you sure?" My voice came out as a squeak. I cleared my throat and tried again. "Are you sure?"

"Yes." His voice sounded distant. "You need to wait here."

"What? No! You stay here. I'll go."

"You can't, Mack."

"You can't fucking tell me what to do. You're on my team, buster, not the other way around." Clearly the stress was starting to get to me.

Aubrey reached out and touched my hair ever so gently. "You're life. Everything about you is life. This place, where we are now, it's all death. You won't be able to enter."

"Screw this place," I snarled and pushed past him.

I smacked straight into some kind of invisible wall. A ward? Here? I growled. I picked at the scab on my index finger until it bled, then thrust it out towards the barrier and stepped forward again. My head crashed against it. I shoved my shoulder into it. Still, nothing. I turned at looked at Aubrey. He was just standing there, watching me.

"I was a vampire, Mack. I've been touched by death." He smiled at me with a tinge of sadness. "And they'll talk to me."

"The dead? They've just been fucking talking to me! In fact, they wouldn't bloody shut up!"

"That wasn't a conversation," he said gently. "I'll find the right souls and find out what you need."

And before I could say anything else, he was gone.

"Fuck!" I shouted out, slamming my hand against the wall.

I began to pace around.

"Come on then!" I shouted to the invisible voices. "Do your worst! What else are you going to say?"

Silence rebounded back at me.

"You think I'm afraid?" I shouted again. "Speak up!"

There was nothing. I couldn't hear a goddamn thing. The place was so silent that if a single feather fell to the ground it would probably sound like a clash of thunder. And then someone spoke.

"You're going to stay here for a while, Mackenzie. John will look after you. You'll be safe here. Try not to get angry or lose your temper. You're going to be on your best behavior all the time. No matter what though, don't forget that I love you with all my heart."

I slowly sank to the ground. My mother. She was dead then, after all. I buried my face in my hands.

*

I had no idea how long I was there for. It could have been five minutes and it could have been five hours. I didn't hear any more voices; I was just alone in the darkness. When Aubrey finally did return, he was so silent that it wasn't until he spoke that I realised he was there.

"Hey Mack."

I scrambled to my feet, beyond relieved to see him. "Aubrey! You made it! Thank fuck."

He smiled at me. "Endor's hiding out in one of the dark planes. Dorchadas."

"I've never heard of it. You're sure?"

He nodded.

"That's brilliant," I said. "We should have come here from the very fucking start."

I cursed myself and my own fallibility. I should have spoken to Aubrey earlier about the vamps. Idiot.

"Come on, then. Let's go." I turned and began walking. When I realised he wasn't following me, I stopped and looked back. "What? Am I going the wrong way?"

"You're going the right way, Mack. Just keep walking straight and don't veer off the path. If you get lost, then call Solus to help."

I stared at him. "You're not coming."

"No."

"Why the fucking hell not?"

There was a kindness in his eyes that I'd not seen before. "I can't."

"What do you mean you bloody can't?"

"Only the undead can walk with a foot in both worlds. I'm not undead. Not any more."

I could feel the blood draining from my face. "I don't understand, Aubrey. Get your arse over here now."

He smiled again. "You do understand, Mack."

No. I didn't. He needed to stop dramatising everything so we could sodding go home. It was just like him to act this way.

"If anyone could just visit the dead whenever they wanted, don't you think they'd always do it?" he said softly.

"But..."

"You can't return to the world of living after you've been here. It's not natural and it's not right. Think about the creatures you've met in the past." He smiled humourlessly. "The wraith, Tryyl. He should have just stayed dead. Think about how much better everything would have been if he had."

"And vampires are fucking natural? Are they fucking right?" I exploded.

"Did you ever think they were?" His voice was calm and even. "They're not. You know they're not." He stood there, watching me from only a couple of feet away. "You brought me back. You gave me my soul and my life whether you meant to or not. I've already lived long beyond my years as it is. This is what's right, Mack."

"You knew," I said, staring at him. "You knew you wouldn't be able to return."

"I don't need to return, Mack. I've already been saved. I even got to enjoy coffee and pizza properly first as well. And we'll always have Russia." He smirked slightly before turning serious again. "I owe you my life."

"Before," I said, "when you were in hysterics…"

"What? You've never been to a funeral and gotten a fit of the giggles?" He raised up one hand in a gesture of farewell. "Now go. Get the council together and go and find Endor. Kill him. And live the rest of your life. You deserve it."

"Aubrey, wait!"

He turned and began to walk away.

"Wait!" I yelled. "Just fucking wait!"

It was too late. He'd already gone.

Chapter Twenty Two

When I finally limped out of the portal, it was still dark. My heart sank slightly. I'd been hoping for a little bit of daylight. Some sun perhaps. The kind that Aubrey detested so very much. My heart sank a little further.

The journey back through the in-between world had been long, and I'd never been entirely sure whether I was heading in the right direction. At least I'd not been plagued with the voices, reminding me of all those who had already died, but it had been arduous and very, very dark. And my mind had been filled with Aubrey. As much as I may once have hated him and everything he stood for, I was going to miss him. More than miss him. I just had to make sure that his sacrifice didn't end up being in vain.

Solus was in the car, exactly where we'd left it. He appeared to be fast asleep. I rapped sharply on the windows and he started, eyes widening when he caught sight of me. I gave him a tight smile, then got in.

He looked at me without saying anything. The events of the last few hours must have been mirrored in my face because he nodded grimly, then turned on the engine and we drove off. It wasn't too long, however, before all hell kicked off.

I was flicking through the radio stations when he popped into my head. None of the sounds I was coming across fitted my mood. I didn't want to listen to fucking pop music. Or the twangs of

Scottish country rock. What I needed was some kind funeral dirge. Something to match how I currently felt.

Mack. Are you there?

I sighed inwardly. *Hi Corrigan.*

You're there. Where the fuck have you been? I've been trying to contact you for days.

He sounded very pissed off. Something gave me pause, however.

"Solus, how long was I gone?" They were the first words I'd spoken to him since I'd gotten into the car.

The Fae flicked me a look with his deep, troubled violet eyes. "About three days."

Three days? Three fucking days?

Mack!

Uh, sorry. I didn't realise I'd been away for that long. I thought quickly. *I need you to contact the council for me. Arrange a meeting.*

I glanced back at Solus. "Are we going to drive back to London?"

He looked at me as if I was crazy. I returned back to Corrigan.

In, say, a couple of hours' time?

It's two o'clock in the morning.

So?

Fine. I'll arrange it. Where are you now?

With Solus. We're going to drive the car back to Fort Augustus, I think, then use a portal to get to London.

He roared in my head. It bounced around my skull, making me wince. Solus shot me a concerned look, but I dismissed him with a quick wave.

What? You're going all Lord of the mighty Brethren on me, are you?

Is it his?

I really was not in the mood for this right now. What in the hell was eating him? *The portal? It's certainly not mine, Your Grumpiness.*

He didn't immediately answer. When he did, his Voice sounded strained. *We need to talk, kitten.*

The diminutive made me swallow. But I still wasn't in the mood. *Which is why I'm asking you to call a council meeting. It's not hard, Corrigan. Just do it.*

I cut him off. Normally I'd be delighted that he was giving me the time of day. Right now I was just too fucking tired.

"Let me guess," Solus drawled, "Lord Shifty is giving you hassle."

I threw him a dirty look. At least he actually looked vaguely contrite.

"Sorry. I can't help myself sometimes. He's just such an easy target."

"If it wasn't for you and your lot," I started, ire rising inside of me, "then things between me and Lord fucking Shifty would be very different."

"You know how badly I feel about that, dragonlette."

"Yeah, yeah," I grumbled, closing my eyes, unwilling to continue this conversation any further.

A moment later, I spoke again. "Solus?"

"Mmm?"

"Thank you for waiting."

"You're welcome, dragonlette," he said quietly.

We arrived back in the small town not very

much later. Solus left the car parked outside the B&B where I'd been staying. When we got out, I sent him a suspicious look.

"Who does this actually belong to?"

"I believe the mages hired it. So they didn't look strange suddenly appearing in bursts of purple light in front of flocks of tourists."

"There aren't any mages here now, are there?"

"No." Solus smirked.

I rolled my eyes. "So you're just going to leave this here and rack up their rental charges?"

"Is that a problem?"

I didn't think a large bill would help improve the Ministry's current state of affairs very much. At my look of disapproval, Solus put up his hands. "Fine. I'll take it to the rental company's office."

I nodded. "I'll just grab my things from my room." At least I'd had the foresight to book it for a week.

Solus dropped me off, then I padded carefully and quietly upstairs. I paused for a moment outside what had been Aubrey's door, then forced down the lump in my throat and continued on.

I was just stuffing the last of my clothes into my backpack when a shadow fell across the doorway. I glanced up, then snarled. The fucking bloodsucker again.

"What do you want?"

"You should keep your voice down. You wouldn't want to risk waking the humans." She licked her lips, making me think that was exactly what she hoped would happen.

"You should get out of my fucking room before I

rip your head off. Don't think I can't take you."

"Now, threats of violence really aren't going to help your cause, are they?"

"They're not threats," I stated flatly.

She stepped inside and sat down delicately on the flowery bedspread, and began examining her blood red fingernails. "So," she said in bored tone of voice, "where is Aubrey?"

"He's dead. So you might as well just quit with this whole thing."

She raised her eyebrows. "If he's dead, then where is the body?"

"Gone."

"So there's no proof whatsoever that you're telling the truth?"

I wondered how much blood vamps had inside of them and, if I killed her, whether I'd be able to clean it up before leaving. Considering that I'd demanded Corrigan arrange the council meeting for within the next hour or so, then probably not.

"I guess there's not, no," I said finally, trying very hard to speak in a low voice and not completely lose my temper.

"Then that's a problem for you."

I stared at her. If I ripped out her carotid artery, then shoved her into the bathroom as quickly as I could, maybe there wouldn't be too much of a bloody mess left behind.

"I know what you're thinking," she said. "You are trying to work out how on earth you could possibly kill me right here and right now, without leaving any traces or waking anyone up."

To be fair, the hate brimmed look I was giving

her probably didn't make that desire so very difficult to work out.

"I think I can probably manage it," I said calmly, although pistons of hot bloodfire were churning through my stomach.

"You probably could. I'm discovering that you can be a resourceful little girl."

Maybe if I just hit her on the head and knocked her unconscious, then I could take her body out with me. Then I could deal with her later in my own sweet time.

"The thing is," she continued, "it may have been me who has met with you, but do not think that I am alone. There are many of us. Kill me and someone else will simply take my place. And they won't be so friendly. Don't forget that we have a hotline direct to your old family friends." She smiled. "Reunions can be such fun. So, find me some proof, or suffer the consequences."

She stood up gracefully, and walked out.

I sat down on the bed she'd just vacated, seething with anger. I was itching to run after her and tear out her throat. The trouble was I knew she was probably right and there were indeed many replacement vamps waiting in the wings. No doubt they wouldn't spend so long dragging their feet on getting Bolux's kids fully involved either. It just wasn't fair she was still hanging around like the lingering odour of stale cat pee when Aubrey was gone. I scrunched up the bedspread in my hands. It wasn't even as if I could offer her any proof of his demise. If I told her he was walking along the halls of the dead, she'd work out that he'd died as a human – and I didn't think she'd take too kindly to the knowledge that my blood could do the same to her and the rest of her undead mates.

I thought about it. Even if the vamps didn't tell the scary power nullifying warriors where I was, they already knew I existed. They were going to find me sooner or later. And if they were anything like their dead friend then it was going to be adios muchachos before I could even swing a punch. But all I had to do was dispatch Endor first and make sure everyone I loved was safe. After that, what happened didn't really matter. I'd go to the vamps and tell them to do their worst. My apparently impending doom was starting to seem inevitable. The least I could do was go to meet my Maker with the same grace and dignity that Aubrey had.

With that decided, I nodded to myself and went out to wait for Solus to return.

*

Two hours later, with the great and the good yet again lining the grand table in Alcazon's private room, I laid out what I – or rather what Aubrey - had found out.

"Dorchadas?"

I looked at the Arch-Mage. "Yep. Do you know it?"

"I know of it." He looked troubled.

"Darkness," the Summer Queen said quietly. "It means darkness."

I rolled my eyes. But of course it did. Spending my days running around in the dark seemed to be becoming a bad habit.

"So," I said, "we need to find a way to get into

Dorchadas without setting off any magical alarm system. And we need to do it fast."

"And when you get in there, how exactly do you plan on killing the apparently unkillable necromancer?" Corrigan's eyes were shadowed, but the taut muscles in his face belied his unhappiness.

I sighed. "I'm working on that. We had it from Balud that he would be vulnerable to palladium." I nodded to the Lord Alpha. "Now we know that's wrong. I sent Alex off to find out what the problem had been. We didn't have much palladium to work with in the first place so it's possible that's why it failed."

"Why didn't you have much of it?"

I could not believe the Arch-Mage had asked that question. Because we were trying not to make you and your bloody organisation look bad in front of the others, I thought sourly.

"We didn't have much time to get any more together," I said.

Thankfully he didn't pass further comment. "I will talk to Mage Florides as soon as possible to ascertain what he's discovered," he said.

I looked over at the Summer Queen. "Can you begin to look into ways to get into Dorchadas?"

She inclined her head. "That is not a problem. It may go quicker, however, if we can work with some mages. That way we can be sure we haven't missed anything. Any traps or warning systems and such like."

I almost fell off my chair. She was volunteering the Fae to work with the Ministry? Fucking hell.

"It's a good idea," the Arch-Mage agreed. "It

would probably also be worthwhile if we can have some shifters and mages work on research for other ways to bring down Endor. Their two different approaches and areas of expertise will complement each other."

I wondered whether I was still back in the in-between world, having some kind of bizarre dream.

"Agreed," said Corrigan, although his eyes were on me.

"Excellent." I stood up, with everyone else following suit. "We don't know when he's planning to strike next, so we need to work quickly. Let's meet back here in twenty-four hours."

"At four o'clock in the morning?"

My body clock was completely out of whack. It must be some kind of heaven-hell jetlag thing. "You're right. Make it ten o'clock tonight instead."

I dismissed the lot of them, and began to head out. Corrigan caught my arm.

"We still need to talk."

His citrus-spicy aftershave made me momentarily weak at the knees. I opened my mouth to answer him, but the Summer Queen interrupted.

"Miss Smith, I have a message to pass on to you."

Corrigan's body stiffened, and he dropped his hand.

"It's really rather important, I believe," she said smoothly, as if she'd not noticed his reaction. "Atlanteia wants to talk to you."

Atlanteia. Oh shit. I stared at her.

"Do you know why?"

"She wouldn't tell me. Only that she would appreciate you paying her a visit at your earliest convenience."

She glided off smoothly. I felt faintly sick. I'd been avoiding even thinking of the dryad since I'd returned from Haughmond Hill. Part of me had hoped that she didn't want anything to ever do with me again because I'd promised her I'd keep her flock safe. Instead their entire species had almost become entirely extinct. And one of them had died at my own hands.

Corrigan had obviously noted my reaction. "I did it too," he said quietly.

I looked at him.

"I killed one of them too. It wasn't your fault, Mack."

Yeah, he could say that as many times as he wished. It wouldn't make me feel any better about it.

"I need to go and see her," I muttered.

"We have to talk," he insisted.

The thought of facing the tree nymph felt like a heavy weight around my neck. "I have to go and see her first," I said. I wouldn't be able to focus on anything else until I did.

"Then I'll come with you."

I blinked. He sighed, and gazed down at me. I could feel myself drowning inside the green pools of his eyes, unable to look away.

"We really do need to talk, kitten."

I swallowed. "Okay then. Let's go."

Chapter Twenty-Three

I had no idea what it was Corrigan wanted to say. It was possible that he was so horribly embarrassed that he'd given so much of himself away on the shore of Loch Ness, he wanted to make it very clear to me it had been an aberration which wouldn't be repeated. I had no doubt a very large part of him still hated me for what I'd done to him.

He didn't speak, however. We travelled the entire way to Hampstead Heath in the back of his ostentatiously gleaming limousine in silence. I was excruciatingly aware of his proximity. Every time his body moved even slightly, I held my breath, wondering whether he was going to start speaking. But he still didn't. And nothing had really changed anyway – Endor was still out there, threateningly at large, and I was still the head of the council and beholden to the promise I'd made to stay impartial by maintaining only a platonic business relationship with him.

The car pulled up outside the entrance to the sprawling park. My legs felt like dead weights, but I forced myself to get out. The pair of us began walking towards the copse of trees where Atlanteia's habitat was located. An owl hooted overhead, and the skitterings of potential prey could be heard rustling in the bushes which lined the path. Other than that, there were no sounds.

"I was so angry at you," he said, suddenly.

I closed my eyes briefly. "I know. I didn't want it

to happen like that. I wanted to explain it to you first. I just didn't get the chance."

"All you've ever done is fight against authority and be independent. You don't do what other people tell you to. All I could believe was that the idea to drop me had come from you." He scowled. "So you could put yourself in the position of council head. Leader of every Otherworld group."

"That's not how it happened. And that's not what my job is."

I stopped and turned to look at him, inwardly pleading with him to understand.

"Yeah, I've spent a lot of time saying fuck off to anyone who's tried to tell me what to do. And look where it's gotten me. I've got no-one. I'm not part of a pack, or the Ministry, or anything."

He scoffed. "You're kidding, right? You're best friends with a faerie, a shifter, a mage, a Scottish bookshop owner and a fucking ex-vampire. I'm the Brethren Lord, Mack, I don't get to have friends."

"I'm not friends with an ex-vampire any more," I said, fresh pain twisting inside me.

Corrigan's face filled with empathy. It hurt too much to think about so I returned to the previous topic.

"Why not?" I asked.

"Why not what?"

"Why don't you get to have friends?"

"Well, I'm hardly going to be best mates with a faerie or a mage, am I? You know things don't work like that. And I can't be friends with the shifters because I'm their fucking boss. I can't tell them all my worries and troubles one minute, then tell them off the next."

I smiled faintly. "So what you're saying is that in order to be a responsible leader, you need to keep your distance." I threw my arms out in a gesture of exasperation. "What do you think I've been doing?"

He blinked at me, then nodded slowly with the light of final comprehension.

"And the three groups are working together in a way that I don't think has ever happened before." His voice was soft. He reached out and gently caressed my cheek with his thumb. "I'm sorry for what I said to you before about never wanting to see you again. I was hurting."

I knew how much it cost him to say that, but I pulled away. "Nothing's changed, Corrigan. We still can't be together. I made a promise."

He watched me carefully. "If we defeat Endor…"

I thought of the bloodsuckers, and the looming threat of Bolux's descendants, and swallowed.

"What about the girl?"

He looked confused. 'What girl?"

"You know. The blonde. The one who called you Corr." I struggled to keep the jealousy out of my voice, but didn't quite succeed.

"I was hoping that if I was seen publicly with other women, it would get back to you. The one time that being in this position and being photographed constantly seemed like a good thing." He appeared momentarily shamefaced. "It was petty. But nothing happened, kitten."

I stared into his eyes. He was telling the truth. And, let's face it, I was guilty of my own petty actions too.

"You're in my head and I don't think I'll ever be able to get you out no matter how hard I try, no matter what stupid shit you pull." He ran a hand through his hair, then shrugged. "I'm in love with you. I think a part of me has been from that very first time when I saw you sparring with Tom on the beach in Cornwall. I want nothing more than to spend the rest of my life with you. Because of you and who you are, Mack. Not for any other reason." There was an odd expression on his face. "It's important you know that."

I could hear my heart beating and I had to squeeze my fingers together into fists to stop them from shaking.

"I love you too," I said simply.

We both stood there, just looking at each other, neither of us touching. A light breeze picked up and floated past; a night bird screeched off in the distance, and the moon hung heavily in the sky, watching everything. Time stopped.

Eventually I broke the reverie.

"Come on," I said, "let's find out what Atlanteia wants."

He nodded, and we began to walk again, slower this time, as if not wanting anything to ruin the mood. Unfortunately, we arrived at her tree far too quickly. The dryad was already there, visible and waiting.

She raised her eyebrows at me. "You brought company."

"He was there too, Atlanteia. At Haughmond Hill." I was still nervous about what she was going to say, even though my bloodfire was singing at what had only just passed between Corrigan and me. I licked my lips. "You can trust him."

The dryad stared at him assessingly, then finally inclined her head. "You should have visited before."

"I..." Damn it. This was a night of truth, not of evasion. "I was afraid," I said. "I killed one of your own."

"As did I," said Corrigan by my side.

Her eyes were filled with sadness. "I know. I also know there was no choice. Your actions, as terrible as they were, saved us all."

"I'm sorry."

I hung my head, and looked down at the ground. Atlanteia floated silently over, her bare feet making no impression at all on the soft ground. She reached out one long elegant arm, and touched me under my chin, raising my head back up.

"You did well, Mackenzie Smith. There is no censure, only gratitude."

A lump rose in my throat.

"We would like to repay your kindness in helping us."

I shook my head. "No. There's no need, really. I don't want anything."

The corners of her green tinged lips crooked upwards. "You'll want this," she said softly. "Remember, the trees see everything. They know what happens and they don't forget. They know where your mother is."

I bit my lip, hard. "She's dead."

Corrigan shot me a quick look. Atlanteia nodded.

"She is. Her final resting place is in Penzance. There is a small cemetery on a hill. You will find her there."

"She's in Cornwall?"

The dryad's answering glance was filled with sympathy. "She did not get far after she left you there."

Pain tightened my chest and the pleasant warmth of my bloodfire turned into an angry burn. "They caught her."

She nodded. "They did."

"She wasn't a Draco Wyr," I said through gritted teeth. "There was no reason to do that."

"By sacrificing herself she kept you safe." Atlanteia blinked slowly. "You and your brother."

I stared at her. Corrigan stiffened.

"He was with your father."

"My father?" The words exploded out of me. "Is he...?"

Atlanteia shook her head. "No. He died years ago in a bar fight. Your brother was placed with a foster family. Humans. We do not believe he knows what he is."

"Where is he now?"

"He lives in Windsor."

"That's so close," I whispered.

She nodded. "Would you like the address?"

I looked at Corrigan, and he looked back at me. Then I turned back to Atlanteia.

"Yes."

"There is also one other thing."

My stomach dropped. One other thing? What more could there possibly be?

"The Voice," Atlanteia said softly, glancing at Corrigan rather than me. "It can be turned off."

My brow crinkled. I had no idea what she meant. Corrigan, however, smiled suddenly and nodded.

"Er, hello? What does that mean?"

"He knows."

"He knows what?" My eyes narrowed. "Corrigan…"

"It's okay," he said, keeping his attention on the dryad. "I'll tell you later."

Hold on a fucking minute. I didn't like being kept out of the loop.

"Relax, kitten," he murmured. "It'll keep for now. Let's go and find your long lost brother."

A wave of nervous panic hit me. Shit, this was real.

"Okay," I squeaked.

*

We arrived in Windsor not long after dawn had broken. The castle, majestic and proud, was bathed in orange and red and gleamed over the entire town like a watchful and protective parent. Corrigan's driver wended his way through the silent streets before finally pulling up outside a row of terraced houses. The only thing remarkable about them was their ordinariness.

From the car I stared at the house my twin brother apparently occupied. Fuck. I was more terrified than I thought I'd ever been. Give me a thousand necromancers over this.

"It's six o'clock in the morning," Corrigan commented. "Do you want to knock on the door?"

"It's too early," I said. "I don't want to wake him up."

"You don't have to do this, you know. We can

drive straight back to London."

I was very tempted. I'd lived this long without knowing him and I could always come back another day. Except I had Endor to deal with. And the vamps. Corrigan touched me lightly on the hand as if to reassure me. Shit. What I was going to tell him about them? I had a funny feeling that just dropping into conversation that they were on the verge of making sure I ended up very dead wouldn't go down too well.

"No," I said finally. "Let's just sit here for a while."

The pair of us watched the house. There were no signs of movement.

"How could he not know what he is? He must have some inkling that he's different." I could boast better fighting skills than most Otherworlders. I could call up green fire at my fingertips. I could transform into a fucking dragon, for goodness sake.

"You grew up in a pack. You know what kind of creatures are out there in the world. If he's grown up thinking he's human then why it would it occur to him to wonder otherwise? Maybe there's a reason why no Draco Wyr have been heard of for centuries. Maybe even they don't know what they are themselves."

"Someone knew. My mother knew."

Corrigan shrugged. "She didn't tell you though. Your old alpha knew, didn't he? He didn't tell you."

Secrets upon secrets upon secrets.

"Would things be better for you if you didn't know?" he asked quietly. "Would you be happier?"

"You can't undo what's already been done. You

can't unknow what you already know," I said. "I have no clue."

I looked back at the house, trying to get an idea of the person who lived inside it from its exterior. It seemed well kept. There was a tidy little garden at the front, and heavily draped curtains covering the front windows.

"Mack," Corrigan said, with a tense note in his voice that made me glance back at him. "There's something you need to know."

That sounded ominous. "What?"

He swallowed. Shit, Corrigan was nervous?

"It was what I actually wanted to talk to you about before," he said.

"What is it?"

"I realised you didn't know when you communicated with me from Loch Ness."

I was starting to feel alarmed. "Corrigan, tell me what's wrong."

"Nothing's wrong." He sighed. "I hope you'll think that anyway."

He was not making me feel any better. He had better hurry the fuck up and tell me what was going on.

"Look. You remember at Haughmond Hill when we…" he paused for a beat, "when we made love?"

As if I'd forget. I nodded slowly.

"We didn't use anything. Any protection. It was dumb, I know." He gave me a little smile. "I guess we got carried away in the moment."

I watched him. If this was where he told me I now had some sexually transmitted disease because he slept around a lot, there was going to be fire.

"I've always been careful in the past. You make me lose all reason, kitten."

He still wasn't getting to the fucking point.

"You used the Brethren address to have some materials sent. From the NHS. We have a secretary who opens all post as a matter of course unless specifically requested to do otherwise. She opened a letter that was addressed to you and then passed it over to me."

The blood tests. I'd forgotten all about that.

"I don't care if it's not even mine," he said, looking into my eyes. "I meant what I said. I love you. No matter what."

A dulled realisation was beginning to hit me.

"No," I whispered.

"You gave blood and the NHS tested it. They were very comprehensive with their findings. You don't have anaemia or anything like that."

Oh God. The strange hot feeling I'd been carrying around in my stomach for days. The increased vomiting whenever I used a portal. The cryptic comments made by Mrs. Alcoon.

Corrigan scanned my face. Don't say it. Please don't say it.

"You're pregnant."

I forgot to breathe. I stared at him and my hands involuntarily went to my stomach. From somewhere outside a door banged. Corrigan's eyes went past me, widening fractionally. I turned to see what it was and realised that the door to my brother's house was open. There was a red haired man standing in the threshold. A woman, looking sleepy, appeared, giving him a peck on the cheek.

Shouts came from within and then a small, equally red haired, boy appeared, hugging the man's legs. He grinned and ruffled his son's hair. The woman scooped up the boy while a similarly sized girl ran out into the garden, giggling. Twins. I watched while the couple leaned in again and kissed, lingering this time. The tenderness between the two of them was patently clear.

"He's so happy," I said softly to myself. "Beedebopdelooolah."

I kept my eyes on my brother as he ambled towards a parked car, unlocked it and waved towards his family. He was so relaxed. There was an ease to his manner which suggested he knew nothing of wild tempers and crazy dragons. I knew nothing about him but I could tell from just looking that this was someone who was contented. Someone who was at peace with the world and their place in it. Maybe he had my bloodfire and maybe he didn't. But even if he did, he obviously kept it well under control. Fire wasn't his life in the way that it was mine.

I blinked away tears. My twin brother got into his car and drove away, while the woman and two children headed back inside.

"Mack," Corrigan began.

I looked back at him. "I have to go."

"Mack, wait."

I shook my head and wrenched the door handle. "I need to be on my own."

And then I was outside and running.

Chapter Twenty Four

Several hours later I was standing in a darkened street staring up at a familiar looking building. Corrigan had tried to contact me with his Voice several times, but I had shut him out. I'd make it up to him later. It was probably better he didn't know what I was about to do.

I touched my stomach very lightly. "I know this is do what I say, not do what I do, but this is not something I want to catch you ever even thinking about. It's a bad thing. The capacity for evil resides in all of us and what I'm about to do could well be considered evil. So don't you dare try anything like this yourself."

I looked back at the house. I knew I wasn't exterminating their entire species. I knew there would still be some left over who weren't there this night. Some who may well want to come after me for this. But I had decided there were no more choices to make. Not now. I'd just have to hope it was enough to make damn fucking sure they were too scared to ever try to really come near me or mine again. I thought briefly of Aubrey. He probably wouldn't have been too happy but he'd have understood. In a way it was revenge for him as well as protection for my family. Then I closed my eyes and thought of dragon.

Fire and blood and anger mixed up inside me. The pain of transformation was fleeting, as if giving a blessing to my decision. I opened my eyes, a red haze clouding my vision as if all I could see was a fine mist of blood. And there would be fucking blood spilt this night. My little match hovered in my mind. I considered it for a second, then blew it out. I wouldn't be needing it.

*

When I arrived at Alcazon, it was still possible to hear the clanging sirens of the fire engines. I completely ignored them, heading straight up to the restaurant and the now very familiar private room at the back. Everyone was already there. Alex and Balud were sitting together at the far end. Good. That meant there had been some progress made on the weapons. Several of the council members were already in deep discussion.

"Do we know whether it was Endor or not?"

I sat myself down and jerked my head towards the attending waiter, and asked him for a glass of milk. I could feel Corrigan watching me, but I didn't look his way.

"It doesn't make sense that it was him. We know he's going after Air next, not Fire."

"And he would need to attack a fire based creature, not just kill them with fire. But who else could it have been?"

A silence descended around the room. Several heads slowly swiveled in my direction. A tall glass was carefully placed in front of me with beads of condensation already forming around it. I leaned over and picked it, taking a sip and idly watching the waiter depart.

"The vampires were attacked this night, Miss Smith. Rather catastrophically."

"Indeed," I murmured.

"Their numbers have been decimated."

I caught a drip on the edge of the glass just before it fell onto the table.

"That is a shame."

"Crazy psycho bitch," someone hissed.

There were several intakes of breath. I merely smiled.

"So," I said, putting down the milk and looking around, "do we have an entry point into Dorchadas or not, then?"

The Arch-Mage stepped in. "We've worked out a way. There are indeed some considerable wards in place to prevent strangers from wandering in, but we think we've come up with a way to stop that from happening. Having the Fae has helped enormously."

Beltran nodded. "We can combine our magic with the mages and focus it in such a way that when they open the portal, there won't be so much as a flicker of attention drawn to it."

"Excellent." I turned to Alex and Balud. "Have you made any progress on the palladium?"

The mage looked remarkably unhappy. I had the feeling it wasn't to do with the fact everyone was pretty much convinced I'd just nuked two dozen vamps out of existence.

"We have."

"And?" I prompted.

"Dude," he said, shaking his head, "we were idiots."

Balud cleared his throat. "It appears I made an error. The document I found suggesting palladium was harmful to necromancers was actually a translation. And it seems not a very good one."

I'd been right all along. I sighed. "Let me guess – there should be an article in front of palladium. It's the Palladium. Not palladium."

The pair of them nodded.

Fucking hell. Three tiny letters had spelled out our failure at Loch Ness.

"So the Palladium isn't as useless as we'd thought," I said. "The question is how does it work?"

Everyone stared at me.

"It's a statue. A tiny wooden statue. It's hardly a fucking machine gun. What are we supposed to do? Hit Endor over the head with it and then he'll collapse and die?"

Nobody answered. I stared around the room. "Well, will somebody fucking find out?"

Several heads bobbed up and down vigorously. Maybe they were afraid I'd set them on fire too. It turns out I was a monster after all; I just needed to have my priorities changed.

"Okay. I need one representative each from the mages, shifters and faeries." I nodded to each one in turn. "We'll enter Dorchadas within the hour."

Corrigan folded his arms across his chest. "You can't go."

I gave him an irritated look. "I'll be fine."

"No, absolutely not." He shook his head implacably.

"Mackenzie..."

I was excruciatingly aware of everyone following our little byplay. "You can't tell me what to do."

I understood his reasons for demanding my non-participation, which meant I was staying calm. That didn't mean I accepted his point of view though. I was pregnant, not helpless.

"We're not going to attack, or do anything that will give away our presence," I said gently. "We're just to do a bit of information gathering. Hence only four people will enter. We can keep a low profile if there are less of us."

"Spying!" Alex interjected. "Cool! If I go along can I get a watch that shoots tranquiliser darts? Or maybe a fountain pen disguised as a gun?"

I raised my eyebrows at him. "You want to come along?"

He shrugged. "I'm not the best person in a fight, Mack Attack, I'll be the first to admit that. But I'm great at keeping hidden and, besides, if Aubrey can step up to the plate then so can I."

"I'm happy for Mage Florides to volunteer himself," the Arch-Mage interjected.

Corrigan stood up. "I will be representing the Brethren."

Of course. I gazed up at him with a mixture of gratitude and exasperation.

"I'm a werepanther. My fur is darker than anyone else's so I'll be better placed to conceal myself in shadows." He jerked his head at me. "Your red hair makes you a target. You should stay behind. It's just common sense."

I growled at him. "I will wear a fucking hat."

The Summer Queen rose also. She clearly wasn't enjoying my banter with the Lord Alpha. "Lord Sol will attend in the name of the Fae."

Corrigan scowled.

"Great." I checked my watch. "Set up the portal. We'll go in thirty minutes."

I drained the rest of my milk. I needed to splash some water on my face to freshen up. Hopefully I could borrow some deodorant or perfume from someone too. The smell of bonfire still clung to my nostrils and I was fairly certain my clothes reeked of baked vamp.

*

Thirty minutes later, the four of us stood together, ready to broach the Otherworldly barrier to Endor's realm. Alex was hopping from one foot to the other. I wondered whether he was regretting volunteering. He gave me a quick tense smile when he caught me looking at him, and continued jumping around. I hoped he wasn't going to end up being a liability.

Solus hooked his arm through mine. "This is simply wonderful. The two of us together, in the dark." He sent me an arch look and a saucy wink. "Why anything could happen."

I could almost see the hackles rising on the back of Corrigan's neck. I pointedly re-directed Solus.

"Have you managed to get a date yet with your Celtic student?"

He suddenly deflated. "No. She has thus far remained immune to my quite considerable charms."

"Imagine that," I murmured.

"It's a war of attrition, dragonlette. She'll agree eventually. It's meant to be."

The Fae was obviously aware of Corrigan

watching us closely because he abruptly flipped back to flirting. He wiggled his eyebrows suggestively. "How do you feel about a threesome?"

I was saved from answering by the crackle in the air, signifying that the portal to Dorchadas was open. Instead of the usual pretty purple flickers in the air, however, these were darker. Nausea rose up through me. I touched my stomach almost unconsciously in some pathetic attempt to prepare myself. Prepare us, I amended silently.

Solus went through first, followed by Alex, with me, then Corrigan bringing up the rear. As soon as I was through, I retched. It was an effort not to groan aloud, but I managed, just, to keep quiet. When I straightened back up, Corrigan was watching me with disapproval.

Alex held something out in his palm.

"What's that?" I kept my voice low and quiet, unsure whether there was anyone around who might hear us.

"Breath mint." When I narrowed my eyes at him, he grinned slightly. "I was in Russia with you, remember?"

"You were in Russia? When?"

I rolled my eyes at Corrigan. He may have been speaking in a whisper, but his annoyance was still obvious. "For fuck's sake. You're going to need to stop doing the whole protective thing. Platonic relationship, remember? And even if it wasn't, I think I've proven I can take care of myself."

A muscle jerked in his cheek. I could see him battling with himself to avoid taking our little spat even further.

Wrong time, wrong place, my Lord.

It's not just yourself any more. You need to show a bit more maternal responsibility.

I just slaughtered half the bloodsuckers in the city. My maternal responsibility is doing just fine.

He snarled in my head. *Were they threatening you?*

Solus cleared his throat. I realised Corrigan and I were facing each other, gesturing expressively with each Voice communication. I guessed it looked pretty strange. I snapped back into the physical world as Alex broke in.

"Which way, dudes?"

Focusing on what we were supposed to be doing, I took a step backwards to stare into the darkness. There was very little to be seen. I was getting so very tired of the dark. Corrigan raised his head and sniffed, then pointed to his left.

"Can you smell Endor?"

He shook his head. "Nothing so specific. But there are living creatures off in that direction."

It was good enough for me. We headed off in single file, Corrigan in front so he could use his superior sense of smell to keep us on track. The ground beneath us was crunchy, making it difficult to tread quietly. I peered down, trying to work out what it was we were walking on. It seemed to be a mixture of materials, different sizes and lengths. There was a curved shape to one that was just like...I looked back up. Okay. We were walking on hundreds and hundreds and hundreds of bone fragments. Excellent.

The air felt clammy and heavy, almost as if a

thunderstorm was about to break. I sucked a breath deep into my lungs. It left an unpleasant taste on my tongue and I made a face. I really didn't like it here.

We'd hardly travelled any distance, when Corrigan halted. I almost went careening into Alex's back, and only just managed to pull myself back in time. I leaned out to my right, trying to see why we'd stopped. There was a faint glow up ahead. Bingo. I crossed my fingers that it was as a result of Endor himself, and not some other nastie we'd have to avoid. Tapping Alex on the back, I motioned for him to veer right, and then for Solus behind me to head left. If we could flank whoever it was, and get close to see what they were up to, then we might just learn something useful. Corrigan turned and looked me. He flashed a sudden grin, and exploded in a mess of ripped clothing and black fur. His werepanther form padded up and he butted his head against my stomach, purring. He might have been trying to look like a cute harmless cat, but the powerful muscles rippling down his black feline body belied his true self. I scratched his ears, then pushed him gently back around and forward.

Corrigan as a werepanther made no sound at all while he picked his way through the path of bones. I, on the other hand, was like a heavy footed elephant in comparison. No matter how gingerly I tried to tread, there was still a sickening noise of crunching under my feet. I lifted myself up onto my tiptoes and began to move more slowly. We didn't have the Palladium with us and we weren't prepared for a fight. It was imperative Endor didn't hear me.

The light grew stronger as we approached. It

was some kind of fire, burning in a small metal barrel. Surrounding it were several free standing walls which oddly appeared to be moving. I strained my eyes. What the fuck was it?

Corrigan spoke in my head, causing me to jump. *Birds. Lots of birds.*

I peered closer and realised he was right. Each wall was covered with them. Different kinds and different sizes. I spotted crows, pigeons, even a peacock. Every single one of them seemed to be affixed somehow through their bodies. Their wings, however, were flapping and free. The lack of sound caused by their continuous movements was beyond eerie.

Air. My returning Voice to Corrigan was grim.

Indeed.

Is Endor there?

He shook his great panther head, stating the negative. Then the smell hit me. I wrinkled my nose; it was blood, lots of blood. You'd have to kill a lot of bloody birds to make the atmosphere smell that strongly. I drew closer to see what it was, and spotted Alex gesturing to me from the other side. There was a stone table close to him with something outstretched on it. I took another step and realised it was a kelpie, spread-eagled and sliced open. Nausea rose again through the pit of my stomach, warring with bloodfire. The kelpies may have double-crossed us, but it appeared that Endor had then double-crossed them back.

Solus appeared silently at the opposite side of Alex. I stopped moving and watched him approach the nearest wall of birds. Their wings continued to beat noiselessly - and uselessly. He stepped up to one and began to stroke its head, his lips moving as he murmured something. Then he took several steps backwards, and made some kind of gesture.

I blinked at him. What was that? Frowning, I moved round Corrigan to get closer. Solus had connected his hands together and was flapping them as if to mimic a bird. I nodded. Okay, yes, I could see the birds. Then he pointed to the fire. I had no idea what he was on about. I was just on the verge of asking Corrigan if he had any idea when he suddenly hissed in my head.

Get down. Now.

I launched myself downwards, only just managing to move my palms to hold my weight and avoid the bones in time. Corrigan was equally down on his haunches, his green eyes slitted. I couldn't see where Alex or Solus had gone. Then I heard footsteps. Oh, shit. I lifted my head slightly and realised that Solus was still bathed in the glow of light from the fire. He was too close to the wall of birds and, even though he was also hunkered down on the ground, he was far too visible. He began to back away, staying low, but the footsteps were getting nearer. A dark shape passed by, barely ten feet away from where I was. It was clearly Endor. I watched in panic as Solus still tried to manoeuver himself around without making too many sudden movements that might attract Endor's attention. All the necromancer had to do was glance over and then he'd see him.

The wall to the far side of Solus began to flap with more vigour and energy than before, drawing my eye away from the Fae. Endor obviously saw them too because he began to stride in their direction. A diversion. The birds were working for us and creating a diversion. Solus scrambled up and managed to back away out of sight just as Endor reached the birds and kicked one of them. There was a sickening crack as its neck broke. The rest of the birds slowed their movements in response. I could feel anger and heat filling me. That fucking bastard. My fingertips tingled. I glanced down, then realised green fire was flickering at the edges of my hands. Quickly, I dropped to my stomach, managing to avoid making any sound, and shoved my hands under my body to hide them. Green flames would be a bit of a fucking giveaway.

Endor moved from wall to wall, trailing his hands over each of the birds. I carefully rose to my knees and stuck my hands under my armpits, then nudged Corrigan with my elbow. He nodded, and the pair of us began to very, very carefully back away. With every single step, I was terrified that Endor would hear us and turn around. Thank fuck he seemed absorbed in his walls of horror, oblivious to anything else. There was one point my foot landed on a bone, causing it to snap. To my ears, the noise was as loud as a foghorn, but Endor didn't register it. It took a few minutes, however, before I could breathe again.

By the time we reached the portal, Alex and Solus re-joined us. I sent a questioning look in Solus' direction and he nodded, but placed a finger to his lips. Then he vanished back through, with Alex following. There was the familiar creak of bones shifting, and Corrigan returned to his human form, standing back upright. He was, of course, fully naked. My eyes travelled down from his face, then back up again. Good Lord. He licked his lips as if daring me to say something. I took a deep breath, composing myself, and gestured towards the portal. He grinned at me with the hint of a promise in his jade eyes, and went through. I swallowed, forgetting to feel nervous at my impending retching and followed after him.

Chapter Twenty Five

As soon as I stepped back through into the real world, the momentary distraction of Corrigan's naked body disappeared. Solus' expression was bleak, and Alex most definitely looked green around the gills.

"Those birds," he whispered. "They were nailed into those walls, Mack. Each and every one of them."

My stomach heaved, and I could feel my knees going. The Arch-Mage walked up next to me, however, and placed a hand on my shoulder. Immediately I began to feel better. Magic certainly had its uses sometimes.

"I hadn't realised," I said grimly.

"There were at least a couple of hundred of them, Mack Attack."

"Three hundred and one," Solus murmured. "Three hundred and one birds."

"It seemed like you were talking to them."

He nodded. "I have an affinity for animals. Most

Fae do."

"And?"

"And we've got a serious problem, dragonlette."

Every member of the council gathered round, even though we were in the corridor of Alcazon. Apparently the time for keeping everything hush hush had long since passed.

"He's drawing small parts of strength from the birds," Solus said, "but they're not his target." His mouth twisted. "They told me what he's after. He's going to kill two birds with one stone, so to speak, and gain mastery of Air and Fire at the same time."

"I don't understand. How will he do that?"

"The phoenix." For the first time ever, I think I saw the Summer Queen appear distraught. "He'll go after the phoenix."

Everyone looked at each other and then suddenly began to talk. The noise rose up in a babble.

"Quiet!" I said, although my voice was lost in the hubbub.

I stared down at my hands, the green fire easily sparking back up, then aimed them up at the ceiling. These people had to learn when to talk and when to listen. Corrigan grabbed my arm, however, with a warning look in his eyes. Some helpful shifter minion had apparently already given him a dressing gown. That was handy. And rather disappointing for me.

They're already afraid of you, kitten. Allow me.

He lifted his head back and roared. The sound was deafening. Ears ringing, I glared at him.

Next time don't do that next to my head. I'm

299

going to be deaf for a fucking a week.

He gave me a little bow. Idiot.

Now that everyone's attention was back where it should be, I spoke again. "That doesn't make sense. Isn't the phoenix immortal? He can kill it, but it will just rise again. That's what phoenixes do." I paused. Or was it phoenixi?

"There's only one phoenix, dragonlette. And you're right, it is immortal. It dies in flame and is reborn in flame." Solus looked worried. "But he's a necromancer, and one who's growing more powerful by the second."

The Summer Queen nodded. "He can trap the phoenix in-between the cycle of life, and draw from it endlessly. It'll be an eternal power source. It won't die, but neither will it live."

"And he'll be more powerful than we can possibly imagine," Corrigan said.

Shit. I chewed my inside cheek. There had to be a bright side to this somewhere.

"There's only one phoenix," I said slowly.

"Yes, dear."

The Arch-Mage patted my hand as if I were a small child. I scowled at him and he immediately dropped his arm and backed off. Huh. Apparently there were some benefits to being a homicidal monster after all.

"There's only one phoenix," I repeated, "so our job is easy. We just take the bird and hide it somewhere. He can't get to it, and we win."

"Except if he can't find it, he'll just switch tactics and pick on someone else," Alex pointed out.

I thought for a minute. "You're right. We leave

the phoenix where it is. But, as there's only one we know where he's going to be. We've surely got a much better chance of defeating Endor because there's no need to be concerned that he'll be off somewhere else."

"That's what we thought last time," Larkin pointed out. "And not only did we really not have a clue, but he hammered us and killed several humans in the process."

"Well, we're out of chances, ladies and gentlemen. If he gets past us this time, then it will be more than just a few humans whose lives will be in danger. The whole world will be at risk if he gains ultimate power over life and death. So the simple fact is that we have no choice but to beat him."

I looked at the Arch-Mage. "The Palladium?"

He pulled it out from underneath his billowing black robes and held it out. I stared at it. I really didn't want to touch the fucking thing if I could help it. Thankfully, Corrigan sensed my revulsion and moved to take it instead. He examined it carefully.

"It's very small," he said doubtfully. "Is this really going to work?"

I glanced over at Balud. He shrugged, his face as blank as everyone else's. "Who knows?" he said. "It's like no weapon I've ever seen."

"So we still have no idea how we can use it against Endor?"

He shook his head. Outfuckingstanding.

I sighed. "Well, we'll just have to roll with it. Everyone better bring their A game in case it doesn't work." I looked back at Solus. "Do we know from the birds when he's planning to attack the phoenix?"

He blinked his violet eyes at me.

"Solus?" I prodded.

"Tonight," he answered heavily. "He's going after it tonight."

My stomach dropped. It didn't give us very much time to work with.

I found my voice. "Where is it?"

"The phoenix? It's at Bird World."

My jaw dropped. "You're kidding me. Bird World? Just hanging out with the ostriches and the parrots, is it?"

The Summer Queen lifted up a shoulder. "Its preferences are a mystery to me."

"How in the hell does it manage to remain anonymous?"

"It looks a bit like an eagle."

"A bit like an eagle? A golden bird that can't die and only looks a bit like an eagle. No-one's ever been suspicious?"

"Why would they? As far as the majority of this plane are concerned, the phoenix is mythological. Like dragons."

"Or shapeshifters."

"Or faeries."

I shook my head. Sometimes the world never ceased to amaze me. "Well, let's get our arses to Bird World then."

Corrigan cleared his throat. "Actually, there's something else we need to think of first."

Everyone turned to him.

Sorry, kitten. It's for the best though.

My gaze hardened.

"If he's going after the phoenix, a mythological bird tied to fire, then Mack needs to stay away."

"Hey! No fucking chance, buster."

"If we prevent Endor from getting to the phoenix, the next logical choice is you. You're a dragon."

"Air and Fire," Solus muttered.

I gave him a dirty look. He was meant to be on my side. "So then it makes more sense for me to be there so I can distract him," I said through gritted teeth.

Corrigan shook his head. "No. You're the last card we'll have. You need to stay away."

"Fuck off. You can't make me stay away. I'm the head of this council, remember?"

"He's right," said the Arch-Mage. "We can't have Endor decide you're the easier target because everyone else is focused on protecting the phoenix."

"Yes, you need to be as far away from Bird World as possible."

I growled at the Fae Queen. "And do what? Stay at home with my knitting needles?"

"You can't come, Mack," Corrigan reiterated

I hate you.

No, you don't.

He was right. I didn't hate him. But I was fucking pissed off at him.

We can't be worried about you and the phoenix at the same time. Having just one target means we have a better shot at really bringing Endor down.

I'm a dragon. You don't think I have a shot?

What makes you strong is your fire. And that's what he needs. Being a dragon isn't going to help, not today.

I tried again. *I have nothing to do with Air. I can't fly.*

Corrigan's face was impassive. *How many times have you tried?*

Once.

He raised his eyebrows. I snarled again.

Keep our baby safe, kitten.

It occurred to me he wouldn't know I was probably carrying twins. That was probably just as well for now.

Corrigan opened his mouth, speaking aloud. "Let's get to this Bird World place and get ready."

Everyone looked at me. I understood my dragon side might be a problem. I didn't have to transform though; I was pretty damn powerful even without that part of me. And I knew I wouldn't let the children I never knew I even wanted get hurt. Even Lord Furry himself couldn't stop me from being there. He just didn't have to know that I was there, that was all.

I pasted on a smile. "You'd better get going then."

Relief flickered across Corrigan's face. I felt a twist of guilt, then ignored it. I wasn't being reckless. I was being smart. He took a step towards me, but I gestured him away.

"Go on then."

"Don't be mad at me, kitten."

"Don't call me kitten."

Amusement danced in his eyes. Feeling the looks from both the Arch-Mage and the Summer Queen, I turned and stomped off, trying to make it look like I was in a petulant fit, rather than running back home to get what I needed for Bird World. It was time to end this necromancer once and for all.

Chapter Twenty Six

I'd not fully appreciated how hot it would be inside Aubrey's fluffy penguin suit. Or how bloody cumbersome the thing would be. I waddled towards the eagle enclosure, trying to keep my eyes open for any of my team or any sign of Endor. The reeking odour from within the costume was really rather remarkable. I was fairly certain there would be some scientists somewhere who could bottle the smell I was being enveloped in and use it to develop an entirely new species. Still, at least it meant when I passed by a small group of shifters, including Lucy, they didn't get a single suspicious whiff it might be me inside the costume.

I flapped my wings and attempted to move faster. I'd lost a lot of time getting back to Clava Books to pick up the furry disguise, make the phone call I needed, then get myself to the theme park. It wasn't as if I exactly had the power to open up my own portals after all. Still, it appeared as if I'd not missed much, judging by the amount of Otherworlders I saw milling around, looking not in the slightest bit inconspicuous. They could at least try to blend in, I thought irritably, as I watched a mage and a faerie accost a couple and demand to see some identification. Like that was going to work.

An itch was starting to bug me at the back of my neck. I twisted my head to try to relieve it, but failed miserably and wondered vaguely whether this was what it felt like to be an actual shifter: hot, sweaty and prickly all over. A small child ran up and hugged my rather enormous and bulging stomach. I patted him on the head and tried to side-step. Unfortunately his parents had already decided this would be an optimal shot for the family album, and I had to submit to several moments of posing before they moved on. I supposed at least I didn't have to pretend to smile.

I quickly shuffled forward, in order to ward off any further photograph hunters, and wished I could see more out of the large penguin head. My peripheral vision was almost entirely obscured. How in the hell Aubrey had ever managed to follow me while wearing this, I had no idea. Considering how awkward the costume was, he hadn't done such a bad job as I'd thought at the time. Right now I wasn't even completely sure I was heading in the right direction.

Aiming for what seemed to be a signpost up ahead, I concentrated on moving as fast as I could. Thanks to the mesh blocking my vision, I pretty much had to shove my face an inch from it to work out that it was saying the eagles were just up ahead. Thank fuck. I smiled grimly and plodded on, flapping my arms in order to make sure that people kept out of my way. Perhaps they'd just think I was trying to fly.

I hit a slight incline in the path and tried to propel myself upwards. It was fine for a few steps but, as the path got steeper, it started to seem impossible. My massive belly kept getting in the way until I was barely managing to inch my way up. I turned to my right and tried side-stepping instead.

It wasn't much better but at least I felt as if I was making some kind of progress. Unfortunately I was suddenly inundated with streams of people exiting from a door behind me – and all walking in the opposite direction. I was banged and shoved and lost my balance, slowly toppling over. I supposed that one good thing was the vast penguin suit cushioned my landing. In fact, I barely felt it. I was, however, now sliding slowly down the path, still surrounded by people, and entirely unable to bring myself back upright.

"Hahahaha! Look at the stupid penguin," someone said.

Great. Yes, look and laugh. Don't try to help the stupid penguin stand back up though. That would spoil all your fun, I thought, annoyance seething through me.

"Here, let me help you," said a smooth and spine-chillingly familiar voice.

Oh, shit. It was Endor. Red began to seep across my eyes, and I felt the burning begin, tearing through my veins and squeezing my heart. He yanked hard on one of my wings, pulling me back to my feet. I stared at him through the penguin's head. What was he going to do now? The one major drawback of this stupid costume was that there was no way I was going to able to either appropriately attack or even defend. He wouldn't want to alert anyone to his presence so, whatever he'd do, it would be fast and silent. Transforming into a dragon in the middle of this throng of tourists would be an incredibly stupid move. But I'd do it if I had to.

Every muscle in my body was tense. But the

necromancer merely patted me on one of my wings and smiled. If you could call it a smile. Clearly he was as good at disguising himself and his true intentions as I currently was. He turned round and continued up the small hill towards the eagles while I watched, shrieking relief pouring from me, along with vast quantities of sweat. For a moment I was frozen to the spot, entirely immobile, then I hopped forward and hooked one wing round a nearby handrail to prevent myself from falling over again and used every ounce of energy I had to rush up after him. Or at least waddle up after him anyway.

When I finally reached what the park organisers had called the 'Eagle's Nest' and squeezed myself through the entrance, I realised just how vast the enclosure was. There was some kind of netting, sure, preventing the birds from just up and flying away, but it was very high up and there were clearly acres of space for the eagles to roam around in. Rocks and scrub were dotted around everywhere to make the birds feel at home as possible. While I appreciated the space, I wondered why the phoenix bothered. A large cage was still a cage.

I slowly spun myself around to get a full view of the area so I could work out where the magical bird actually might be now that Endor had disappeared from view. Without the benefit of communication with anyone, I didn't have a clue where to head. Then I had an idea. He wouldn't like it when he found out the truth, but if it meant having the chance to save his sorry hide from Endor it'd be worth it.

I opened up my Voice to Corrigan.

Hey, I said, keeping it light. *What's happening? Has Endor shown up yet?*

Hi kitten. His opening was soft, and made trippy little butterflies flap around in my tummy. *There's no sign of him yet.*

Oh. Well, he was about to show his face any minute now. I could hardly tell Corrigan that though. *Do you have enough people to cover the area?*

We've got hundreds dotted throughout the park. We won't miss him.

That's what you think, I thought desperately. *Where's the phoenix?*

I kept my fingers tightly crossed.

Safe.

Goddamn it, Corrigan, safe where? *That's good to know.*

Yeah. I can see why it chooses to live here. It lords over all the other birds. The actual eagles seem to treat it as if it's some kind of god.

Interesting. I swivelled all the way around again. Towards the middle of the enclosure was what appeared to be some kind of fake mountain, rising up out of the ground. There was nothing else around that was even remotely of the same size. If I were a god, that's where I'd hang out. I began to waddle towards it, hoping that a penguin mascot wandering around the eagle enclosure wasn't too weird.

So how are you? Are you still mad at me?

Um...*I understand why you want me to stay away.* Just like I hope you'll understand why I didn't, I thought.

A voice suddenly came over the Bird World

tannoy. "Ladies and Gentlemen, boys and girls, the falconry display is just about to begin. If you make your way over to the North end of the park, you'll be wowed by the skill and mastery of these birds and their keepers."

A surge of people abruptly headed for the Eagle's Nest exit. There were going to be virtually no tourists left in this area. What better time was there than now for Endor to strike?

Kitten, I have to go.

Corrigan suddenly sounded strained and tense. I was relieved that he'd had the same thought as me and I wouldn't have to find some way of letting him know that Endor was already there. I took a deep breath. We had to succeed this time. There was simply no other way out.

And then I saw him. He was striding out from behind a grassy outcrop. Or grassy knoll, I thought sardonically. He wasn't trying to conceal himself, however. He walked right up to the mountain and outstretched his arms. Fuck. I began to waddle over in his direction; he was at least two hundred feet away, but I had to get there. I looked up and spotted Corrigan emerging from within the tower of rocks, along with many others.

"I don't know how you knew I'd be here," Endor boomed at them, "but you know it's futile. You can't beat me. Haven't you learnt that by now?"

No-one bothered answering him. Instead several withdrew weapons, and the mages among them sparked up blue flames.

"Where's the dragon?" Endor taunted. "Or has she worked out that it would be pointless to face me? You know you can't break my wards without her."

I shuffled forward faster, cursing my lack of mobility. Endor sent out huge thick streams of black towards the Otherworlders. I watched horrorstruck as they approached, then almost collapsed in relief as the black fire slammed into a ward. At least the mages had thought to construct one. It was obvious, however, it wouldn't last for long. Already it was shimmering blue – an indication it was weakening. A few more hits like that and it would be broken.

There were some hurried voices to either side of me as the few remaining tourists were being ushered out due to what sounded like 'preparations for a later show'. I nodded my head to myself. That was smart. A faerie began to head over in my direction, no doubt to tell me to do the same. I gave him a wave and continued forward. I was hardly inconspicuous dressed like this. With any luck, the faerie would think I was one of them and would leave me alone. Fortunately it seemed to work.

Someone broke away from the main group and began running towards the necromancer. It was Tom. My heart in my mouth, I tried to yell at him to get back, but my voice was muffled by the thick fabric of the penguin's head. One thing the necromancer had been right about was his wards: without my blood, they were unbreakable. Tom was about to be slaughtered in front of my eyes. I was too far away to do anything. I watched helplessly as he sprinted forward. He was toast.

Several mages began throwing out blue fire towards Endor, distracting him. They may have been powerful streaks of Protection enhanced magic, but they bounced off him with barely a sizzle. I tried to run, but the costume just wouldn't let me. Then, all of a sudden, when Tom was barely ten feet away, he threw something towards him. It was some kind of liquid, but I couldn't make it out clearly. It slapped into Endor and his ward with a tremendous spitting hiss, instantly breaking it. Then Tom was running back to the relative safety of the mountain, dodging a spray of returning black fire as he did so. My blood. He'd thrown my blood. They must have somehow gotten it back from Tarn. I wondered what the UnSeelie Fae had demanded in return and hoped the price wasn't too high. My relief was overwhelming, however.

With Endor's wards broken, the mages were free to hit him with everything they had. Despite that fact, however, their streams of blue flame seemed to be doing little damage. Again and again, they smacked into Endor's body. All he seemed to be doing in return was laughing. I was still more than a hundred feet away. I couldn't move any faster without taking off the costume. The trouble was I couldn't let Endor know I was there. Corrigan had been right about that: if the necromancer knew where I was I would simply provide too easy an alternative. If he didn't turn round though, he wouldn't see my fat penguin shape coming until it was too late.

Sweat was dripping off me as I pushed myself forward. Endor attacked the mages' own ward again, this time with a stronger bolt. There was another sizzle, as it too was destroyed. Now it was a level playing field: no magical protection in either direction. With a roar, a group of shifters already in their were forms burst forward, fur and fangs flying. Endor took them down with one strike, as if he were simply at a bowling alley and leisurely knocking down some pins. I snarled deep within my costume.

The Fae were next. They swooped down, with speed and elegance. Several reached close enough to hit him, dancing away before he could take a shot. He produced something from within the folds of his cloak, however. Something long and sharp and pointy, and fended them off with ease.

Then, without warning, the sky darkened and there was a rumble of thunder. Nearby trees began to shake, their leaves rustling dramatically in the sudden heavy wind. Everyone looked surprised. A bolt of lightning shot out from the clouds above, landing scant inches away from Endor.

"Again," I whispered, "again."

Taking the opportunity, Corrigan leapt down. There was something small and brown clutched in his hand. I fucking hoped he had some idea about how to use it. The sky boiled overhead, and ropes of harsh silver rain began to beat down mercilessly. There was another strike of lightning. Then another.

I was getting close. I pushed and pushed and pushed. The rain was making my costume wet and heavy. I shoved my wings up to the head and tried to get it off. It wouldn't budge though. Without the traction my fingers offered, the stupid costume was stuck to me. But I was almost there, and so was the Lord Alpha.

Corrigan flung himself at Endor, swiping at him

with the Palladium. A mage to the side sent out more blue flame, arcing it through the now dark sky. It hit him on the side of the face and, finally, the necromancer seemed pained. Solus, coming out of nowhere, leapt at him feet first, kicking him on the other side. We were winning.

Endor shot out more black fire, catching both Solus and Corrigan. Each of them was clearly in pain, but it didn't stop them and they continued their attack. Then he began to mutter something. An indigo dark cloud was rising, enveloping all four of them and concealing them from sight. What it was I had no idea. With only a few feet between me and where Endor had been, I flung myself through the cloud and into the heart of it. I kicked out with my penguin feet, and rolled, trying to connect with the necromancer and knock him off balance. But whatever he was conjuring up, it was making the air difficult to breathe.

I continued rolling until I was clear of the choking haze. The rain was making it difficult to see, but I just caught a glimpse of Endor striding out from the dark haze. Where Corrigan and Solus were, I couldn't tell. Hearing a shout from up ahead, I looked back at the mountain to where Endor was obviously heading. Someone up there was pointing out at the sides. I twisted over from where I was lying and realised what Endor had done. He'd conjured up some kind of dead army out of nowhere. We were hemmed in on every side by the shapes of rotting skeletons. Okaydokey then.

Streams of Otherworlders ran up and engaged them. The dark sky was being lit up by the force of the mages' magic and, everywhere, shifters and faeries were getting up and close to the dead. But Endor was at the foot of the mountain and already beginning to climb. His cloud of darkness continued to hang where he'd been. I'd have to go back in and get Corrigan, Solus and the fucking Palladium.

Twisting in the other direction, I rolled myself again, this time into the cloud. I held my breath, forcing my body round and round until I hit something. It felt like a body – and it was complete inert. Every single good intention I had completely broke as a furnace of bloodfire lit inside me and roared. The penguin costume split open as I transformed. A mini hurricane spun through the cloud, forcing it to dissipate. Solus was at my feet. I scooped him with one clawed arm, and looked around for Corrigan. He was unconscious, lying face down. Roaring, I sprang forward and picked him up in my other hand. Then I looked upwards and jumped. And this time I flew.

It was beyond anything I'd experienced before. Exhilaration sipped through me and I felt as light as a feather. I didn't have time to appreciate it, however: I had to get them to safety. In a flash, I was by the Eagle's nest exit where I carefully laid down their inert bodies and then twisted back. A skeletal shape ran towards me but I flicked my tail round, easily catching its midsection. The thing collapsed in a pile of bones. Then I lifted up, stretching out my neck and flew back to the dark cloud.

Lying there, on its own in the driving rain, was the Palladium. I stared up at the mountain for a second. Endor was almost at its summit. I scooped the statue up in my talons and, without pausing, sprang upwards. I roared, just as another bolt of lightning struck in front of Endor, forcing him to find another path. Breathing in deeply, I took as much oxygen into my lungs as I could. Then I spat it out in huge wall of flame that engulfed the necromancer. I pulled back slightly to watch the results of my labour. Shit. It didn't seem to be affecting him. He laughed and shouted up at me in the air.

"Did you not think I'd come prepared?"

His lips began moving, then there was an almighty shudder. I looked behind, my mouth dropping as I realised there was another dragon right behind me. Except this one was all bones. He'd called up a fucking dead Draco Wyr to beat me. Endor laughed again. There was a flicker of golden fire and I could suddenly see the phoenix, rippling with magnificent plumes of red and gold and silver. Endor was stretching out his hand to catch it. Behind me the skeleton dragon screamed. Screw that. I dropped down, flapping my wings, and concentrated on my match and my grip on the Palladium.

My bones snapped and my flesh shifted and then I was naked, in the middle of a thunderstorm with only a wooden statue in my hand. I sprang forward and tapped Endor on the shoulder. His head turned, and an irritated scowl lit his face. The dragon above us screamed again and swooped down, but I didn't pay it any attention. I just gripped the base of the Palladium, and rammed it down Endor's throat.

He choked, eyes bulging and tiny veins popping. His fingers clawed at his throat and his mouth. I used the base of my hand to shove it in further. I felt the roar of the dragon behind me as its jaws opened, and then Endor was on his knees with the fight completely drawn out of him. He collapsed on the stones thudding down as every flicker of life left him. The hollow sound of bones crashing onto stone came from behind me, and, in front, a large golden bird blinked. I could have sworn it was smiling.

Chapter Twenty Six

I found the change of venue refreshing, even if the Summer Queen and the Arch-Mage were patently unimpressed at having to sit on battered white plastic chairs. The air was clean and fresh, with the heat of summer still clinging on. I swatted lazily at a fat bee, and surveyed the council. The dead were buried and, while the mourning was not yet over, and the wounds were still fresh, there was the sense that they had not died in vain. Small comfort, I supposed, to their loved ones. I was fully aware that had it been Corrigan who had lost his life at the Eagles' Nest, then I would not be finding it so easy to recover.

"Are we sure he's dead?"

At Haughmond Hill, Endor had recovered seconds after receiving what should have been a fatal strike to his heart. I needed to be certain this time.

Beltran nodded. "We have divided his body into five parts."

I couldn't help wincing. Euurgh.

"And those parts have been separated and burned at different points across the British Isles," added Larkin. "He ain't coming back."

"The clean-up operation?" I asked. "At the Eagles' Nest?"

"All done and dusted," the Arch-Mage said. "The Queen herself glamoured the Bird World staff, and no-one is any the wiser. The enclosure opened again yesterday morning."

I smiled in approval. That was good. "Where's the Palladium?"

"We removed it from his body. It's safe at the keep."

Corrigan looked good, despite the curving black scar that now ran from his ear to his chin. Normally, his shifter ability to heal would preclude any scars from forming. Something about Endor's dark cloud of necromancy had changed that. I didn't mind it though. It added to his ever present air of danger, as if he may just pounce on someone at any second. I hoped he was going to pounce on me.

"And we've spelled it to ensure it won't be removed," said the Arch-Mage with a look of satisfaction.

"The phoenix?"

"Happy. We've even had some communication from the kelpies. It appears they regret their earlier actions and wish to make amends."

I snorted. "I bet they do."

"So what happened to the sky?" asked Beltran. "That storm wasn't natural."

Lucy nodded. "Yeah. And it wasn't of Endor's doing either because every bold of lightning seemed to be directed at him."

I smiled smugly. "That was Vasily."

The entire gathering stared at me.

"He's Russian," I said airily, as if that explained everything. "He normally prevents storms so he can help farmers. Well, he actually normally drives like a demon taxi driver, but he used to prevent storms. I just asked him to come and do the opposite. He was happy to oblige."

Corrigan grinned at me. "Nice."

The squeak of wheels announced Julia's arrival. She beamed at me, then turned to everyone. "Ladies and Gentlemen, the service is about to begin."

I stood up. It was over. Endor was dead, the council was finished and I was fully absolved of my responsibilities. I touched my stomach for a moment and glanced towards Corrigan with a tiny smile. His eyes crinkled back, then we walked out towards the courtyard.

I breathed in the heady scent of him, and his hand lightly brushed against mine, making my bloodfire sing.

"Who'd have thought it?" he said. "Faeries, mages and shifters all together at the same wedding and no-one's started arguing yet."

I grinned. "The wedding's not started yet." I looked over to where my date was waiting patiently. "I should go."

Corrigan scowled. *I don't understand why he is here with you.*

I have a promise to keep. There's nothing between us, my Lord.

He growled, a low deep sound from within his chest.

Down, boy. You should go and find your sister.

I veered off. Cherniy Volk held out his arm, and I hooked my hand round it.

"Thank you," he murmured.

"I meant what I said," I reiterated, "if she really doesn't want to see you..."

"I'll back away and leave quietly. You have my word." I looked down and realised the werewolf's hands were shaking.

We strolled into the great hall. Rows upon rows of chairs were laid out, pretty white and pink flowers strung at the end of each. I felt someone's gaze on me and turned round. It was Anton. I hadn't seen him since he'd thrown me out of Cornwall last year. So much had happened since then, but it didn't outdo half a lifetime of mutual hatred. His expression was guarded and wary, making me pray he wouldn't take this opportunity to cause a scene. The last thing Tom and Betsy needed was their wedding day upstaged by that prick.

I turned back to Volk just in time to see a fist flying in his direction and connecting with a painful sounding crunch against his nose.

"Where the fuck have you been?" It was Leah, Corrigan's sister. Then she leapt up, hooked her legs round his back and began to kiss him. Okay, then.

I backed quietly away, and left them to it, finding myself a seat on the right side of the aisle. It was strange being back here in Cornwall. I had thought it might be too painful, that the memories of the life I used to lead here would overwhelm me. Instead, however, it was almost the opposite. I wasn't indifferent – far from it. It just felt more like a fond nostalgia for a part of my personal history which was now over. A chapter that was finished.

"The past is a foreign country," quoted Mrs. Alcoon, sitting herself behind me. She must have telepathically picked up on my mood. "They do things differently there."

I looked around the room. "Yes, they do."

She leaned forward. "Slim has been released

from his duties with the Ministry. He's going to come and work at the bookshop full-time."

It had kind of seemed to me that he was already there full-time, but I held my tongue. "That's good."

She grinned. "He'll look after me in my dotage."

I had a feeling she would be the one doing the looking after. It would no doubt involve tea. Lots and lots and lots of tea.

More and more people began to wander in and take their seats. Originally, the wedding had been planned for a far smaller number: the Cornish pack, naturally, some of the Brethren and, well, me. Somehow the bonhomie between all three Otherworld groups had extended the guest list quite considerably, however. Looking around, the sense of camaraderie was clear. Rather than choose to segregate themselves, every row contained a mix: a pure melting pot of mages, faeries and shifters. Half of them probably didn't even know Tom or Betsy, but that kind of wasn't the point. It felt like a new beginning for everyone. Fortunately, before I became too maudlin and sickly-sweet, the music signaling the arrival of the bride and groom kicked in. The chattering died down, and everyone turned to watch them enter together, with smiles which must have stretched from ear to ear.

*

Johannes had managed to designate himself as the official photographer. Everyone milled around outside as he fussily arranged groups of guests first one way, then another. I was distracted by his amusing suggestion that Solus and Corrigan place their arms round each other's backs in a gesture of bromance, when Anton appeared by my side. I stiffened involuntarily, and had to force myself not to step away and put some distance between us. For a long time, the pair of us stood there in an awkward silence before he eventually spoke.

"So you're not human after all."

"No," I said shortly. Anton had frequently used my theoretically human status as an excuse to treat me like shit. "Does it matter?"

"I suppose not." He sighed heavily. "Look, Mackenzie, er, Mack, whatever you prefer being called, for what it's worth, I'm sorry."

You could have blown me down with a feather. "Pardon?"

"I'm sorry. I was horrid to you."

I stared at him. "You were a fucking wanker to me."

He nodded. "Yeah, I guess I deserve that. Not that you were particularly a bed of roses." He grinned. "Well, perhaps the thorns…"

He had smiled at me – with a genuine smile. I was utterly flabbergasted.

"Er…"

"You seem a lot mellower than when you lived here."

"You seem a lot mellower than when I lived here, Anton."

He laughed. "Yeah. You'd think that responsibility would make a person more stressed and angrier. Instead it's had the opposite effect."

I glanced up and noticed Corrigan watching the pair of us, as if ready to defend my honour at any minute. I flashed him a smile of reassurance.

"I should go," said Anton, "it wouldn't do to piss off the Brethren Lord, now would it?" He patted me on the shoulder. "You could do worse than him, you know."

He walked off, leaving me open-mouthed and staring after him. Damn. I guessed I wasn't the only person with the capability to change.

Solus wandered over in my direction, lifting his fingers towards me a half salute. "So what gives, dragonlette?"

"Hmmm?"

"You're different. Not just because Endor has gone. There's something else."

I shrugged. "I have no idea what you're talking about."

He raised his eyebrows slightly. "I was chatting to Mrs. Alcoon earlier." He leaned in towards me, and lowered his voice. "So what do you think a cross between a panther and a dragon really looks like?"

I could not believe Mrs. Alcoon had told him. I opened my mouth to say something, but he just grinned and patted me on the shoulder. "If you ever need a babysitter..." He turned and left. I snorted to myself. As if.

Breaking into my thoughts, a cherub fluttered up and offered me a glass of champagne. My mouth dropped open a little bit further. I shook my head. It actually had a golden harp strapped to its back. Surely...?

"We used a few spells to spice up the occasion," said the Arch-Mage, walking up.

"Oh." That made more sense.

He raised an eyebrow. "You're not partaking?"

"What? You mean the champagne? Um, no. The bubbles give me a headache."

I wasn't sure whether he believed me or not. I shrugged inwardly. I wasn't going to announce my pregnancy by telling the fucking Arch-Mage before anyone else, even if my old Scottish friend was doing half that work for me. Then the Fae Queen drifted over in a haze of honeysuckle and glowing warmth. Excellent.

"I believe congratulations are in order," she said.

I coughed. "Excuse me?"

"With your success. We knew no-one else could lead the council. We were right." She swept her arm around the garden. "Look. Everyone's here and having fun. Together."

"Oh, right, yes. Thanks," I said.

"So we need to consider what the next step is."

I stared at her.

"The way we are all working together now means that there is no end to what we can achieve. What do you think the council should focus on next?"

My tongue was cloven to the roof of my mouth. She could not be serious.

The Arch-Mage smiled. "You don't seem happy with the vampires, Miss Smith. We can always start with them. Get rid of them all from our little island for good? Just say the word."

I found my voice. "We've done what we set out to do. Endor's dead. There's no reason to keep the council going."

She arched her eyebrows. "Dear, if we don't keep the council going, we'll lose everything we've achieved. We need to sustain our momentum."

"My fucking name is Mack," I hissed.

She looked rather taken aback.

"And if you want to continue the council on, then that's great. But you'll need to elect a new head. I'm done."

Her gaze hardened. "Let me guess. You'd give up the chance to create harmony across every facet of the Otherworld for a werepanther. Men like him are nine to the dozen. You'll find someone else."

Not a chance, sister.

The Arch-Mage butted in. "She's right. Just think of all the good you can do."

"Find someone else," I repeated through gritted teeth.

"But why should we when you are already so very capable?"

I dug my fingernails into my palms. My blood was boiling. Before I did something I truly regretted, I turned and walked away, pushing through the crowds of people. I reached the fringes of the keep's boundaries and just kept on going, my thoughts a maelstrom of seething anger. How dare they? I had done what they'd asked of me. It wasn't fair to do this. Someone else could fucking take the council leadership on if they thought it was so bloody important. I kicked at the ground, scuffing it and sending clods of dirt fling up into the air. In one fell swoop the pair of them had completely destroyed my sunny mood. Screw them.

I continued stomping along the well-trodden path, cursing aloud. Fire coursed through my veins and I was aware my vision was starting to cloud into red. I shook my head to clear it. I wasn't going to lose control. Not because of them. I forced myself to take deep calming breaths as I marched. Get a fucking grip, Mack, I told myself.

Before I realised it, I had emerged out from the canopy of trees. I looked around. The sea stretched in front of me, glittering invitingly in the sunlight. I was high up, on top of the cliffs that overlooked the beach. To the other side, I could see the little village of Trevathorn, sitting snugly at the edge of the bay. If I looked down, I'd be able to see the spot where John had died. I sat down heavily and crossed my legs. How in the hell was I going to get out of this?

There was a rustling behind me. Fuck. Someone had obviously seen me storm off and decided to check whether I was okay. I really just needed some alone time. I craned my neck round to tell whoever it was to go away, then scrambled to my feet and spun round fully.

It was a young man. He looked achingly familiar. I guessed I'd not intimidated the vamps as much as I'd hoped. Fear shivered up my spine. It wasn't just me I had to worry about any more - but the bloodfire that had been roiling around in my system had vanished. Shit.

"You killed my brother," he said.

"I didn't. He was trying to kill me."

He spat. "So it was self-defence?"

"No!" I put up the palms of my hands in a conciliatory gesture. "A vampire killed him."

"You work with them?" The disgust in his voice was evident.

Oh, for fuck's sake. "No," I said. "They were

trying to blackmail me. I'm sorry about your brother, I really am."

He stared at me with dead eyes. "You're a Draco Wyr."

"Yes, but, come on. All that stuff between our ancestors happened hundreds of years ago. There's no reason for us to hate each other. Let's be sensible about this."

"Fuck you."

He launched himself at me, slamming my body into the ground. I tried to call up my bloodfire, tried to get even a spark of green fire to defend myself, but it wasn't working. I lifted up a knee instead and connected with his groin. He rolled off and groaned, then stumbled back up to his feet.

"Just for that, I'm going to make your death as slow and as painful as possible."

I pulled myself half upright, just in time to allow him to kick me in the face. Salty blood filled my mouth, and I coughed.

"You don't want to do this," I said, trying again.

"I'm sorry, I couldn't hear that in between all the gurgling. Maybe this will help." He shot out a punch, although this time I managed to just jump out of the way in time.

Okay. I didn't want to hurt him, but I would defend myself and the babies growing inside me any way I could. I was still a fucking good fighter, Draco Wyr skills or not. I jumped up in the air, somersaulting and landing to his left, and smacked out my hand, catching him on the bridge of his nose. Blood gushed out. He scissor kicked me in return, the heavy heel of his boots crashing into my chest. I fell backwards onto my elbows.

"Your kind is unnatural," he snarled. "You should not exist. You're disrupting the balance of nature."

Through the haze of pain, I felt dull recognition at his words. They were almost what Aubrey had said. Almost what I'd felt about Endor. Maybe he was right. A weak flicker of heat lit up my belly. I couldn't let him hurt me any more though; I couldn't risk losing my children. I pulled up my legs and tried to scuffle backwards. Then a dark shape came flying out of the trees. Corrigan.

The others are on their way.

Relief shot though me. Thank fuck. Maybe one of them could talk some sense into this guy. He half turned, however, and clocked Corrigan's fast approach.

"I guess it won't be so slow after all." And he grabbed me by the material of my hem-line, yanked me up and pushed.

My hands scrabbled at the air as soon as I realised I was falling. I was going backwards off the cliffs, down to the rocks and the churning sea below. Corrigan howled and flung himself after me. No. Air rushed past me as I gathered speed. Tears were beginning to form in my eyes and then, just as I thought it was all over, my bloodfire flared and I transformed in midair. My body extended into its dragon shape, and my wings flapped. Corrigan landed on top of me, his claws digging into my scales for purchase, as I gained control and swooped round to rocky cliffs and over to the beach.

It was hardly what you'd call a smooth landing.

But it was a darn sight better than what the alternative had been. I concentrated on shifting back to human form. This was a public beach – but better to be found naked than to be found as a dragon. The smooth fur of Corrigan's werepanther equally dissipated, until it was just his hot bare skin against mine.

"Who the fuck was that and why did you take so long to transform?" He pulled up slightly and stared down into my eyes.

I sighed. "It's a long story, but essentially he and all his family are sworn to kill the entire race of Draco Wyr. And when they're next to me, all my powers seem to fade away. I can't do anything. No fire, no dragon. Nothing. I guess when he pushed me over the cliff I eventually got far enough away for everything to start working again."

He glared down at me. "And you were planning to tell me this when?"

"I just told you now!"

"For fuck's sake, Mack! I can't keep you safe if you keep running into danger and keeping secrets from me!"

Oh, that stung. I pulled myself out from under him and stood up, placing my hands on my hips. "Keep me safe? Hello, your Lord fucking Mightiness. Who saved your sorry arse at Bird World? Who saved you from being smashed against a pile of rocks just now?"

Corrigan smirked up at me.

"What?"

He started to laugh.

"What?" I repeated.

"You're magnificent when you're angry. Can you always be naked when you get pissed off? It's so much more entertaining."

Heat flooded my cheeks. He leapt to his feet in one lithe motion, and cupped my face, leaning in for a kiss. I pulled away.

A hurt expression flitted across his face. "What's wrong?"

I looked down. "The Summer Queen and the Arch-Mage…"

"I saw them talking to you," he said grimly. "Let me guess. They want you to stay on as head of the council. Which means you can't be with me."

I nodded miserably. "I pretty much told them to fuck off. And I mean it, I do, but…"

"But they can be very persuasive."

"I won't do it, Corrigan."

He smiled at me. "I won't let you. Not this time. Come on." He tugged at my hand. "Let's face them together."

Like Adam and Eve, we both walked hand in hand up the dunes and into the trees, wending our way up the train back to the top of the cliffs. We were just at the edge of the woods, when I spotted a huge group of people. Bolux's descendant was on the ground, with two large shifters standing over him. Everyone else was staring down over the edge of the cliffs. Someone – I couldn't tell who – began to cry loudly.

"Shit." I started forward. "They think we're dead."

Corrigan grabbed my arm and pulled me back. "I can turn it off, Mack."

I stared at him, confused.

"I can turn off the Voice for good. They'll think I'm gone. We can leave together. Now. We'll be done with this forever."

"You mean...?"

He nodded. "If you want to."

"We'll be free," I said slowly. "No-one else will come after me if I'm dead."

He watched me.

"Our children will be safe."

Corrigan touched my cheek.

"But they need us. You're the lord Alpha. What will the Brethren do?"

"They'll find someone else. It's a fucking pain in the arse job as it is, kitten. I'm not going to miss it."

"But Mrs. Alcoon..."

Then I thought of what she had said about Slim going full time. She'd been letting me know she would be fine if I went.

I looked out through the veil of leaves. Someone was turning round. Solus stared right at me. He mouthed something. 'Go'. He was telling me to leave, to do what Corrigan was suggesting. Alex was next to him, and he also flicked his head round. Solus nudged him and said something. The mage grinned, then lifted up one surreptitious hand, as if in a wave, and returned to gazing at the sea.

"We'll have ruined their wedding day."

"They'll get over it."

I turned back and looked directly into Corrigan's eyes. "What if we don't make it? As a couple?"

"Do you think we won't?"

I shook my head. No.

"We're in this for the long haul, kitten, no matter what. But this is your decision. We leave now and never return, or we go and tell everyone that we're okay. Make a choice."

Epilogue

On a small island on the west coast of Scotland, where the houses are quaint, the air is clear, and the only way in or out is by ferry, lies a small tight-knit community. They notice when strangers arrive, and notice when they leave. So when the new young couple came to live, eyebrows were raised. They bought the old lighthouse keeper's cottage and, for the first few months, kept to themselves.

A few islanders, admittedly, thought they were rude and standoffish to begin with. It quickly became clear that wasn't the case. They were simply in love. And when the woman's body began to swell and she later gave birth to a set of beautiful twins, one boy and one girl, those wagging tongues were silenced. They integrated themselves bit by bit into the community. The man helped old Adams re-build his roof when the winter storms blew half of it away. The woman volunteered at the small primary school, helping the local children. The problems with vanishing sheep from the farms in the north abruptly stopped, and old wives' tale about staying away from the dark caves close to the harbour no longer seemed to matter now that the wind no longer howled through them in the middle of the night.

So if occasionally more strangers abruptly appear out of nowhere and just spend a bit of time watching the couple, then smile to themselves and leave, no-one says anything. And if, when the moon is up, there are strange marks left on the beach, it's prudent not to comment on them. Besides, the tide washes them away quickly enough. Sometimes it's easier if you let a few things just slide without question. Because although they may live on an island, no man is an island, and for communities to work and co-habit in such an isolated spot you sometimes need to live and let live. Sometimes.

About the author

After teaching English literature in the UK, Japan and Malaysia, Helen Harper left behind the world of education following the worldwide success of her Blood Destiny series of books. She is a professional member of the Alliance of Independent Authors and writes full time, thanking her lucky stars every day that's she lucky enough to do so!

Helen has always been a book lover, devouring science fiction and fantasy tales when she was a child growing up in Scotland.

She currently lives in Devon in the UK with far too many cats – not to mention the dragons, fairies, demons, wizards and vampires that seem to keep appearing from nowhere.

You can find out more by visiting Helen's website: **http://helenharper.co.uk**

Made in the USA
Middletown, DE
14 June 2022

67164966R00201